VÁMONOS!

VÁMONOS!

a novel by
Bill Stephens

FRANKLIN
SCRIBES
PUBLISHERS

Vámonos! © 2013 Bill R. Stephens

Published by Franklin Scribes Publishers. Franklin Scribes is a register trademark of Franklin Scribes Publishers.

Franklin Scribes books may be purchased in bulk for educational, business, fundraising, or sales promotion. For information please email: SpecialMarkets@franklinscribes.com

Publisher's Note: Vámonos! is a work of fiction. References to events, establishments, organizations, locals, and real people living or deceased are intended merely to equip the fiction with a sense of authenticity and shadings of local color. They are used fictitiously. All other names, characters, places, and all dialogue and incidents portrayed in this book are the product of my imagination.

First Edition

Shout Out to Author:
Stephens dot Billy @ ATT dot Net

Library of Congress Cataloging-in-Publication Data

Summary: Skeets and Jesse, two offbeat, C & W musicians, flee Austin, Texas, on a Don Quixote-esque journey of redemption in the Mexican Desert. The reader experiences (in spite of the playful tone and often thigh-slapping humor) mankind's foibles arrayed, illegal immigration illuminated, greed uprooted and foiled, and despotic political oppression confronted and vanquished – all without a single gunshot. Then there is wonderful Josefina, the Mexican burro, who shows us that if we are steadfast in our faith, practice meticulous hygiene, and stay the course; we can achieve our dreams, even though we might get diddled along the way.

Authors Note: Italicized Conversation in Vámonos! is Spoken Spanish.

ISBN 978-0-9886433-0-7 (softcover)

Printed in the United States of America

To my wife, Kay, who toils tirelessly so I can write.

PART ONE

"CAMINANTES DEL MAYAB"
"Mayan Wayfarer" Guty Cardenas (Composer)

Chapter 1

Skeets Hollaran knew the woman's gaze had all the makings of a life-altering event. The pretty blonde at the table of three ladies stared at him like a coyote circling a fawn. He'd been on good behavior for about three months since Gena threatened to throw him out of the small duplex they shared for what he knew he was about to do again.

Skeets found singing in the bar of Rancho-O-Rita Bar & Grill, Home of the Flaming Chicken Fried Steak just outside Austin, Texas, a humbling experience. He'd wiggled his way onto the tiny stage that barely held a stool, his guitar, the microphone, and himself, and sung to an unappreciative audience for months. Add lousy pay, patrons hungry but not for music, and the smell of chicken fried steaks as they bubbled in burned grease, all mingled with a pall of cigarette smoke, and Skeets had himself a disagreeable venue. "But a gig's a gig," he kept repeating.

The blonde's amorous interest proved to him once again that he held his thirty-five years well. Lean and tanned from Harley-Davidson motorcycle riding, he wore over-length stovepipe jeans rumpled on his boots, a big belt buckle, pearl-snap buttoned western shirt, and a big hat. Gena had interrupted fifteen years of uncomplicated one-night stands with women just like this blonde in bars just like the Rancho-O-Rita. Gena's loving care and support topped everything he'd ever experienced. He glanced again at the blonde and shook his head involuntarily and thought, *a man who might even considers a dawdle with that woman cannot be good enough for Gena. But that's the problem isn't it? Gena deserves better than me.*

Close to midnight, he'd just finished the song written by a friend to celebrate his divorce, "Darlin', If You Really Loved Me, You'da Married Somebody Else." Skeets had included the song on his only CD, and the single release made it to the top forty of C&W and rested at number thirty-nine for one week – his closest brush with fame. The dealership held his Harley hostage for an unpaid one-hundred dollar repair bill, and he now relied on friends for rides. With one song left in the final set, he had to find a new friend real quick or he'd have to thumb it back to town.

The blonde and her two lady friends seemed more interested in drinking than chicken fried, and they listened to his music with interest. The blonde – who looked to be in her late-twenties – had maintained predatory eye contact with him most of the evening. He launched into his final song, "Baby, If You've Had Too Much, I Can Pop Your Clutch" and sang to the blonde. She smiled with recognition at the song that had made Skeets semi-famous around Austin. He put his soul into the song, and, for once, those muddy chord progressions that always cramped his fret fingers came so easily he felt truly gratified.

He put his guitar into the case, stepped from the stage, and settled up with the bartender. For the first time since he could remember, his bar tab did not consume his entertainment fee. An event of this magnitude could not go uncelebrated, so he moved to the ladies' table. "You ladies put up with my singing all evening, least I can do is buy you a drink."

The blonde pulled back the empty chair next to her and patted the seat. "Best offer we've had all night. Sit down and rest yourself."

He turned to the bartender, made the universal circular motion for another round, slid the chair closer to the blonde, and sat. "You ladies university students?"

A snicker circled the table as the three looked at each other to see if they could pass for UT undergrads. Unconvinced, the blonde shook her head. "Nice try, but college is a distant memory."

The drinks arrived, and Skeets passed them around and paid the bartender. He held his glass and saluted the women, "You coulda fooled me about the college thing. Oh, by the way I'm Skeets Hollaran." He doffed his big hat as he introduced himself.

The blonde smiled in appreciation of his gentlemanly gesture. "I'm Sue. Meet Janet and that's Fran." The other two nodded at the introduction. The three sipped their cocktails and studied him.

His practiced eye had already picked up on the wedding bands. "Girls night out?" He smiled at the three and took a pull from his scotch and water.

They chortled whisky giggles, and Sue explained, "Our husbands went fishing at the coast."

Janet and Fran spoke almost in unison. "So we decided to do a little fishin' our own selves." They broke up in uncontrollable laughter.

Skeets looked around the bar and shook his head. "You've got one nibblin' around the bait now, but I don't see many other fish in this pond."

"What're three gals and a guy to do?" Sue feigned perplexed irony.

"I'm headed down to the Dillo Doe and do a little picking and singing with my buddies. Why don't you gals join me? There's usually a pretty good group there right about now."

The three looked at each other and nodded. "You're a smooth-talking dude, Skeets Hollaran. We'd follow you anywhere." Sue tossed her hair and stood.

As she unfolded from her seat, Skeets saw an even more impressive slender figure. She stood eye to eye with him and carried her body with the grace of a super model. "Ladies, I'd give you a ride 'cept I expect my friend who brought me to swing back by, but if I'm not here, he'll know where to find me."

"Not to worry, we've got room for one more." They laughed again and Sue grabbed Skeets' hand and jerked him toward the door so hard that he barely grabbed his guitar.

The pink script "Dillo Doe" neon sign with its armadillo and antler-less deer, an Austin icon for decades, always gave Skeets a warm feeling. The classic honky-tonk dated back to when Willie, Waylon, and the boys were happy to get any kind of gig. The size of the room gave the place a comfortable air, and the large stage accommodated as many musicians as wanted to sit in for the late night jam sessions. Musicians without gigs and those finished with their paying jobs gathered about midnight after the dancers got tired. The music lovers pulled up their chairs and enjoyed what Austin's picker-singer-songwriters had to offer. Skeets and every other musician knew that singing cover songs to this crowd would get you shunned.

He hoped his buddy, Jesse Suarez, piano man for the Royal Flush, would show up so Skeets could show him largesse at the bar with the night's net receipts from the Ranch-O-Rita. Jesse's Harley could be counted on for a second-seat ride to Gena's place. As luck would have it, Jesse didn't show, so Skeets paid more and more attention to Sue, who had driven him to the Dillo Doe in a brand new BMW. He communed with the ladies at the table between songs until his turn to sing again.

When Skeets finished his newest song, "Darlin', I Really Don't Think So" and returned to the table, the two musicians he'd enlisted as wingmen sat next to Janet and Fran ready to cut them out of the herd as instructed. Now he could focus his charm on Sue and a ride home.

"You guys go ahead and make yourself comfy here." Skeets grinned as he pulled up another chair and slipped it in between Sue and the closest interloper. He leaned forward and gestured toward the other two ladies. "Have you two met Janet and Fran?"

The four nodded and smiled at each other. Skeets turned to Sue. "So when does the babysitter have to get home?"

"No kids. No babysitter."

"You're all alone and waitin' patiently by the window watchin' for your man to return from his big adventure."

"Yeah, something like that."

Skeets gestured toward her friends, now absorbed in relationship building with the musicians. "Your friends are enjoying themselves enough they wouldn't mind us splitting?"

"They're big girls. They can take care of themselves." Sue leaped up.

"You mind giving me a ride?"

"I've thought all evening about just that." Sue reached for his hand and pulled him up.

Skeets turned to the other four. "Listen, Sue has offered to give me a ride home. Great to meet you. Have an enjoyable evening." With that he doffed his hat, collected his guitar, and trailed behind the tall blonde as she towed him out the door.

The Beamer hummed over Loop One west of Austin. Skeets adjusted the radio to a C&W station when the conversation sagged. Sue turned to Skeets and with a wry smile asked, "You mind if we make a small detour?"

"Ma'am, It'd be plum rude of me to deny a sweet person like yourself anything she desires."

The Beamer slowed to a stop early the next morning in front of Clyde Volmer's house a half block from Gena's duplex, a ploy both to disguise the location of his real digs and to avoid an encounter with Gena. As the Beamer roared away, he stood on the curb and took inventory. His guitar case leaned against his leg, and he recollected that he put his guitar in it. His shirt smelled of beer, scotch, expensive perfume, tobacco, and body odor. Sixty-three bucks still languished in his pockets as near as he could make it. Before Gena he'd have called it a pretty successful night. But now remorse settled over him like a morning fog. *Why do I keep pushing Gena away? Keep trying to save her from me?*

Something heavy hit the ground at Gena's duplex and interrupted his reverie. He looked around to see a garbage sack sail across the lawn and explode onto her front yard next to the first, and the contents splayed everywhere. Before he could react, a third sack flew threw the air and slammed onto the ground with similar devastation. Except this time he saw his motorcycle helmet tumble across the yard and heard the shout, "You miserable shit."

"Christ almighty, what's going on?" He grabbed his guitar and trotted toward the duplex as fast as his weariness allowed. He slid to a stop in the driveway, breathing hard, in full view of his digs. The front yard looked like the scene of a natural disaster. Everything he owned lay before him.

Gena nailed something to the front door with her back to him. She turned, saw him in the driveway, and threw the hammer at him as she shouted, "You miserable shit." By the time he dodged the hammer and recovered, she had leaped into the driver's seat of her black Pontiac LeMans parked in the driveway, and cranked the engine.

Skeets threw down his guitar case, ran to the car's window, and banged on it until she rolled it down. "What's happening? Why are you doing this?"

"Why am I doing this? Why am I doing this, you piece of shit? You stay out all night screwing God knows who, and you ask me 'Why am I doing this?'" Her anger dissolved into one tear that hung in the corner of her eye. "You promised this wouldn't happen again. That you had changed. Get away from my car, you lying bastard."

"Whoa. Where did you get the idea that I screwed somebody? I played down at the Dillo Doe until two o'clock. Jesse never showed up, so I had to walk home." He half-squatted and leaned against the car to get down to her eye level.

"Walk home my ass. It takes five hours to walk three miles?" Her engine caught and roared over her voice.

"I saw Clyde's light on, so I stopped in for a cup of coffee. Honest. Call him and check it out." He squirmed a little and hoped Clyde would cover for him.

"God, Skeets, you're so pathetic. I mean you're clueless. You reek of perfume and sex and lie through your teeth. You're worse than pathetic. You're hopeless." With that, she dropped the gearshift into reverse, and spun the tires as she backed out of the driveway.

Skeets jumped back to keep from getting impaled on the radio aerial. "Christ, Gena . . . ." The Le Mans burned rubber, roaring away as her hand protruded through the window and displayed an unfriendly sign.

He watched the car careen out of sight, then turned and surveyed the front yard. A sobering sight, to be sure. The thought that his thirty-plus years of breathing had produced fewer hard goods than could cover a patch of grass the size of a parking space. If he'd been the spiritual kind and eschewed materialism, it might be redeemable in heaven, but Skeets and spirituality didn't mix, and redemption for him seemed out of reach.

A few Merle Haggard LP's, Willie Nelson tapes, one George Strait CD, one Garth Brooks CD, and a book called *Guitar Chords Made Easy* had satisfied his cultural cravings. He managed to keep his wardrobe uncomplicated: two pairs of cowboy boots (one needed new soles), five pairs of jeans (knees out of two and three dirty), three pairs of socks with holes, six western fake mother-of-pearl, snap-button shirts, five Harley-

Davidson tee shirts, a motorcycle rain suit, a scuffed up pair of motorcycle leathers, a helmet, a fringed leather jacket, and a pair of black leather gloves – that was it. In staples and hard goods, his inventory listed a few toiletry items, a broken down suitcase, a bedroll, and the 1990 Harley-Davidson Soft Tail Springer currently still at the dealership for repairs since he lacked the one-hundred dollars to ransom it.

PK, Gena's tomcat, moved through Skeets' belongings and sniffed each and then stared into infinity before he moved to the next item.

Skeets sagged to a cowboy squat beside his meager net worth and contemplated his failure. His life to that point had never demanded an inventory or reckoning of this type, certainly not in the heat of an August morning, hung over, crotch itching, and sleepless. If given to emotion, he might have cried over his condition. Not for the lack of worldly goods, but over Gena Koster who apparently had signed his execution certificate.

Nothing in his life had any validity except Gena Koster. Beautiful, talented, intelligent, charming, and long suffering, the reality of her warm, compelling love made him feel ashamed and undeserving. So much so that he tried almost full-time to save her from himself. Now that he'd succeeded, the thought left such a void that he fell forward on all fours, desperate. In the past when he felt lonely or out of sorts he'd think of Gena's big smile, and it all got better. When they made love, he marveled at her compact, beautifully proportioned body and her soul-stirring tenderness and warmth that transcended physical desire. He could never believe himself worthy of her. Now it seemed she agreed.

He began to pick up his belongings, opened the George Strait CD, and found the ten twenty-dollar bills he had folded and placed there for a rainy day. This day qualified. He put the bills in his pocket, just as PK, short for Pussy Kat, after an extended olfactory examination, backed up to Skeets' motorcycle helmet, and laid down a line of piss. Skeets, never a cat lover, even less a PK lover, and already stressed by current events, leaped over his things and guided a sharp toed cowboy boot right into PK's tenders. PK rolled end-over-end, yowled, and came to a crouch under the lone shrub at the side of the house to contemplate life's disappointments. Skeets cursed as he hopped around and tried to rub PK's pee from his boot onto the grass.

PK's privates snapped back to their anatomically correct position like the rubber-banded ball on a Fly Back Paddle after he completed his first full rotation. As a rule, tomcats do not consider it wise to dally about and analyze the source of a significant blast to their most sacred parts. PK, no exception, moved away quickly to a secure location and thereby reduced the chance of a second shot to the already offended privates and to ruminate on the condition of cats in general.

Skeets gave up trying to clean his boot and stood surrounded by his life history and wondered if things could get any worse. He looked at the duplex door, and things got worse. He could read the title of a note nailed to the door in the fashion of another famous reformer, but he had to move closer to read the rest.

NINETY-FIVE FECES

1) *You are a slob.*
2) *You are devoid of respect for your fellow man.*
3) *You care nothing about the feelings of others.*
4) *You are self-absorbed.*
5) *You are ungrateful to me for paying all the bills.*
6) *You are a slug.*
7) *You wouldn't know a good thing if it bit you in the ass.*
8) *You couldn't write a hit song if your nuts were in a vise.*
9) *You have the morals of a goat.*
10) *You hate cats*

From here on it began to get personal. But a little promise bloomed near the end.

94) You make me ashamed that I ever loved anyone like you.

95) The fact that I still love you cannot compensate for the burden of your being a complete zero.

GET SCREWED (AGAIN) - Gena Koster

Skeets stared blankly for a long time after he read his life's litany. Then he looked around like someone leaving a whorehouse and wondered who watched his embarrassment. He moved to the steps, and sat down on the porch. His head rested face down, cradled in the notch formed by his hands, while he considered his plight. Even he knew a defining moment when he saw one. Knew it from his groin to his soul. Everything ached at the thought of his loss, a loss explained only by his delinquencies. He knew he didn't deserve Gina from their first kiss -- a scurrilous love thief with no conspicuous redeeming qualities. Now the thought of his dereliction left him so miserable, escape seemed the only possible comfort. To run fast and far. To redefine himself. To atone for sins committed against one of God's most perfect gifts. His life was a cesspool with regeneration nowhere about.

Something rumbled in the back of his consciousness and forced him into the present. Jesse Suarez's Harley made an unmistakable noise to anyone within a five-block radius. Within seconds, Jesse roared up the street. When the bike turned into the driveway, Skeets saw an unusual collection of baggage and a bedroll strapped to the machine. He made no visible movement as he watched Jesse dismount. Jesse showcased his Hispanic heritage well, tall, brown skinned, with black hair combed straight back, and piercing black eyes. He was the son of a high school teacher mom who insisted on complete literacy and perfect pronunciation of both English and Spanish. He'd had to practice the piano hours each day and study for spelling bee competitions in two languages. Mrs. Suarez insisted on college, but he chose freedom at high school graduation and refused higher education. His natural musical ability and his practiced piano technique landed him a job with a band, and ever since, he had been in demand by a succession of more talented bands.

Jesse gestured toward the debris on the lawn as he pivoted off his bike and pointed skyward. "A good day to air out your things, good buddy?" No answer so he tried again, "A bad hair day? I mean you're lookin' semi-homeless."

"Where the hell were you last night?"

"Whoa. A bit testy aren't we? Why do you ask?"

"If you'd been at the Dillo Doe, this wouldn't have happened." Skeets gestured around at his things.

"Why do I doubt that my presence in a dingy bar would be healthy for your connubial relations?"

"If we'd been pickin' and drinkin', I wouldn't a gone home with young Mrs. Beamer, and I'd be indoors right now."

"Somehow I feel this apocalyptic event to be inevitable." Jesse sat on the opposite side of the stoop. "What with your propensity to shit in your nest and all." After a long pause he continued, "Besides, I am somewhat inconvenienced myself."

"How so?"

"It seems my last three rent checks bounced, and when I got home from my gig last night the landlord had changed the lock."

"You had a gig?"

"Yeah, the keyboard man for The Clearwater Boys was puking his head off. They asked me to sit in."

"Good bucks?"

"Four hundred. They were desperate." Jesse held four fingers up.

"Free drinks?" Skeets eyes brightened at the thought

"Desperate."

"So where'd you crash?"

"I slipped the lock, and went to bed. So this morning when the prick came to clean out my things -- there I was."

"Did it get ugly?" Skeets squinted against the morning sun.

"Physical even. He called the cops and admitted to me he had already turned the checks over to the D. A. two weeks ago. I came by to explain my impending absence." Jesse kicked the step and looked off to the south.

"You're hittin' the road?" Skeets attempted to rise but settled back instead.

"No choice this side of criminal prosecution."

"Mexico?"

"Where else, *compadre*?"

Skeets' mind went into hyper-drive. *Mexico. Redemptive opportunity at every turn in the road. A pilgrimage of atonement. A cleansing catharsis of the soul the purification of which would make him worthy of the Gena's clemency. A pivotal spiritual event. Sin seared from the soul by Mexican desert sun. And finally, absolution.* "Mind if I ride along?"

"My soul soars like the eagle." Jesse's arm extended in a gliding movement.

"I won't be much fun."

"The Skeets I grew up with never let a little thing like heartbreak keep him down too long."

"It will be a religious pilgrimage . . . for me."

"No shit." Jesse looked doubtful.

Chapter 2

Gena Koster downshifted and powered around the corner onto Airport Boulevard and headed toward IH 35. Both upper and lower levels of the Interstate were jammed. "Shit." she shouted aloud, accelerated through a yellow light, and continued until she swerved left, bounced over the train tracks, and blasted her way onto 45th heading west toward Guadalupe.

Trees and small, refurbished homes blurred past her window; still lowered from the finger she gave Skeets. She knew Skeets loved her, but she also knew Skeets. To know him brought the sure knowledge that he had trouble understanding monogamy. She'd met him when she took a job as a cocktail waitress at the Dillo Doe three years ago while still a sophomore at The University of Texas. Few of the entertainers at the Dillo Doe interested her, but the attractive singer whose face had softened over three decades of disappointments, and who seldom missed the late night jam sessions intrigued her. She loved his parody songs that spoofed C&W. But when he sang his serious songs, almost with apology, the lyrics opened a hole in the center of her soul through which he crept word by word.

She was an avid reader since childhood and could rhapsodize over poetry before high school. This love for poetry pushed her toward Country and Western music, the only music left in which lyrics played any meaningful part. Of course C&W had plenty of "My heart's a breakin' and my balls is achin'," songs, but to her, a Jerry Jeff Walker/Jimmy Buffet lyric like "Railroad Lady" should be studied in school. Skeets' lyrics held the same magic. They stayed only friends for about a year, as women who required no commitment seemed his only interest then.

At Guadalupe Street Gena squeezed through the light and swerved south and headed toward the UT campus where she was already late for a meeting with Professor Higdens, for whom she worked as an assistant. Her agitation grew at each red light until she screamed and pounded the steering wheel in frustration.

Parking was its usual problem, so she wheeled right on 24th and spun her wheels as she turned one block onto San Antonio Street behind the University Co-op. She slid to a stop in the apartment parking place of a car-less friend who worked at the Dillo Doe.

Gena looked up and saw Lizzie Ortega step onto the apartment balcony, curlers in her black hair and a cup of coffee in her hand. "Why do I think there's trouble in paradise?" she called down as Gena opened the car.

"I threw the no good son-of-a-bitch out this morning." Gena accented her remark with a door slam that rattled the windows of the apartments.

"I wondered if there might be repercussions from last night." Lizzie took a swig of coffee from her mug.

"Last night? What about last night?" Gena craned her neck to read Lizzie's expression.

"Skeets spent most of last night at the Dillo Doe with a tall skinny blonde. I was busy, so I don't know if they left together, but they both vanished about the same time." Lizzie took another pull on the coffee. "Come on up and cool down a little before you face the world."

"Cool down. I'm not gonna cool down. I'm gonna get my rifle and hunt that bastard down. Tall skinny blonde, my ass. I'll show him tall and skinny." She had to breathe, and some reason filtered in with the air. After a pause she added, "Besides, I'm late for an appointment with Higdens."

"Doctor 'Lovelorn'?" Lizzie laughed. "You both might be better off if you postponed."

"You're right. Looking into those needy eyes while he tries to hold my hand and counsel me about graduate school won't be easy today." Gena took her cell phone from her purse and pressed a speed dial number. "Dr. Higdens? Right, Charles. OK, Hig, listen, I've got a personal problem, and I need to reschedule. Right. I'll call you tomorrow, okay? No, I'm fine. I just need to get a few things done today. OK, talk to you tomorrow."

Lizzie waved her friend up. "See how easy that was?"

"Got anything to drink up there?" Gena started up the stairs without an answer.

Lizzie pulled two beers from her fridge, popped the tops, and handed one to Gena, who had slumped onto the apartment couch. "So, what's the latest chapter in the unending saga of Skeets Hollaran?"

"I woke up about four o'clock this morning, and he wasn't home. The longer I sat there, the madder I got, so I gathered all his stuff, which didn't take long, stuffed it into garbage bags, and threw them into the front yard. I admit I got a little sappy when I saw how pathetic his stuff looked, but I didn't weaken. Just before I left home I wrote out "Ninety-Five Feces," nailed it to the door, and broke off my key in the lock so the bastard couldn't get in."

"Ninety-Five Feces?" Lizzie raised her eyebrows.

"Yeah, Martin Luther's theses, remember? I listed ninety-five of Skeet's major shortcomings and nailed those suckers to the front door." Gena made a hammering motion.

"Give me an example."

Gena recited the litany as Lizzie howled with pleasure. When Gena finally wound down, Lizzie said, "Hell hath no fury like an English major scorned."

"I'd rather use the hammer on *him*, though." Gena made the pounding motion again.

"So what's next for you two love birds?" Lizzie chuckled.

"No next. Skeets Hollaran and his mister friendly are finished. How dumb can I be to hang around this long?" The rhetorical question made her grimace.

"You had two years of training as you watched him do what he does best. You should've known better than to get involved." Lizzie held her finger perpendicular to the beer bottle's neck and held up the cross as if to ward off Skeets. The phone rang. "It's probably my lover boy. He's got a big plan for us tonight after work." She went to the kitchen to take the call.

Gena listened to Lizzie's love talk to her boyfriend. She remembered the early days together with Skeets. The imprint of that love still clouded her thoughts even after all of his transgressions. She had quit the Dillo Doe toward the end of her junior year and taken a job grading papers for Dr. Higdens and tutoring. Her friendly encounters with Skeets slowed to those times she went to the Dillo Doe to see him. As she walked home from class that summer, Skeets roared up behind her on his recently purchased Harley-Davidson. He coasted to a stop then racked his pipes and leered. "Want a piece of candy, little girl?"

"I never talk to strangers." She continued on her way.

"I bet your mother told you never to get into strange vehicles, right?" He eased the clutch out to move at her speed.

"Right."

"What did she say about gettin' *onto* strange vehicles?"

"It's pretty strange."

"A Harley?"

"No, that she never mentioned that particular peril." She stopped and pondered the consequences. "So . . . I guess you got me." She squealed and leaped on the cycle, her skirt almost to her waist. Traffic slowed considerably and fell in line to follow the only Austin rush-hour traffic thrill in recent history.

On the trip to Barton Springs Park she put her arm around him for the first time, and she was sold on two-wheeling.

They lay in the grass within sight of the topless sunbathers, but neither showed interest. They talked, soothed by a breeze that rustled the grass and rattled the live oak leaves overhead as they lay on their backs and listened to the cicadas sing. She kissed him first. She rolled over and suspended her head above his and slowly lowered it until her lips touched his. She lingered, then moved on exploring his face and settled again at her starting place. Her tongue darted over the surface of his lips, and then she pulled back to admire her work

He seemed confused. Even a little agitated. "I'm gonna have to report this to your mother, little girl." He laughed nervously.

"She warned me about nasty old men." She smiled

"You shoulda listened. Us old guys are the very worst kind."

"Yeah? I've heard you biker guys are harmless."

"Now that might be an exaggeration."

"If that's the case, you might as well tell her about this." She again lowered herself over his lips and pressed a little harder and sent her tongue deep into his mouth to search for a response.

The response came like flash-flood water. He rolled her onto her back and held her close while he returned the kiss, firm and hard. He explored with his hands. She writhed and bit her lips and then convulsed to lie, eyes closed, dreaming.

The next day he called, apologizing. "Listen. I sort of got out of line yesterday. I guess it had to be the mood of the moment."

"Maybe I brought out the worst in you." She grinned into the phone and felt his tone and demeanor melt his attempt to regain poise.

"I hope I didn't do anything that would, you know . . . mess up our friendship." His unease poured through the phone.

"Maybe we should get together and sort this thing out?"

After a pause he said, "You know . . . I think . . . I have an out-of-town gig for the next couple of weeks. Maybe I'll call you when I get back." He hung up without further explanation.

She set the receiver on the phone and shouted, "Gotcha."

The next year his graduation presents to her were the duplex on which he'd paid the first month's rent and a song he wrote for her.

Gena drained the beer bottle and looked at Lizzie, who had returned from the kitchen. "It was the song that did it. I'm a sucker for a good lyric."

"That's right. 'The song.' I forgot about that." Lizzie rolled her eyes back in recollection and began to beat out time:

> *Can there be anything more precious*
> *Than a moment of your time,*
> *To read your eyes and feel your smile*
> *And know your love is mine*

Gena joined in on the verse:
> *A hundred loves behind me*
> *And an empty life ahead*
> *You took me in and loved me.*
> *With nothing asked or said*

You took me in and showed me
My cheating days are gone
Now time with you is all I want
My whole life long

Can there be anything more precious
Than a moment of your time,
To read your eyes and feel your smile
And know your love is mine

Gena slammed the beer bottle on the coffee table. "The no good lying bastard."

Lizzie sat on the couch next to her. "Some men drink. Some men gamble. Some men cheat with other women. And then there's Skeets."

"Skeets doesn't gamble." Gena shot back defensively.

Lizzie tried not to laugh out loud, but the convulsions erupted. "Maybe we should say a little prayer of thanks."

Gena's face clouded, then opened with a flickering smile. "It's not funny. I'm very disturbed here." A chuckle bubbled up. "I'm serious. He did me wrong."

"I think there's a C&W song somewhere in all this." Lizzie no longer tried to control her laughter.

Gena laughed but more subdued. "How can I sit here and laugh when the bastard boffed another woman last night?"

"You don't know that."

"What do you mean, I don't know that? He didn't come home last night. I doubt he spent the night in church."

"Yeah, but don't you think you should at least give him a chance to explain?"

"Well, maybe."

"Come on, Gena, if the phone rang right now and someone said Skeets got injured in a motorcycle accident, you'd be out the door in a flash, and you know it. Right?"

Gena looked away and shrugged agreement, but her cell phone rang before she could answer.

Chapter 3

After Jesse Suarez's roar died in the distance, Skeets stuffed clothes into two pairs of blue jeans with their legs tied, and the rest he put into the sad looking suitcase. He hefted these and his motorcycle gear and trudged up the street to Clyde Vollmer's home.

Clyde, his neighbor, a little paunchy at age sixty with gray hair accelerating into extinction, nevertheless still presented himself well. He opened the door to a bedraggled Skeets who held all of his worldly possessions. He leaned on the doorframe and looked Skeets over. "Son, you look low enough to sit on a cigarette paper and swing your legs."

"It's not been a good morning, Clyde." Skeets came in and set his belongings on the floor. "I reckon I'm as welcome up at Gena's as a fart at a party."

"Moving days are never pleasant." Clyde nodded toward Skeet's stuff. "I saw you offload from a BMW out front this morning, so I reckon last night's little peccadillo didn't go over so well with Gena."

"You have a marvelous gift for understatement, Clyde." Skeets looked down as he scuffed something imagined with his boot.

"I heard Jesse's scoot comin' and goin'. What's up?"

"Jesse's gone to pick up my bike." Skeets pointed in the general direction of the Harley-Davidson dealership.

"Is he gonna ride them both back Roman style?" Clyde pantomimed a two-horse rider.

"Very funny, Clyde. He didn't want to unload his bike to give me a second seat, so he's picking mine up, and then we'll ride back to get his. We're blasting off to Mexico as I'm now unencumbered and without an abode. I wonder if you'd stash part of my stuff while I'm gone." Skeets motioned to his belongings.

"You're hittin' the road? Not stayin' to fight another day?"

"Don't think there's a choice this time."

Clyde reached down, picked up the suitcase, and they moved toward the kitchen where Clyde poured two cups of coffee. They settled at the table, and Skeets handed the "Ninety-five Feces" to Clyde. Clyde read the bill-of-particulars and howled at each new insult posted against Skeets. "I don't think she missed much."

"I'm afraid I've torn the rag right off the bush this time." Skeets covered his anguished look with his hands.

Clyde stared at his friend for a moment and all the mirth left his face. "Skeets, let me tell it to you straight. Gena Koster's the only real thing you've ever had. I've known you and your folks since you were a pup and Gena for more'n a year. If you run off without any effort to get her back, you deserve every bad thing that's gonna happen to you. I mean, think about it, son, this is not something to take lightly."

Skeets continued to hold his head in his hands. "I truly don't think there's much hope right now. Maybe when I get back I can try again, but I doubt it."

"For God's sake, son, lie to her. Tell her you spent the night here. Tell her anything. Get on your knees and beg. And if she'll take you back, then see if you can grow up enough to show her the respect she deserves. Here's a phone, call Gena and forget this Mexico crap." Clyde picked up the phone from the table a thrust it toward Skeets.

"I tried all that lying stuff, and it didn't work." Skeets moaned in reply. "I truly don't deserve Gena. I've known that all along, but I hung around anyway hopin' I'd change. Try to get it together and be the man she wanted me to be. It's hopeless. When I get back . . . maybe . . ."

"That may be too late. Trust me, it won't be no trouble for her to find somebody to take your sorry ass's place." Clyde sat the phone in front of Skeets.

Skeets reflected on life without Gena. The thought was so sobering and painful he closed his eyes and hoped it would go away. When he opened them again, Clyde still stared at him and pointed at the phone. The pain persisted. "You think I should call her? I'll bet she won't even answer."

"Try it." Clyde pointed again at the phone.

Skeets slowly picked up the phone and dialed Gena's cell number. Seconds before voice mail clicked in, he heard her voice. "Clyde, is that you?"

After a pause Skeets answered. "No, it's me. I'm calling from Clyde's."

"Oh, if I'd known that, I wouldn't have answered."

"Listen, I guess we've got a situation here." Skeets summoned all of his creativity and people skills, but before he could continue, Gena interrupted.

"No Skeets, *we* don't have a situation. *You* have a situation. You can't keep your dick in your pants." A long silence.

"Now, Gena, don't jump to conclusions. I know I didn't get home last night, but I can explain."

"Explain? You can explain my ass. What lie are you going to trot out this time?"

"No, really, I've been here at Clyde's. Jesse didn't come by the Dillo Doe, so I had to walk home. I saw a light on in Clyde's, so I stopped in and passed out on his couch. I overslept this morning." He waited to see how this story played out.

"Funny thing, Skeets, Lizzie bartended at the Dillo Doe last night . . ."

"Lizzie bartended last night? I didn't see her." Skeets' shocked expression caused Clyde to shrug a question?

"There's no way you could've seen her since you only looked at the skinny blonde you poured drinks down."

"You've talked to Lizzie?" Skeets slapped his forehead with his empty hand.

Clyde shook his head asking, "What? What's she saying?"

"Actually, I'm in her apartment right now." Gena's voice trailed off but left the power of retribution in its wake. After a long silence, she asked, "You still there?"

Skeets brow knotted as his mind whirred. "She said something about a skinny blonde?"

"Yes, Skeets, the skinny blonde you left with."

"She saw me leave with a skinny blonde?" Skeets again pounded the palm of his hand to his forehead in disbelief as his shoulders sagged.

Clyde stood and paced. "Jesus, Skeets, what's she saying? I think you're messin' this up here."

"Give it up, Skeets. Did you pork the skinny blonde or not?"

Skeets thought of all the lies over the past two years. All the stories to cover up his failures. All the times he wanted to tell the truth. The truth that she deserved someone better. That he disappointed her to prove his unworthiness. That she should send him packing.

Her voice sputtered over the phone again. "I'm waiting."

He held the phone away from his ear. "Yes. Yes, I screwed the skinny blonde."

Clyde stopped in his tracks and spun on his heel. "Good God, man, I can't believe you just said that."

"What?" Clyde heard Gina without the phone. "You admit it. You don't have enough respect for my feelings to lie about it? God, Skeets, that really hurts. It's one thing to cheat on me, but it's something else completely to brag about."

"I'm not bragging about it. I'm *confessing.* I made a very big mistake. I thought for once I would own up to it and hope you would forgive me." Skeets jumped up and paced until the phone cord jerked him back.

"*For once?* How many other times were there?" She sounded like a siren.

"I'm just saying that I love you, and I want you to forgive me. I want to be a different person in the future."

A long silence followed as Skeets listened and hoped.

"Skeets, you don't deserve me."

The level of hurt in her voice caused him to slump back into his chair. "I know that. I know I need to be a different person." He heard Jesse pull into the driveway and rack up the motorcycle's pipes.

"Is that Jesse's bike I hear?"

"No, he picked up my bike for me." He waved his arm back and forth and tried to wipe away this interloping subject.

"What brought that on?" She had gained control of her voice again.

"We're riding to Mexico." He gestured toward the south.

"Mexico? What are you going to do in Mexico?"

"I need to get away and think things through." He rubbed his forehead and gestured futilely. Clyde sat back at the table and now held his head in his hands.

"Yeah, well I've already thought things through. I think we should not see each other again." After a pause, Skeets heard the phone click off.

There was a knock at the kitchen door. "Come on in, Jesse," Clyde hollered from his chair.

Jesse stood in the door for a moment and looked back and forth between the two dejected figures. "Did I interrupt a funeral or something? What's up?"

"Lover boy just made an unimaginable screw up running damage control on the phone with Gena." Clyde got up and poured a cup of coffee for Jesse.

"Hey, good buddy, you're holdin' that phone like it smells bad." Jesse took the coffee from Clyde and sat in the vacant seat.

Skeets looked at the phone held away from his ear, then lowered it into its cradle. "Well, Clyde, that went *really* well."

"Qué pasó?" Jesse shrugged the question.

"Let's just say that Gena didn't beg me not to go to Mexico." Clyde shook his head in disbelief. "He told her the truth."

"That's right, I told her the truth."

"You told her the truth?" Jesse's eyebrows arched at the idea.

"Nobody tells them the truth, Skeets. They don't want the truth." Clyde shook his head at Skeets' apparent naiveté.

"Well, Mr. Veracity, we better load our gear, 'cause you just became homeless for good." Jesse pointed toward Skeets' stuff in the front room.

"What? Can't a guy do the right thing? Tell the truth? Try to be a better person?"

"You can never tell women the truth about infidelity, if you want to hang around, that is." Clyde ran his hands through his hair as if removing something repugnant, like the truth.

Jesse shook his head. "That's right, good buddy, it's the worst possible thing you could have done."

The three sipped their coffee and considered the events of the day. Finally, they stood, moved into the living room, and considered the detritus of Skeets' life, who moved around it like a rock climber looking for a handhold. "Clyde, you have a box I could put this stuff in?" When the box arrived, he dumped everything from the suitcase into the box and picked out a few toiletries, and started, not too carefully, to fold the clothes he'd stuffed into the blue jeans.

"That's the ugliest suitcase I've ever seen. Ugly. Uhhhgly." Jesse kicked the scuffed vintage cloth-covered suitcase. "We better buy you a genuine Harley-Davidson duffel when we pick up my bike, 'cause we might gross out the entire population of Mexico with that thing."

"Actually, they won't even let him in unless he leaves it at the border." Clyde nodded agreement.

"We're talkin' serious loss of style points when we show up at the Harley place with that bag." Jesse nudged the suitcase again for emphasis.

"Ok. Ok. God forbid my mom's old suitcase will get me arrested by the Harley-Davidson style-police."

Bike loaded and extra-stuff box stored in the garage, they returned to the kitchen table. "So, you guys have a plan for this great expedition?" Clyde asked.

Jesse nodded. "I thought we'd ride south."

"Oh, now that's a plan," Clyde said with excited irony. "I mean, do they give you the big *bienvenidos* at the border, or do they want to see a little paperwork before the *abrazo.*"

"What paperwork?" Skeets looked uneasy that his travel résumé extended no further than San Antonio, Dallas, Houston, and a couple of trips to Boys Town in Laredo.

"You know, maybe a passport, title to your bikes, and maybe even insurance." Clyde's voice had an edge to it.

"They never wanted any papers when we rode to Boy's Town." Jesse leaned back and lifted his coffee cup.

"Somehow I think the Mexicans might be a little more interested when you ride further south than the nearest whorehouse." Clyde hesitated. "You guys seem a little light on preparation for your great adventure."

"Maybe they can tell us what we need at the dealership when we pick up Jesse's scoot. Besides, they must still have the title to my bike, 'cause I sure don't have it." Skeets grinned.

Jesse got up. "I guess we'll find out when we get there."

With all Skeets' stuff stowed on his bike, Jesse had to strap Skeet's guitar on his back in order to second seat. The two voyagers mounted up, and Clyde stepped back, examined the overloaded motorcycle, and shook his head. With the bedroll strapped to the front fender and the ugly suitcase on the back fender sissy-bar, the bike looked horribly diseased. The two riders and the guitar rounded out a truly sad visage. "You know, as ridiculous as you guys look, and as much as I think this whole trip's a mistake, I'd sure like to go with you."

Chapter 4

A fierce blue South Texas sky was splattered with indifferent, fair-weather cumulus. The heat stifled anything stationary, but at eighty-five miles per hour Skeets had the illusion of comfort. They settled in, contented as pigs on ice, for their long ride as the Austin city limits sign faded in their rearview mirrors. They rode staggered and impersonated seasoned road hogs. Skeets' style deficit healed when they ditched his mom's suitcase in favor the Harley duffel now strapped along with his guitar case to his bike's second seat and sissy-bar. Skeets felt every bit the troubadour.

Light traffic in San Antonio allowed them to clear the Alamo City in record time and head south on IH 35; Laredo in their sights. The shape-shifting landscape kept Skeets' interest. Austin's live oak-studded limestone hills sighed and lay down on the coastal plain of San Antonio, where oaks and elms metamorphosed into mesquite that diminished from thirst under the torturous sun until it remained the endless expanse of scrub brush that is Southwest Texas.

Skeets, a newcomer to long distance motorcycling, felt alive but somewhat mesmerized by the subliminal stimuli of

"Harleying." Those random occasions when motorcycles, like horses galloping in unison, fired in sync as they picked up the load of a hill climb, sent a thrill that pulsed through his groin into his soul. He looked around the landscape as it blurred past, drew in the smell of sage goaded into bloom by a recent rain shower, and nodded satisfaction as the problematic day faded from memory like smoke signals. By God, Harley riding was a purgative for the soul.

Mid-afternoon, Skeets gave the hand signal to pull off into the Burros Locos Cantina just south of Encinal. The sign offered the essentials – beer, food, gas. Two gas pumps stood like sentinels in front. Awash with the multicolored beer signs of any cantina south of the border, a clay tile roof, and concrete burros with sombreros beside the entrance made them feel they had already arrived in old Mexico.

The two gassed their bikes and moved them to a parking place near the front door. They strapped their helmets to the handlebars, put on their Harley-Davidson bill caps, and Skeets grabbed his guitar. Several bobtail trucks and pickups were parked in the lot dominated by an eighteen-wheeler whose Peterbilt 379X tractor and semi-body shimmered in iridescent, clear-coated black. Someone had crafted the rearview mirrors with great skill and effort into the pointy ears of a wolf, and the front grill had a cavernous, toothed, growling wolf's mouth extended by means of paint over the sides of the truck's hood. The headlights metamorphosed into fire-breathing nostrils. A translucent material appliquéd around the edges of the windshield transformed it into a mean-eyed predator's stare. "El Lobo" painted in gold adorned the tractor's door. Even at rest, engine idling, the truck emitted the low growl of a malcontent carnivore.

"Man, that's one bad ass looking truck." Jesse pointed in the El Lobo direction.

Skeets gestured toward the truck. "That thing adds new meaning to 'eat where the truckers eat', right?"

"Right now I'm hungry enough to eat the trucks."

Skeets heard billiard balls click, and the aroma of masa tortillas, fajitas, and onions sizzling on a flat grill made his knees weak when he pushed through the door. He saw Jesse salivate. "I think you're gonna enjoy this, good buddy."

Their eyes adjusted to the dim lights and they saw several vagrant types, who lounged around tables and played cards or shot pool. A tall, slender Anglo sat at the bar and nursed a beer. A toilet-brush mustache festooned the upper lip of his rangy, handsome face. A grimy, straw cowboy hat with the brim curled almost to the crown sat atop his head. A tank top showcased a wolf head tattoo on his arm at the shoulder. Faded black jeans over black cowboy boots completed his fashion statement. He watched in the bar mirror as they looked him over and lifted his beer bottle in a salute. They nodded in his direction, and Jesse said under his breath, " El Lobo, ya think?"

The proprietor returned from the back with a plate of food for the bar-sitter. He turned his attention to Skeets and Jesse, smiling. "*Buenas tardes, amigos.*"

Skeets pointed toward the cash register. "We're eatin' . . . pay for the gas now or with the food?"

The proprietor pointed toward the tables still smiling. "Take a seat. *Un momentito.*" He held up his thumb and forefinger pressed together, sign language for "just a minute."

They dragged chairs from a table some distance from two groups of card players and sat facing the bar. Skeets' guitar rested in the third seat. The proprietor stood tableside before their chair seats warmed. "What can I get you, amigos?"

"Two beers and a bunch of whatever we smelled comin' through the door." Skeets pointed in the direction of the food still steaming on the counter.

"We're double hungry, *amigo*, so don't be shy with the *comida*." Jesse rubbed his stomach for emphasis.

"Fajitas and a beer. You got it." The proprietor returned to the bar and brought them two longneck Coronas wrapped in deli paper with a lime wedge in the mouth of each.

"You think they charge extra for the lime?" Skeets held the lime up for the question.

"My dad always used lime. Mexican tradition. Germs grew in ice bins in old times that didn't even have scientific names. So folks sanitized the mouth of beer bottles with lime and salt. I guess they got used to the taste of lime in their beer." Jesse demonstrated with his lime before he downed half the bottle.

Skeets tugged with his thumbnail at the deli paper as it sogged up from condensation on the bottle. "You think we'll get into Mexico? The guys at the Harley-Davidson Dealer seemed pretty firm we needed a bunch of papers and shit."

"It'd have taken us another two days to get it all together. We'll just put the old *mordida* on them. They'll let us in."

"Yeah, but we're not flush with *mordida* either." Skeets rubbed his fingers together in the traditional request for a bribe. "I didn't understand why we needed to give them a credit card receipt for vehicle duty either."

"If we had a credit card, we might give a shit. Anyway, we're about forty miles north of *"Mordidaville."* Jesse gestured somewhere south. "We'll find out soon enough."

A stocky Mexican pushed his way through the front door and looked around the room like he'd seen his wife's car parked out front. A black Stetson sat atop a square, mustached face and dark eyes squinted into the dimness. Short, with a Santa Claus transplant bulging over his big silver belt buckle, his arms and legs nevertheless seemed firm and strong. Large gold rings on his fingers shined like headlights; a heavy gold chain and coin hung from his neck and flashed a semaphore through the dimness. When he smiled recognition at Skeets and Jesse, three gold crowned teeth glistened like the headlights on an Edsel.

"You know ol' Goldfingers over there?" Skeets pointed but did not raise his hand.

"No, but I think we're gonna have the pleasure."

As the man moved in their direction, he caught sight of El Lobo at the bar and nodded. Lobo watched with interest in the bar mirror but ignored the salutation. As he approached the table, the newcomer held his arms up as if he expected a giant *abrazo*. "*Son ustedes los puercos?*"

Jesse sat up. "Hey. Easy with the pig talk, dude."

"What did he say?" Skeets asked.

"He called us pigs."

The man waved his hands and spoke in broken English. "No. No, amigos. The Harleys. The Harley hogs. You the Harley guys?" He pointed out the front door.

"Oh. Yeah, they're our bikes." Jesse settled back in his chair.

Uninvited, the man pulled back the fourth chair and sat. "Man, I've always wanted a Harley, you know guys, *una motocicleta chingona. ¿Sabe?* You guys goin' to Mexico?"

"We're headed that direction," Jesse replied.

"*Me llamo Redondo.*" The stranger tapped his chest and repeated, "Redondo." He held out his hand to Jesse, who pointed to his partner.

"That's Skeets, and I'm Jesse. You travel in Mexico?"

"I'm Mexican. *Vivo en Monterrey.*" His gesture indicated the size of the city. "Where you goin' in Mexico?"

"We don't know." Skeets shrugged.

"We're not sure we can even get into Mexico." Jesse pulled on his beer.

"You don't know if you can get into Mexico, and you don't know where to go if you do?" Redondo shook his head in disbelief. "*Muy loco*, guys."

"We left in a hurry." Skeets sounded a little defensive.

"Why you can't get over the border?"

"People told us we need paperwork to get in with our bikes. We hope a little *mordida* will get it handled."

Redondo leaned back in his chair, and his loud laugh caused bar patrons to check out the disturbance. "Man, you gringos are *locos*. You think you can bribe your way into Mexico?"

"It's been done before"

"Forget it, *hombre*. Those days are gone." He continued to chuckle as he took a swig from the beer the proprietor delivered to him without ordering. He quit laughing, rocked forward in his chair, and looked at the two with a conspiratorial eye. "Unless you know the right people."

"We don't know any people -- right or wrong," Skeets blurted out their collective lack of border-crossing savvy.

"You're screwed, man." Redondo's irritation at their stupidity glowed from his face. "It takes years to learn who to deal with at the border."

The proprietor brought plates heaped with steaming fajitas and tortillas to their table and went back to the bar for more beers. Redondo stood up "You *hombres* enjoy your *comida. Hasta pronto*." He turned and walked to the back of the room and sat with a table of card players who greeted him as a friend.

Skeets and Jesse hoisted their third fajita taco before either spoke. "Man, this is good stuff." Skeets came up for air and a slug on his beer bottle.

"Totally righteous, I'd say." Jesse hefted his fourth taco.

El Lobo stood at the bar and shook hands with the proprietor after he paid his tab. He nodded in their direction as he walked toward the door. A moment later a roar from his diesel rattled their beer bottles across the table.

The meal wound down and Jesse and Skeets called for their check. Before it arrived, Redondo appeared at their table again. This time Jesse motioned him to sit, and Redondo called for another round of beers.

"I been thinkin' about you guys getting' into Mexico." Redondo read their eyes for a response before continuing. "You're headed for Laredo, right?" The two nodded. "Impossible, man, no way."

"You already told us." Skeets wondered about this guy's interest.

Redondo leaned forward and lowered his voice. "There's another way, about the same distance, and the border people *son más simpáticos*. The bridge goes into Nuevo Leon at Columbia. You take the Camino Columbia Toll Way west about twenty miles south at Callahan."

Skeets asked, "You think we can cross there?"

"*No solos*. But I can help you." He leaned back, took a draught on his beer, and waited to see if the hook set.

"A kind offer, but how can you help us?" Something about this guy Skeets didn't like; maybe the glare from all the gold.

"Yeah, it's hard to imagine why you'd help us." Jesse rocked back in his chair.

"I like Harley guys, man. Help out a couple a biker dudes." He opened his arms in a gesture of embrace big enough for them both. "And maybe you guys could help me out, and buy gas for my truck."

"We gas up your truck, and you get us into Mexico?" Skeets' skepticism registered about six degrees above bullshit.

Redondo leaned forward and motioned for them to do the same. He talked in a hushed tone. "I have friends at the border. I cross the border a lot. And I do business with the border guys on both sides. They know I don't haul drugs, so they never check my truck. We'll load your bikes in the truck, and when we're past the 30 kilo checkpoint inside Mexico, we unload 'em, and *vamonos*."

"You just smuggle us and the bikes into Mexico. Right?" Jesse shook his head in astonishment.

"Easy, man, I don't like the word 'smuggle.' It's against the law, man." Redondo hissed. He called to the barkeep for another round of beer with tequila shots.

Skeets asked, "What do *you* call it?"

"I make their paperwork easier. They appreciate it, *amigo*." The shots arrived and he motioned for the other two to join him as he shot the tequila in one gulp, bit the lime and chased it with beer. He stood and held his beer out for a toast. "I gotta go soon. I cross right after the night shift comes on. You guys think it over. I'll stop by on the way out." He turned and went back to the table of card players.

Three rounds of tequila and beer warmed their insides, and warmed them to the idea of taking up Redondo's offer. "I mean, what can happen? They catch us, they'll just throw us out, right?" Jesse slurred a little as he spoke.

"Yeah, either that or throw us in the *hoosegow*." Skeets, still not sold, hated the idea of turning tail and running back to Austin. Another round of tequila arrived, and Skeets shot his with lime and salt.

"Sounds like our only way in, man. Remember, spontaneity is the soul of joy. We're after joy and adventure, right?" Jesse emptied his beer bottle. "This'll damn sure be an adventure, okay?"

Redondo stood at the table again. "What's the verdict, *amigos*?"

Skeets stood and staggered a little as they headed for the door. "Let's go pump some gas."

The two motorcycles followed Redondo's truck, a nondescript white, twenty-foot GMC bobtail with no markings and a Texas license tag covered with mud. They turned onto a dirt side road about eight miles south, and Redondo stopped and got out. He unlatched the rear door and raised it to reveal an empty cargo bay with a row of benches down each side of the truck bed. The unmistakable stench of stale urine assaulted them.

"Jesus, your truck smells like a bouquet of assholes." Skeets held his nose.

"Yeah, I hauled goats yesterday." Redondo pulled out a cargo ramp attached under the truck body and motioned for them to load their bikes. They roared up the ramp one after the other. Redondo brought rope from the cab, and they tied the bikes to the side of the truck.

Jesse threw a loop around the handlebar and one on the sissy-bar and lashed these to a cargo rail that ran along the truck body. He shook the bike for a test and then jumped from the truck. Skeets still toiled over his bike while he spun a web of security rope. Jesse watched for a while, then pointed at Skeets bike "Hey, good buddy, I think you're getting' a bit extreme. Your bike looks like a cocoon."

"A beautiful machine like this falling over and getin' all scunt up would bum me out." Skeets started to put another rope on the bike.

"*Vámonos, hombres.* We gotta go." Redondo made a threatening gesture and stomped back to the truck cab.

Skeets stepped back from his bike and admired his work. He handed Jesse his guitar and clutched the rear door pull-down strap as he jumped from the truck. Jesse swung the door latch into place. "Let's go have an adventure, amigo." He handed the guitar to Skeets, and the two walked to the truck cab and crawled in just as it lurched forward.

Redondo stopped just before the town of Callaghan and told them to get out. They followed him to the rear of the truck. He opened the door "Get in and be quiet. They hear something back here when we cross the border, and they'll be all over you guys *como olor mierda.*"

"Your truck smells like stink on shit, hombre. We didn't sign on to ride back here." Jesse's nose curled as he spoke.

"How you think I can get somebody in without papers." Redondo motioned to them to get in the back of the truck and mumbled under his breath, "*Idiotas.*"

They looked at each other, shrugged, and crawled into the back of the truck. Skeets turned back to Redondo. "How long will we be back here?"

"Not long, amigos. We'll be turnin' onto the toll road soon." His gilded smile glistened as he pulled the truck door down.

They heard the latch swing into place, and the rattle of a lock. Redondo shook the door testing it. "I'd swear that asshole locked us in here. Hope you're not afraid of the dark." Jesse gave a nervous chuckle.

"You feel semi-stupid right now?" After about thirty minutes Skeets' voice came across the dark void of the truck at a volume necessary to reach Jesse over the din of the as the truck rattled over something other than a toll road. The bikes slammed against the truck body oblivious to the spaghetti strung around them.

Jesse, sat on the opposite bench and held his hand in front of his face. "It's blacker'n ol' Coalie's ass back here. The bastard shoulda told us we'd be ridin' steerage back here in the piss soaked black hole of Coahuila."

The truck lurched through what had to be the pothole of the century, and Skeets slid off the bench and landed on his butt with an audible thud. "Goddammit that's it. I'm outta here." He grabbed the bench, pulled himself up, and worked his way back to the rollup door. He tried the handle. It wouldn't budge. "The bastard did lock us in."

"This sucks, man." Jesse moved to the front of the truck and pounded on the wall behind the cab. "Hey, asshole. Stop the truck and let us out." The truck lurched on, interrupted by major potholes and sharp turns. He balanced himself as best he could and tried to shove his boot heel into the truck cab with no success. He moved to the back of the truck, he said, "Let me see if I can open it." The truck stopped before he could try, and he heard Redondo open the cab door.

"I don't know about you, but I'm in favor of feedin' this motherfucker a serious amount of boot leather." Skeets groped in the darkness as he tried to find Jesse. Redondo rattled the latch handle as he unlocked the door, and the door flew up as light flooded into the cavity. The late afternoon light blinded them like the dawn of man. When they focused, Redondo stood away from the truck and brandished an XXL-sized pistol.

Chapter 5

"*Bienvenidos, amigos.*" Redondo pushed back the brim of his hat with the pistol and adjusted a coil of rope on his shoulder. "Welcome to Mexico."

"If I didn't feel stupid before, I can report dumb-ass creeping over me like psoriasis right now." Jesse motioned in the direction of Redondo "We stopped for a little target practice?"

Skeets looked around for any signs of civilization. The truck stood in a clearing, and mesquite and scrub brush stretched into tomorrow. The mud-rutted road ended right at the edge of the world. "Why do I think we're not in Mexico?"

"Trust me, *amigos*, Mexico's just the same except more flies. Now get down *con mucho cuidado. ¡Ándale.* I don't want to shoot you."

They stood motionless and considered all the reasons Redondo might need to shoot them. They all came down to one -- the Harleys. "Easy with the pistol, dude. We don't want you to shoot us either." Their hands went up in unison like charismatic churchgoers.

"*Ahora*, gringo assholes. I got no time to fuck with you." The pistol had drifted from side to side now came erect and pointed at their crotches. "I'm gonna shoot you *pinche pendejos* right now." He cocked the hammer on the pistol.

"Whoa. Whoa. Easy does it. We're gettin' down." They hopped flatfooted from the truck with hands held high.

Jesse's foot twisted, and he tumbled on the ground. He sat up and rubbed his ankle. "Right now I wish I'd watched more of those Kung Fu movies."

Redondo motioned with his pistol for Jesse to get up "*Arriba. Arriba. Quítense las botas y los pantalones.*"

"What's he want?" Skeets reached down to help Jesse up.

"You'll be dismayed to learn he wants our boots and blue jeans off." Jesse looked down and kicked at the dirt.

"What?" Skeets couldn't comprehend "I mean, is this son-of-a-bitch gay or something?"

Jesse tried to put double-bass in his voice, as much as possible with a gun pointed at his groin. "Hey, man, look, if you want our bikes, just take them. You don't have to go through all this pistol waving, *machoñ*. '*Quítense las botas y los pantalones*' bullshit."

"I can shoot you in the legs, or you can take off your pants. *Es igual.*" Redondo pointed the pistol from leg to leg.

"You didn't happen to bring a boot jack did you?" Skeets glanced at Jesse as he fell to the ground and grabbed his boots. Boots off, they dropped their jeans and presented their honky-tonk musician's pasty pallor in the late afternoon sun.

"*Y los calcetines.* Redondo again motioned with the pistol barrel toward their Fruit of the Looms.

"He wants the underwear too." Jesse looked helpless.

Skeets almost pleaded with the *pistolero*. "Come on, man, you don't want our Jockeys. We've been ridin' all day in these skivvies. They've got skid marks, man."

"*Apúrense.*" Redondo squeezed off a shot just to the right of Jesse's feet.

The pistol report packed such motivation, the two leaped from their briefs. They stood devoid of all poise, one hand up, the other shielded their southern regions, and endured an anxious pause while Redondo reveled in their distress. Jesse whispered to Skeets, "I feel a draft, man." Redondo pulled the coil of rope from his shoulder and threw it at their feet.

"This bastard's got more ropes than a circus tent." Skeets growled more to himself than Jesse. They stood and awaited further marching orders, masculinity at parade rest.

"Two choices, *es.* I can kill you right now, or you can tie yourselves to that tree." He pointed his pistol toward a large mesquite that stood in the clearing. *"Me da igual. "*

"How do we tie *ourselves* up?" Skeets looked back and forth from the tree to Jesse.

"Pendejos. You tie up him, then I tie you up." Redondo fired another motivational shot next to Skeets' toes that sent him to his knees where he grabbed for the rope. He bounced up, spun Jesse around, and threw a loop over one of his hands.

"Easy, man, I need a little circulation here." Jesse wiggled his hands and tried to loosen the rope. Skeets stretched the knot to make more room.

"OK, *amigos*, get over to the tree." They spaced themselves with their backs on opposite sides of the tree. Redondo wound the rope around them and the tree. He began at their crotch and progressed upward until the end coiled under their chins with little room to breath, and cinched it off. Animal-howl laughter echoed out into the scrub when he stepped back to admire his work. "Like I said, assholes, I always wanted a Harley. Now I got two." He turned, rolled the rear door down, picked up their clothes, threw them into the truck cab, and leaped in after them. His laughter soared above the truck noise as he bounced down the dirt road and into the distance.

The truck faded into the silence that cloaked the mesquite tree and its captives. After a time, Skeets turned his head from side to side to ease the rope and squeaked out a raspy, "Is it time to be joyful yet?"

"It might be time for introspection, review of past transgressions, and overall personal evaluation."

"I don't think I can handle it twice in one day." Skeets' voice trailed off as he remembered the morning's revelations. God, what a difference a day makes. I could be slidin' under sheets, for a snuggle with Gena, and feel the pure joy of her complete acquiescence, he thought.

Jesse tugged at the ropes to test them. "Man, I forgot this all started today. It seems a lifetime ago. This morning we were two underachieving Austin C&W musicians with Harleys and our lives in front of us. Ten hours later we're strapped to a mesquite tree, airing out our private parts, watching our bikes disappear over the horizon God knows where in South Texas. It doesn't seem fair."

Skeets took his turn and strained at the ropes. "The first cat turd I found in my sand box taught me life'd be difficult and often unfair. As other turds followed, I became distrustful of the world and its inhabitants, a negative trait I've tried hard to overcome."

"If you consider our current condition, we've both strayed into semi-lethal gullibility." Jesse looked at the ground in the fading light. "Those mutant red ants walkin' around our feet, licking their chops, looking up at our balls like they're super-sized Mexican *piñatas* bother me the most." He did his best rendition of the South Texas Shuffle and tried to redirect the ants' attention.

"If the pesky little devils decide to come on up for a scrotum sandwich, we might be moved to rip this mesquite out by its roots." Skeets stared down at the crowd formed at his feet and tried a little footwork of his own. The interlopers fell back to safety. "In the excitement I forgot about all the beer we drank. I've needed to piss for hours."

"Likewise." Jesse agreed

"I remember Gulliver put out a fire for the Lilliputians, but was under-appreciated for his efforts."

Jesse's voice had a hopeful lilt in it. "You think those red-faced Lilliputians down there would be as put off by a fusillade?"

"On the count of three."

"They'll never know what hit 'em."

In the subterranean vaults where red ants dwell, and from which they sally forth each day to range over vast areas in hope they might find a seed or miserable scrap of plant to return to the nest for daily sustenance, urban legends persisted. Each time someone complained about their hard and unfair life in this barren land, someone else trotted out the old myths.

The most persistent story told of how God had, on one occasion and without any understandable reason, dropped a heaping load of meat almost on their doorstep. Gone were the days of foraging all day for a dry, tasteless bit of grass. With almost no effort, one had only to stroll a short distance and have all the meat he wanted, then just tear off a huge chunk to carry back to the wife and kids.

Pure renaissance reigned in the nest. A time of happiness and plenty. At least until some started to demand the best parts of the meat and stake out claims and force others onto parts where only small shards of meat still hung on the bones. An angry God sent huge, evil beasts that descended from the sky on wings large enough to blot out the sun. They devoured the meat with their rapacious beaks and claws. *Their meat.* Thousands came out to defend their meat, but it was hopeless. When the evil beasts had stripped the bones of all but the most meager amount of meat, they flew off never to be seen again. Hundreds swarmed over the bones to look for even tiny bits of meat, when a furry evil beast appeared and dragged the bones and those on it away to an unknown place.

In the town meetings that followed, and on all the twenty-four hour cable news channels they prattled on endlessly about what went wrong. Some felt the greed of a few caused God to punish all. Others felt they did not thank God enough for the meat he sent them. And so the argument raged on for as long as any remembered.

Most did not believe how God had sent back the meat again. Others rushed out and came back astounded by the two mountains of meat (one white meat – the other dark meat) right on their doorstep. They were determined not to mess up again, so they approached with great caution and tried to know what best to do. Hundreds, maybe even thousands, ringed the meat while they waited for someone to tell them how to proceed. They all agreed on one point. They needed a world-class blessing before they crawled onto the banquet table.

No one knows how it happened, but right in the middle of the blessing, the heavens opened, and a torrential flood of the most vile, distasteful water rained down on them. Caught by surprise, most immediately washed away, others clung to some bits of grass but were grossed out. They too floated away as they tried to keep their heads above the foul flood.

The nonbelievers who remained in the nest felt put off by the evil smelling survivors of the flood and insisted they remain outside until they dried off and no longer stank. The survivors milled around the entrance to the nest, as each wondered why God made life so difficult and unfair.

Skeets and Jesse discovered they could rotate their waists to redirect their streams with pinpoint accuracy. When their ammunition ran low and went dry, the area below showed Middle Eastern devastation. "Score: Gringos 675 – Ants 0." Hollowness rang in Jesse's laughter. "I guess we have a bigger problem though."

"I'd say so. Unless Redondo caters this event, our quality of life will go down pretty quick." Skeets tried the ropes again before he settled back.

"Any suggestions?"

"I'm a little short on ideas since my knife's still in my pants. And by the way, Redondo at this very moment, has our wallets, money, and, most important of all, my guitar." Skeets angrily tugged at the ropes again.

"Step One we need to get loose. Then we worry about Redondo and those things." Jesse joined in the escape attempt.

"Maybe we can rub the rope against the tree bark and wear it in two." Jesse moved his hands as far as possible to one side, grabbed a circle of the rope, and began to rub it against the tree. "It's not real easy. See if you can find the same rope I'm rubbing. Then we can take turns."

The full moon descended and Skeets' rubbing still ground into the silence of the night. "Hey, man, wake up. I'm toast here. Time to rubba-dub-dub. Jesse. Come to, bro, we've gotta keep rubbing."

Jesse's sleepy voice came from the other side of the tree. "Sorry, man, I guess I dozed off. Been a trying day. Get some sleep yourself." He grabbed the rope and started to scrape.

"Thanks to Ms. Beamer last night, I'm going on twenty-four hours without shut-eye." Skeets listened to the rubbing. It sounded aboriginal – eerie as it spread into the night. The moan it produced drew several curious animals near the clearing. Skeets heard them scurry around in the brush just out of sight. But the rhythmic sound soon put him to sleep.

About an hour into his watch, Jesse thought he heard voices. He stopped scraping— antennae up.

Two crouching figures crept into the clearing. They gasped when they saw Skeets who hung limp on the ropes, genitals arrayed. They grabbed each other and dropped to their knees while they whispered prayers. Then they rose to a half crouch, reached into the mesh *bolsas* they carried and drew out *machetes* that glistened in the moonlight. They still crouched as they moved toward the dead man on the mesquite tree.

Chapter 6

Alfonso and Beto had crossed the border the way other members of their family had for decades. Just west of Columbia, *El Rio Bravo* slowed in a wide shallow flanked on both banks by thickets of mesquite trees. On a moonless night they waded across with their bolsas on their head and followed a trail marked only by mesquite trees trampled to grow parallel to the ground.

Tonight moonlight bathed the two figures as they crept toward the dead man. A short distance from the tree the corpse hung on, one reached out to halt the other. They stood, watching for sounds of life. They saw none. Alfonso whispered, "*¿You think we could be blamed by the police for this terrible murder?*"

"*That's very possible.*" Beto nodded.

The two men turned to leave, still staring at Skeets, when a voice spoke as if from heaven. "*¿WHO ARE YOU AND WHAT DO YOU WANT?*" Jesse's voice projected dramatically.

"*¡Saint Mary, Mother of God!*" They released their *bolsas* and machetes, dropped to their trembling knees, and crossed themselves.

The voices woke Skeets, numb and stiff from hanging on the ropes, and a few seconds passed before he raised his head and saw the two penitents on the ground in front of him. "Hey, guys, glad you could come."

The dead man brought to life by God's voice paralyzed Alfonso, who fell forward prostrate, arms outstretched. This "*miracle*" provided a thunderbolt of inspiration to Beto, and he leaped up and almost ran out of his *huaraches*. He had seen enough miracles for one moonlit night.

"Jesse, you still there?" Skeets wiggled the ropes.

"Is that a rhetorical question?"

"Just checking, since I've been out of the loop, so to speak." Skeets wiggled and tried to get circulation going in his extremities again. "It seems we just ruined a couple a illegal aliens' evening."

"How's that?"

"One just fainted, and the other just set a new South Texas record in the scrub brush hurdles. There's good news, though." Skeets watched as the unconscious one stirred.

"This side of the tree could use a little good news."

"The unconscious one has a machete lying beside him."

"That's good news?"

"Absolutely. You just have to talk him into usin' it on these ropes and not on us."

Skeets and Jesse shuffled down the double-rutted ranch road in the bright moonlight. Alfonso, *muy simpatico* with their plight, seemed embarrassed by their nakedness. He gave each a pair of *huarache* sandals, a size too small, and a pair of briefs, several sizes too small, from the two *bolsas*.

Skeets and Jesse's privates, now acclimated to the great outdoors, complained in their new cramped quarters. Combine this with the *huarache* blister-machines on their feet, and it was slow going. Conversation provided their counterirritant for discomfort. "Where are they from?" Skeets asked as he tried to keep the conversation alive.

"Guanajuato, wherever that is." Jesse busily shoved a tree limb along the ground.

Alfonso had cautioned them about the rattlesnakes. "They come out at night and warm themselves in the ruts of roads." He said he recently stepped on one, which caused him acute bowel function but no lasting harm. Jesse used a machete and whacked off a bushy tree limb for the old Indian custom of pushing the limb along the ground in front of them as sure-fire rattlesnake repellant.

They found Beto at the road-fork where he and Alfonso needed to veer north toward economic opportunity. He looked at Skeets and Jesse in wide-eyed surprise and relief. He asked Alfonso, "¿*They're not ghosts?*"

Jesse said, "*Amigos, you saved our lives, and we're grateful.*"

"*It's no problem, señor.*" Both Alfonso and Beto held out their hands in a gesture of friendship.

Skeets told Jesse, "Tell them if we get our bikes back, we'll go to Guanajuato, return their clothes, and tell their family they're safe in Texas."

After the translation, handshakes went all round, and they parted company.

About an hour later as they dragged themselves through the dusty South Texas countryside, Skeets thought out loud, "If we have anything left, we should give those *hombres'* families a little something."

"First we have to get our bikes back." Jesse threw the rattlesnake wand away as the road in front of them became more visible at first light.

The rising sun bleached the moon, which still hung above the horizon, and Texas brush country came alive. Skeets wished he was less tired, less hungry, fully clothed, better shod, uncrotch-chafed, and still a Harley owner, so he could enjoy it. Dew formed during the night and hung in sparkling droplets on the prickly pear cactus thorns. Large yellow and orange blossoms trimmed each prickly pear pad and transformed a clump of the lowly cactus into a brilliant fiesta of color. White wing doves rested in the mesquite trees and rehearsed their cooing before they headed off to work. Ripe red berries festooned the agarita bushes, and tiny flycatchers flitted from branch to branch, feasting. A roadrunner with a hapless lizard in its beak burst from the brush onto the roadway and blasted away from them, evoking his roadrunner heritage.

Skeets drew in the heavy scent of the purple sage blooms. "Gena grew up down here. She told me it can be beautiful, but I found it hard to believe it." The guajillo bushes and cat's claw cactus still bloomed, and he saw honeybees work their magic as they harvested the nectar. "I swear, there's a song out here in all this outdoor thing."

"The only thing I see without fangs, thorns, claws or horns, is a rock." Jesse snorted his displeasure.

"I'm afraid our compromised condition has muzzled your muse." Skeets chuckled while he tired to raise Jesse's spirits. "You're right though. It'd be hard to get pickup trucks, trains, cheatin' love, whiskey, cigarettes, and prison time into a song about the great outdoors."

"Don't forget a verse about us buying gas for the guy who stole our bikes." Jesse stubbed his great toe that stuck out of its *huarache*. He hopped and cursed on the other foot for a couple of steps. The uproar startled a covey of blue quail, and they ran across the road. Their top notches gave them the look of plump Londoners in top hats chasing a double-decker.

They'd walked for a time in silence. Then Skeets stopped and held out his hand to halt Jesse. "Hear that? An eighteen-wheeler. We're getting' within sniffing distance of a highway."

"Wish I'd dressed for the occasion." Jesse gestured at their scant wardrobe. "What are the chances of Mom, Dad, and the kids picking up two flashers?"

The thought of rescue spread a soothing balm over Skeets' blistered feet and chafed crotch and quickened his pace. He heard the intermittent sound of traffic, and his hopes soared. Skeets and Jesse topped a small rise and saw their road "T" with a perimeter road that ran beside a high fence. Behind the fence they saw a four-lane divided highway. The sight of asphalt spurred them into a trot.

"Man, the closer we get to the fence, the higher it gets." Skeets strode up and stood by the fence, which dwarfed him.

"You didn't happen to bring wire cutters, did you?" Jesse felt the heft of the woven-wire, deer-proof fencing. "I can't believe any rancher could afford a fence like this."

Very few cars passed since they saw of the road. "Why isn't there more traffic on a great road like this one?" Skeets wondered aloud.

"This has to be the toll road Redondo talked about. Now if we can just get over this fence without leaving part of us behind." Jesse took an exploratory leap to no effect.

The two continued to walk south beside the fence and looked for a way over. About a half-mile later, they discovered a construction timber about twelve feet long beside the perimeter road. "They must've used this to build the concrete drainage culvert." Skeets pointed toward the structure.

"Man, finding something like this can make a guy believe in divine intervention." Jesse hoisted the timber upright, and the two tilted it over so the end rested on top of the fence. "Short of a couple of splinters, we can shinny up this pole to the Promised Land and not leave our balls behind."

Skeets went first and, except for a tricky maneuver at the top, dropped heavily on the other side of the fence without incident. With no one to steady the pole, Jesse's ascent was more treacherous, but shortly he joined Skeets on the business side of the fence, and they continued on south while thumbing a ride. As predicted, motorists shunned the two dirty, half-dressed hitchhikers like they were Amish whores.

The sun beat down as they walked beside the highway. They came to the only tree on their side of the fence and took advantage of its shade for a brainstorming session. Skeets pulled a stem of buffel grass and chewed it for a second. "I swear to God from now on I'll pick up every hitchhiker I ever see, even if they're bare ass naked and carrying an axe."

"You'd think one of these bastards would've used his cell phone to report two semi-naked crazies on the road, and the sheriff would be here by now." Jesse sailed a rock across the road in disgust.

"Maybe if we mooned a few cars they'd report us, and we'd get picked up by the constabulary for indecent exposure." Skeets adjusted his hat down over his eyes and leaned back against the tree. After a pause he added, "Truthfully, we'd best consider if we're even goin' in the right direction."

"It's a pretty sure bet the bastard took our bikes to Mexico." Jesse pointed south.

"Mexico's a big country. What makes you think we could find them even if we made it across the border?" Skeets paused a moment. "Forget pants and shoes, we don't even have enough money for a pay phone, and I doubt our sad story will mobilize the *policia* into action. We should just admit our bikes are gone and try to go back to Austin and get on with our lives. Christ, I'll even have to borrow a guitar."

Jesse sailed another rock into space. "I'd truly love just one good crack at that miserable son-of-a-bitch, Redondo, though."

"Likewise, but I guess this is why people buy insurance."

"Yeah, I guess so."

The two got quiet while they considered their options. A distant rumbling growl bored into their consciousness. They looked at each other and then back toward the distant ridge to the north and saw an eighteen-wheeler plow through the horizon and start down the gentle slope toward them. Even at a distance they could make out the face of an angry wolf. They jumped up and ran to the roadside leaping and flailing their arms and legs like style-challenged madmen.

Black smoke billowed from the twin exhaust pipes that protruded like devil's horns from the wolf's head when El Lobo downshifted to slow his truck. Gradually he applied the brakes, and the black beast slowed, rattling off engine backfires like a Gatling gun. Growling, it came to a shuddering stop filled with moans and hisses fifty yards past Skeets and Jesse. The Wolf Wagon panted on the roadside as they reached the tractor door. Skeets opened the door, and a voice with the timbre of a bear at the bottom of a well greeted them. "You boys doing a little jogging, or just workin' on your tan?"

"Mister, we got more problems than a soap opera." Skeets stepped up on the running board to see El Lobo better.

"I can see that. You better hop in and tell me about it." A smile like a watermelon slice broke under his mustache.

Once inside, the Wolf Wagon crept forward with a growl as El Lobo wound up through the gears. "I saw you two talkin' to Redondo in the Burros Locos yesterday."

"You know Redondo?" Jesse leaned forward to see El Lobo's reaction.

"Only by reputation. He's one of the worst 'coyotes' on the border." He finally shifted into his running gear, and the Wolf Wagon lurched forward.

"'Coyote'?" Skeets' forehead twisted into a question mark.

"Coyotes smuggle illegal aliens into this country. The poor bastards save their money for months, even years, and give it to Coyotes to bring them into the U.S. The worst smugglers take the money and just dump the guys out in the desert. Folks around here think Redondo's the coyote that left those thirty people to suffocate to death over by Del Rio. He unhooked the trailer and abandoned them when he thought a patrol plane spotted him. He's a bad *hombre*."

"Tell us about it." Jesse slumped back in the seat in resignation.

After proper introductions, Skeets and Jesse delighted El Lobo with their 'Really Big Adventure' with Redondo.

El Lobo quit laughing and frowned. "I don't know how you guys survived. He must have liked you, or else you'd a had a bullet in your head and been dinner for the real coyotes last night." He grinned at the two and added, "I guess he got your bikes into Mexico for you, though."

"But now we have to find them, right?" Jesse's voice held little hope as he turned to watch Southwest Texas blur past the truck window.

"Look, I dropped off a load in Laredo last night and picked up one for Mexico City this morning." El Lobo explained. "I use the Columbia Bridge for the same reason as Redondo. These folks are more hospitable, so I can get you into Mexico if you want to go."

"I'm just not sure what we do after that." Skeet's sounded doubtful.

"There's a cathouse and cantina on this side of Anahuac about forty miles inside the border. I've stopped there a few times for a little R&R. Redondo's been there a couple of times and acted like he owned the place. So I asked somebody. They said he does. It's probably where he collects his customers before he heads for the border. I'm going by on my way to Mexico City."

"If you drop us off, we'd like to open up a can of 'whip-ass' and pour it all over him." Jesse's voice crackled with the excitement of revenge.

"We'd be happy to pay you if we had any money," Skeets added.

El Lobo laughed. "I can drop you off all right, but I'll warn you, the place crawls with coyotes and drug dealers, and they all pack *pistolas.*"

"We hope we can have a shot at getting' our bikes back."

"I'll give it to you, boys. You've got guts to go up against this guy and his *amigos.*" El Lobo shook his head in wonderment. "If you want to go through with this, here's the plan."

El Lobo lent them blue jeans and money, and let them out after they crossed the bridge. They bought shoes in a small shoe store on the main street of the dusty little town while El Lobo cleared his load through customs. Late in the afternoon they reconnected and headed south again.

As they rode along, Skeets looked around the truck cab at the unusual amount of communications equipment Lobo had on board. Two CB Band transmitters, a short wave transmitter, a satellite phone, cell phone, a radar Fuzzbuster, and something called a satellite transponder gave the dashboard the look of an airliner cockpit. "Man, I'm not sure Air Force One has all this radio stuff."

"I've got a ham radio setup at home, and I talk to my old lady at night. Down here in Mexico things can get pretty dicey. It's always good to know what's up ahead and to be in touch with what's happening around the country." Lobo pointed ahead. "We'll come to the customs and immigration check point about eighteen miles from here, so you'll need to hide in the sleeper cab until we're past there. If there's a line of trucks, it might take awhile, so be patient -- and be quiet."

"They won't search the sleeper cab?" Skeets opened the sleeper door and looked inside.

"People and drugs don't get smuggled *into* Mexico. If you hand me those two cases of beer, I'll put them on the passenger seat and they'll 'confiscate' them." Lobo pointed in the direction of the beer.

Skeets climbed back into the sleeper and handed Jesse the two cases of Lone Star beer. Jesse placed them on the passenger seat and joined Skeets.

They'd bounced along without speaking for a time in the darkness of the shuttered sleeping cab, when Skeets said, "Have you noticed we've spent a lot of time in dark places as our lives spin out of control?"

"If you mean do I hate to be locked up in a black hole and to wonder what will happen next, the answer's yes." Jesse shifted around and tried to get his legs comfortable.

They felt the Wolf Wagon begin to growl and hiss as it decelerated and slowed to a stop. They heard only the low growl and vibration of the idling engine. Nothing. More nothing. Skeets' whisper hissed across the darkness. "What the hell's going on?"

"He told us to be patient."

The door to the sleeping cab opened a crack and Lobo's voice rumbled in. "I also told you to be quiet. There're four trucks ahead of us. It'll be a while." The door closed again and locked.

"Shit, we're locked in again." Skeets voice echoed a hint of claustrophobia.

"There's just something about being locked up that makes me crazy."

"I guess there's a little good news this time."

"I have trouble with the 'good news' part." Jesse sounded a little shaken.

"Look at it this way. It can't be much worse than the last time."

The two fell silent, and the darkness, low rumble and gentle vibration soon lulled the sleep-deprived adventurers into restless sleep.

The door opened and Lobo's voice rumbled in again. "Welcome to Mexico, amigos."

The two stirred, and Jesse replied, "We've heard that one before."

Lobo pulled the door to the sleeper full open and switched on the overhead light. "You'd best be puttin' yourselves together, 'cause Redondo's cantina's right up there."

Chapter 7

El Lobo sat in the cab of the truck and reconnoitered the parking lot and exterior of Redondo's Cantina, as the Wolf Wagon growled its unrest. He turned to Skeets and Jesse. "Put a couple of concrete burros with sombreros in front, and it could be the Burros Locos Cantina back in Texas." Open fields surrounded it on three sides, and a cheap motel-like structure attached to the rear of the cantina.

"He runs a motel too?" Skeets pointed to the building behind the cantina.

"That's where the whores live and work. Most of them try to work their way across the border on one of Redondo's trucks. By the time he takes out their room and board, they'll need a walkin' cane to make the trip." El Lobo shook his head at the injustice.

Occasionally a pickup truck pulled into the parking lot, but few left. Business was good, judging by the number of SUV's and pickups in the lot. "These guys don't drive junkers." Jesse pointed around the lot at all the late model vehicles. "They didn't get these rides working in the fields."

"Smuggling's very profitable." Lobo nodded agreement. "Most are stolen out of Texas, and I'd bet half of those trucks have an automatic weapon hidden in them."

"So you say we've brought our fists to a gun fight, right?" Jesse's face glowed with frustration at being outgunned. "God, I'd like to serve up a bunch of shit soup to that bastard."

Skeets elbowed Jesse and pointed. "Look over there."

"Where?"

"At the far side of the parking lot. That's Redondo's truck parked beside that livestock pen." Skeets pointed again at the white, bobtail Ford truck barely visible through the slats of a livestock trailer parked beside it.

"Let's go see if our bikes are still in it." Jesse opened the door and jumped to the ground before anyone could respond.

"Easy, amigo, we better have a plan." El Lobo's voice carried the authority of a drill instructor.

"Any suggestions?" Skeets stopped before he followed Jesse out of the cab.

"That truck's locked for sure. I've got a bolt cutter in my toolbox behind the cab. One of you should put on a poncho for disguise, sneak over with the bolt cutter, and check out the truck." They nodded agreement on the plan and followed Lobo to the rear of the cab. He held out the cutter and poncho asking for a volunteer.

Jesse grabbed the poncho. "I look more authentic in one of these." He hid the bolt cutter under the poncho and headed across the road and into the parking lot. His cowboy hat and poncho made him every bit the *campesino*, so he didn't need to skulk around. He strolled up to Redondo's truck as if he'd made the last twenty-four payments on it and tried the driver-side door. When he found the door locked, he reached under the poncho apparently digging for the keys. Instead he pulled out the bolt cutter, bashed in the driver's window, reached inside, and unlocked the door.

Skeets and Lobo stood beside the grumbling Wolf Wagon and watched Jesse. "Jesus Christ, the guy's crazy" Lobo dropped down behind his truck in a reflex action.

Skeets leaned on the truck fender watching the drama unfold. "No, but I think he's pretty pissed off." After he pulled their purloined boots, jeans and skivvies from the cab, Jesse waved them at Skeets and Lobo like the flag raising on Iwo Jima. He rolled the boots and skivvies in the jeans and set them on the driver's seat. Then, with the bolt cutter, he moved around the truck, and whacked off the valve stems from each tire. It caused a great rush of air with the sound level of an elephant farting in the "Cave of Winds." Jesse ran to the rear truck door and attacked the padlock with the bolt cutter. The crack of the broken lock shank sounded like a rifle shot even over the Wolf Wagon's growl. He rolled up the rear door and leaped like a man possessed. On the second try, he disappeared into the truck, and Skeets and Lobo ran to help.

Nobody saw Jesse's assault on the truck, so Skeets and Lobo arrived unnoticed. When they reached the truck door, Jesse had untied his bike and struggled with the spider web of rope Skeets had used to lash his bike to the truck. "Man, I told you your bike looked like a cocoon with all this rope. Get up in here and help unravel this mess." Lobo unlatched the loading ramp and slid it from under the truck body. A loud squeal and grunt startled them. The three whirled around and saw, for the first time, the two hogs in the cattle pen next to the parking lot. A big tusker boar and a younger but still impressive sow eyed the three with the look a hog gets when it knows the difference between a hog and bacon.

They worked together and rolled the bikes, one by one, down the ramp. To start the Harleys would stretch their luck so Skeets and Jesse pushed them toward the Wolf Wagon. Lobo carried their clothes and Skeets' guitar.

When they reached the road, the headlights of an approaching truck caught them, and the pickup slowed like it might turn into the parking lot. Skeets and Jesse threw their legs over the bikes as if to start them, and the truck, which must have slowed to look at the Harleys, sped up again and continued down the highway. Once on the other side of the highway, they parked the bikes out of sight behind the Wolf Wagon and changed out of Lobo's jeans into their own.

Skeets felt his pocket. "Hey, man, my wallet's still here."

"Mine too," Jesse shouted.

They turned to Lobo and almost said in unison, "We can pay you back the money you loaned us."

El Lobo had gone to the truck cab and brought back a clipboard on which he wrote while they finished dressing. "Keep it, amigos. I think you'll need it more than me. Judging by your luck up to this point, you might need more help down the line also." He handed Skeets a sheet of paper with a bunch of numbers on it. "Keep my phone numbers, my CB call numbers, and my short-wave band frequency and call numbers at the ready. I like you guys, so if you need help, contact me, and maybe we'll have more fun. Us Gringos got to stick together, right?"

Skeets and Jesse looked at each other with the same question. How could they ever pay back this guy for his help? Finally, Skeets blurted, "Not all our luck's bad. Those two hombres helped us get loose, and then we met you."

Jesse reached out for Lobo's hand. "Amigo, we can't thank you enough for your help. But if you're ever in Austin, we'll give you the keys to the city, and I guarantee we'll have a bunch more fun." Jesse pulled Lobo toward him into an *abrazo*.

"Any idea where you're headed?" Lobo asked.

Skeets shook hands with Lobo. "To Guanajuato."

"Why Guanajuato?" Lobo raised his eyebrows.

"We have to return the clothes our other two amigos loaned us and tell their families they're in the U.S. and fine."

"Lot of guys would just forget about that promise and go about their business. You're makin' good on your word. I like that." Lobo nodded approval. "I'd get on those bikes and get as far as you can from here. Keep your bikes hidden when you're not riding, cause Redondo will come after you without a doubt."

Skeets and Jesse followed Lobo to the cab. Jesse shuffled his feet. "I love your truck, man, but it's sure enough different."

Lobo smiled from the cab window. "Customizing's a hobby of mine. But the Wolf comes in handy down here cause there's lots of superstitious folks. Even bad guys are afraid of the Wolf, and most leave it alone. It's a mean-looking bastard, ain't it?" The Wolf Wagon roared its agreement and growled onto the highway.

Skeets strapped his guitar to his bike, swung his leg over, and settled into the seat. Jesse still stood beside his bike and kicked at the ground with his boot. "Man, we can't just ride off into the sunset and not leave that Redondo bastard something to remember us by."

"Since we don't have explosives, what do you suggest?" Skeets crossed his arms and expected the worst.

"I look at it this way. We took two hogs out of the truck, so we should put two hogs back into his truck. It's only fair, right?" Jesse looked for agreement from Skeets.

"I don't know how 'fair' it is, but it could be mighty stupid if the bad guys show up during our hog roundup." Skeets looked disgusted. "I think we should ride like the wind and put distance between us and another brush with death."

"Ah, come on, man. How hard can it be? We just run those hogs up the loading ramp and pull the door down, and that's it. Think about the look on Redondo's face when he rolls up the door, and stares those hogs in the eyes. I would almost hide in the bushes and watch, just to see the look on his face." Jesse already laughed at the thought.

"You know this idea ranks right up there with buying gas for the guy who stole our bikes, right? I'm not too sure how many of your adventures I can survive." Skeets knew the hog pen was the only way he could get Jesse to budge.

They started the bikes, idled into the parking lot, and parked them out of sight of the cantina front door. At the pen they looked at the two semi-unfriendly hogs. "I think all the rope you used on your bike will come in handy." Jesse crawled into the truck to get the rope.

"So what's the big plan?" Skeets still looked at the hogs staring from across the pen.

"We'll just drop a noose around their necks and lead them up the ramp. Right?" Jesse made a lariat out of the rope. "You keep them distracted, and I'll go around the pen and lasso the sow first."

"I think I'm lookin' at two hogs here who won't completely understand nor agree with our plan. They don't seem to be leash-trained." Skeets continued to look at the hogs.

The door of the cantina opened, and two *borrachos* staggered out leaning on each other, and laughed so hard they doubled over slapping their thighs until a cigarette coughing spell forced them to sit on the cantina steps to catch their breath. Once under control, they both lit cigarettes and sat woozily and gazed at nothing in particular.

When they realized the drunks could not see them, Jesse and Skeets returned to their pig rodeo. Each time Jesse approached, the hogs moved away. Finally, in desperation, he opened the gate to the pen and moved slowly toward the sow, and then did his best imitation of a calf roper. More by accident than by skill the lasso caught the sow around the neck, but when Jesse tightened the noose, the indignant sow made a break for the gate. The force of her charge almost jerked Jesse to the ground, but he recovered enough to run after the sow until he reached the parking lot gravel. When he set the heels of his muddy cowboy boots to stop the porcine missile, he found himself gravel-skiing through the parking lot behind the porker.

After a tryst with his favorite employee, Redondo felt magnanimous on his return to his cantina. He passed the cantina's tequila freely to his *amigos* and never allowed anyone to drink alone. During dinner and the following card game, he talked endlessly about the two *Gringo idiotas,* and how he'd stolen their two Harleys. The tequila had worked its magic on both Redondo and his friends, and they all registered about three degrees above belligerent.

One of his *amigos* said, "*Cabrón, you keep talking about Harleys, but we ain't seen no Harleys.*" Others chimed in and all accused Redondo of stretching the truth.

Meanwhile, back at the corral, Skeets thought he should close the gate before the boar escaped and turned just in time to evade the full brunt of "ol' Tusky's" charge by leaping straight up spread-eagle while the boar charged between his legs and knocked Skeets off balance. He fell forward caught the hog with a leg-lock around the throat and dropped belly-down on the hog's back. Out of sheer terror he grabbed the hog's tail, and found he was backward bare backing his way across the parking lot atop a boar hog trying for the world speed record.

Inside the cantina Redondo tried to stand. Failing, he addressed his entourage from his chair. "*You pinches think I'm lying? I'll show you lying. I'll show you fucking Harleys, cabrónes.*" He tried again to stand.

One of his amigos tossed back a tequila shot. "*We ain't seen no Harley hogs, man.*"

Redondo finally made it to his feet and stood weaving. "*I'll show you Harley hogs, amigos.*"

Jesse's sow turned toward the cantina at the end of the trucks and SUVs, and he desperately held the rope to keep from sling-shoting off the end. She hung a right between the front row of vehicles and the two drunks, who watched the sow fly past with gravel-skiing Jesse behind. They glanced at each other to see if the other just saw what he just saw. Tusky had taken the road less traveled and reached the other side of the parking lot and hung a left in front of the cantina from the other direction. The drunks watched the hog and backward bareback rider with equal interest. Each took a long pull on his cigarette and then glanced at the other's reaction to recent events. They nodded at each other, and one said, *"Es un gran pig rodeo."*

The pig rodeo sow had completed a circuit around the parking lot with Jesse skiing behind, when she remembered better times back in the livestock pen and made straight for the stockade. Slowed by exhaustion and befuddled by not finding the gate, Jesse seized the occasion and threw a loop of rope behind her back legs and another around her neck. Then he dragged her up the loading ramp into the truck and rolled down the door.

Skeets' luck dwindled, as the boar's tail was too difficult to hold. He grabbed the only other protuberance available before he fell off of the hog—the boar's bulbous balls. This produced an immediate attitude adjustment in the hog. His first attempt to dislodge the ball-napper produced a level of pain that slowed him to a confused, grunting halt in close proximity to Redondo's truck. Jesse, returned from his ski trip, ran over and slipped a noose around the boar's head. Skeets dismounted but did not give up his ball-grip advantage. They administered a Pavlovian training exercise. A step forward by Tusky reduced the pain in the rear, and before long the porker loaded, and by the look of relief on the hog's face, not a moment too soon.

They slammed the door down, closed the latch, and both turned to lean and rest against the truck. Skeets spoke first. "We'll just drop a noose around their neck and lead them up the ramp,' right?"

"What do I know about hogs, man? I mean, those bastards got attitudes." Jesse pulled his Harley-Davidson bandana out of his back pocket and wiped his hands and face.

"So does this mean I have veto power over your next big idea?" Skeets looked at Jesse, who chose not to answer the rhetorical question. Together they shoved the loading ramp back into its place under the truck.

"Now can we get out of here?" Skeets said over his shoulder as he walked to the bikes.

Redondo got his balance and staggered toward the front door. The others made their way as best they could behind him. After he kicked two drunks off the steps who kept asking when the pig rodeo would start again, he staggered toward his truck. He had trouble focusing, but it looked like the truck had flat tires. He stopped and held his hand up to the followers, then listened to strange sounds from inside the truck.

Tusky the boar hog had recently suffered a series of setbacks that made him wonder from where all his bad luck had come. He had for all his years been the best at avoiding becoming bacon. Hogs came, and hogs went, but Tusky had outsmarted the system. He learned early when any hog went up the ramp into one of those rolling boxes it never came back. He decided to supply the big demand for ramp volunteers, and he took it upon himself to provide as many new pigs as possible. The word around porkdom, even among other boars, was don't stand still too long, or ol' Tusky will top you and bang away with no invitation at all. In addition to the fringe benefit of longevity, Tusky enjoyed his work to the point he never applied for job enrichment training.

The problems started when all of those pretty young sows he had enjoyed took to the ramp and left only this one sow that Tusky found particularly unattractive. Middle aged and willing enough, the sow still did not interest Tusky. He waited for new sows to appear, but instead he found himself rudely herded into a pen with the ugly sow. Now she followed him around all day talking dirty.

The indignity of a two-legger on his back while he frantically struggled to unload the burden was bad. But having his balls squeezed by an unseen force was too much for any hog to bear. Now he found himself inside the dreaded rolling box, in pitch darkness, with the ugly sow talking dirty again. He swore to whoever up there that caused life to be more difficult than necessary; given the chance, he would exercise extreme diligence to right the wrongs that found him in his current condition.

Redondo paused for a moment at the back door of the truck while his *amigos* gathered around him for the great unveiling. He thought he had padlocked the latch on the back door, but he shrugged it off before he unlatched and rolled up the door. Two hogs of determined countenance and bristled necks stared at the group. Redondo shook his head in disbelief and mumbled, "*Milagro.*"

This *hombre* answered Tusky's prayers, and, true to his vow, he lunged forward in full flight and buried his tusk in Redondo's forehead.

Chapter 8

Skeets took the lead as he and Jesse blasted south, away from Redondo's Cantina. The dark, narrow back road flashed through his headlight at a terrifying speed to any sane person. Visions of Redondo in hot pursuit spurred them into the night hoping to outrun bad luck this time.

Skeets felt wild and alive. The cool night air mingled with smells of plowed earth and newly mown hay. His nerves tingled with excitement from recovering their Harleys, coupled with the sound of rolling thunder between his legs. It excited him like the first time he made love to Gena. He shook his head. God, how he'd screwed up the best thing he ever had.

He signaled for Jesse to pull over when the lights of Anahuac came into view. "I don't suppose you brought a Mexican road map?"

Jesse smiled and shook his head. "Do I look like a geography teacher?"

"Should we just keep headin' south?" Skeets gestured down the road.

"Let's ditch Redondo. Go another direction."

"Which direction?" Skeets shrugged.

"Turn on the first highway you see."

Skeets looked for a highway, any highway, as Anahuac materialized from the darkness on each side of the road. Ahead, a road sign announced Highway 22 to the town of Don Martin and underneath the words *"Presa de Don Martin."* He signaled a right turn, swung the corner, and missed a pushcart vendor by inches. The vendor stopped to shake an angry fist at the motorcycle and then had to dive for safety as the second devil machine roared past him. Skeets watched the angry man in the rearview mirror as he stood up and shook his fist while he put his sombrero back on.

Night closed in again as the lights of Anahuac faded behind them. Skeets followed the hole his headlight stabbed into the blackness and fought back his gnawing anxiety. He had no idea where to go or how to get there, and the fear of Redondo painted everything behind him. Only Jesse stood between him and total isolation.

The tiny village of El Quarenta appeared on their left, too small to have a PEMEX gasoline station. Skeets signaled to keep going as he hoped for a bigger town. Half an hour later the lights of the small town of Don Martin beckoned them. Skeets looked at his watch and waved to pull into the local PEMEX. As they filled their tanks, Jesse asked the teenage attendant about a place to eat.

The attendant pointed down the road. *"There's a cantina just past the dam with really good fish."*

"There must be a lake here, because he says a cantina just past a dam cooks good fish." Jesse pulled the gas nozzle from his tank and screwed the cap back on.

"What about a place to stay?"

"The story of two Harleys parked outside a dingy motel in Don Martin might make it all the way back to Redondo's before morning." Jesse yawned and stretched. "I tell you what, though. We may have gas for the bikes, but I'm running low on energy after these truly adventuresome two days."

Chapter 9

The Sabinas toll booth attendant pointed to the sign posting the price of admission to the four-lane *cuota* toll road to Monclova. Skeets shouted over the motorcycle engine, "You've kidding, right. That's twenty bucks U.S. for two motorcycles." The attendant shrugged. Skeets dropped his kickstand and walked back to Jesse. "Twenty bucks is a lot of money."

Jesse looked at the road map. "We could take the free road, but who knows what that's like."

"Screw these guys. Let's save the money." Skeets got on his bike, pushed back out of the toll both, and the two rode off to find the free road. Sabinas was their first Mexican town of any size. Stop-and-go traffic and exhaust fumes engulfed them along with a cacophony of horns, burros braying, boom boxes, Mexican *conjunto* music, and playful children screaming. Pedestrians jaywalked at the slightest whim. Twice Skeets had to skid to a stop to miss children that darted in and out of traffic. He raised his helmet visor at a traffic light. "I can't see any street signs. Not that they would help, 'cause I've got no idea where we're going."

"Not to worry, bro. I'll ask the locals where the highway is." Jesse moved ahead and half a block further pulled to a stop where two girls stood in the street and apparently waited for a ride. One taller than the other, but from what Skeets could see, they both were classic Mexican beauties with sepia skin, round eyes and finely chiseled features. They wore blue jeans and peasant blouses, and the taller girl had well-groomed black hair, which cascaded almost to her waist. He could hear only bits of their Spanish conversation. The two girls erupted into embarrassed laughter and surprised him when they shook their fingers at Jesse like had said something naughty.

He heard them say, "*No. No. señor,*" as they held their hands to their faces and again laughed aloud. He saw Jesse motion them to get on his Harley; and heard more flustered laughter. Jesse reached back, patted the seat behind him, and then held out his hand to the closer girl. She resisted for a moment then leaped on the bike like a seasoned Harley babe. The shorter girl trotted back to Skeets' bike to climb aboard but stopped when she saw his guitar had beaten her to the second seat.

"*There is a problem, señor,*" she said, laughing and pointing to the guitar.

Skeets reached around, unstrapped the guitar, and helped her aboard. The pretty girl, about eighteen or nineteen years old, had shoulder length hair. She had a ready smile of brilliant white teeth, and he nodded his approval and thought Jesse had good taste in guides. Then he shook his head and purged thoughts that would compromise the soul-cleansing essence of his pilgrimage. "Here hold this." He handed the guitar to the girl and accelerated away to catch Jesse about a block down the street.

Skeets noticed an old red pickup truck in his rearview mirror racing after them. He caught up with Jesse who apparently enjoyed the directions communicated by his rider. The pickup truck gained on them and almost rammed Skeets, but instead swerved into the other lane and pulled alongside. Inside the three agitated boys, about the age of the girls hollered and made threatening gestures. One hung out the window and grabbed at the girl on Skeets' bike. The girl made rude gestures at the three pickup guys and pounded Skeets on the back shouting, "¡*Vámonos, hombre!*"

The pickup now tried to crowd Skeets off the road. "Holy shit." he shouted and rolled on the throttle. The bike shot forward between the truck and Jesse's bike and startled Jesse as Skeets roared past pointing back at the pickup. Jesse pulled next to Skeets, and they ripped through cross streets, dodging traffic at the intersections. The girls squealed with glee and flicked off the boys in the red pickup as they receded behind them.

Skeets' girl signaled him to turn right after a curve in the road hid them from the pickup, but the bike slid in the dirt on the pavement when he leaned for the sudden turn. They both screamed, and he released the throttle and the brakes and straightened the front wheel. The bike righted itself just in time for Skeets to see a *topes* speed bump. No time to brake, so he rolled on the gas. The bike vaulted into the air and soared a full bike length before landing. He struggled to regain control after an almost calamitous fishtailing crash-landing.

Jesse had learned from Skeets' near miss and slowed for the turn without leaning the bike as radically, but he slowed too much to jump the speed bump. His kickstand crashed on the bump and knocked the retainer spring loose. The kickstand dragged on the pavement like a broken leg. He couldn't steer the bike with the stand down, so he slowed and searched for a place to stop. He looked around hoping to see no red truck full of angry Mexicans. "Shit. Man, this sucks." He tried to signal, but Skeets disappeared around the next corner and failed to see Jesse stop.

"*My uncle has an automobile repair garage in the next block.*" The girl pointed past the next intersection

"Now I call this divine intervention." Jesse rode as fast as he dared and held the stand up with his heel, to what he hoped was a safe harbor for repairs. Before he turned into the driveway, he let the girl off and pushed the bike into a backyard crowded with several cars in various states of disrepair.

A balding, portly man came out to greet them who wore the confused expression of a man needing business, but shocked to see his niece cavorting with a gringo on a motorcycle.

"¿Maria, what are doing on that motorcycle?"

Maria ran to hug her uncle. Jesse stood by the bike with his best smile on while the girl tried to explain how these two gringos offered her friend, Lola, and her a ride home while they showed the *Norteños* the highway out of town. Jesse smiled through all the accusations and recriminations. The man finally approached him and looked as if he desperately wanted to slap the shit out of Jesse. Instead, he asked in passable English, "What's your problem, señor?"

Jesse said, "Listen, I didn't mean to get Maria in trouble."

The indignant man held up his hand to stop Jesse. "What is the problem with your motorcycle?"

Before Jesse could answer, the roar of a Harley, a girl squealing, horn honking, and boys shouting zoomed past the front of the shop. Jesse feigned disinterest, but the man turned and wondered about the disturbance. "*Señor?*" Jesse tried to return the man's attention to the problem at hand. "*Señor, if I can borrow a pair of pliers, I'll fix my kickstand.*" Jesse pointed with his boot to the offending stand.

Maria's uncle stooped to review the problem, then stood to shout at one of his mechanics, but the sound of a Harley, a girl's excited squealing, more horn honking and boys shouting speeding past from the other direction drowned him out *"¿What the hell is happening out there?"* He moved toward the driveway to find out, but Maria grabbed his arm and reminded him of the problem at hand.

Meanwhile, Jesse had borrowed the pliers from the mechanic and scooted under the bike to replace the spring. *"Señor, would you mind holding the bike vertical?"* The uncle reluctantly returned to the bike and pushed it upright so Jesse could raise the stand and replace the kickstand spring. Once again, the uproar passed down the street. The uncle fidgeted and wanted to see the commotion but instead held fast to Jesse's bike. He gave a stern look at Maria, who shrugged. *"I don't know what's happening, Uncle."*

Jesse stood and returned the bike to the kickstand and pulled out his wallet chained to his belt. *"¿How much, señor?"*

"Nothing, nothing." The uncle waved off Jesse's offer to pay and craned his neck to see down the driveway. He turned to tell Maria something, but she had leaped onto Jesse's motorcycle.

"Gracias, amigo." Jesse started the engine, executed a tight-radius U-turn, and accelerated out of the driveway.

The uncle shook his fist and shouted, *"Alto.* Stop. Bring back my niece, you gringo piece of shit."

As Jesse cleared out into the street, he saw Skeets approach from the other direction but no red pickup. Jesse made a U-turn and slowed for Skeets to catch up.

The two stopped at the intersection to the highway, and Skeets raised his helmet visor. "Jesus Christ, man, where you been? I thought I'd never lose those assholes in the truck. I think they ran out of gas, or they'd still be stuck on my ass."

"Broke my kickstand on a speed bump and had to fix it." Jesse pointed back in the direction of a heavyset, balding man running toward them.

"Hurry, hombre." Maria pointed in the direction out of town.

Jesse took the lead again, and they blasted out on the highway with the two girls waving and shouting at each other.

They were about to leave Sabinas, and Jesse wondered what to do with the girls, when Maria tapped him on the shoulder and pointed to a colonial style building with an enclosed parking lot. The sign announced, *"Hacienda Norteños-Comidas Especiales.* They parked the bikes out of sight behind the *Hacienda,* went inside, and took a round table toward the back of the restaurant. Local lunch customers were scattered around the dining room.

Skeets leaned his guitar against the table and held a chair out for his passenger, a courtesy she appreciated. He took a chair an arm's length away, and she slid her chair next to him. The motorcycle ride must have vibrated her into frenzy, as she couldn't keep her hands off him. He looked at the girl, then at Jesse. "Why didn´t you just ask a policeman how to get out of town?"

"Down here, man, you gotta make split-second decisions. Besides, you've made a real friend out of Lola." Jesse pointed to the girl plastered to Skeets.

"Lola?"

"Oh, you've not been introduced to our guides. *"Maria and Lola, this is my friend Skeets.* Skeets, meet Maria and Lola." Jesse made grand gestures with the introduction, and the self-conscious girls twittered.

"Who the hell were those guys in the red pickup?" Skeets asked somewhat irritated.

Jesse, the interpreter, posed the question to Maria and Lola and, after several minutes, gave the answer. "Two of the guys are idiots who think they're Maria´s and Lola´s boyfriends, but the girls can't stand them. The other guy's Lola's brother."

"Oh, that's great. That's just great. We have two jealous lovers and a brother after us for abducting these girls?"

"And an uncle." Jesse winced.

"An uncle?"

"I fixed my bike at Maria's uncle's garage." Jesse pointed to Maria, who got up with Lola to go to the restroom.

"So we've abducted two Mexican girls, we have at least four angry Mexicans chasing us, not to mention wonderful Redondo, after half a day we're only thirty miles closer to Alfonso and Beto's place in Guanajuato, and we sit here like King Shit without a worry in the world. Is that about it?"

The waiter brought the four Margaritas they had ordered. Jesse grabbed one. "A margarita will help our attitude."

"We need to get our asses out of here while we still can. Christ, Jesse, we can still throw a rock and hit Texas. Besides, I'm not supposed to chase pussy down here. I'm should be cleansing my soul. Remember? 'Sin seared from our souls by desert sun.'"

"Man, we've been on the road a long time, and I'm horny as a Mexican traffic jam."

"Jesse, we've been on the road for two and a half days."

"That's a long time, man." Jesse picked up his Margarita and drained it.

Skeets followed suit, gulping his down out of frustration. He glanced out the window as he sat the glass down. "Jesus H. Christ." He pointed out the window at a red pickup followed by two other pickups with young Mexican men stacked in them like cord wood that stopped in front of the Hacienda. He pulled out his wallet and left a twenty-dollar bill on the table, grabbed his guitar, kissed Lola on the cheek, and headed for the back door. Jesse leaped up and trotted behind.

They belted out from behind the building on their bikes, and executed sliding turns onto the highway and headed south at full throttle. Skeets could see three pickups full of angry Mexicans waving their fists in his rearview mirror as they pulled out from the hacienda.

Chapter 10

Skeets' felt the grizzly grin of death on his face as he and Jesse screamed down the free road center stripe out of Sabinas to Monclova. The slow traffic, mostly trucks, which teetered from overload, flashed past on both sides – often at the same time – as they three-laned the road. They crouched, racer style, below the potential guillotine of truck rearview mirrors. Sanity returned as their adrenalin ebbed. The panic gone, Skeets felt they had outrun their militia of Mexican antagonists, and he dropped back into the right hand traffic lane.

He soon realized the scale of the mistake they had made when they took the free road. Only the sleek, big-company eighteen-wheelers and late model cars could afford the toll road, shunting all the junkers to this narrow, crooked two-lane road. These old trucks trundled along at thirty to fifty miles per hour depending on the slope of the road. Progress was slow even in desert straight-aways where both he and Jesse passed slower vehicles with little difficulty. When road curves and oncoming traffic held them behind the ancient trucks, the exhaust fumes stifled them.

They found the speed bumps in this no man's land even more maddening. They stretched across the highway and brought traffic to a stop. As vehicles crept over the speed bumps, vendors of everything from Chicklets to *chicharrones* to rattlesnake skins assaulted them. In desperation, Skeets passed on the road's shoulder when trucks slowed for speed bumps. Small towns preferred an array of *topes* rather than speed limit signs. Skeets, Jesse, and everybody else halted every block to crawl over the bumps. They felt a spiritual pull every time a speed bump aligned with the door of a bar or cantina, so he often stopped and honored the urge with a shot of tequila.

They fought their way around trucks grinding their way up the foothills and the Sierra Gloria Mountains until they saw Monclova. The city sat high on a mountain, its huge foundries belched the bad breath of steel making. Later, in the fringe of the city about dusk, a speed bump alignment occurred at Cantina Vista perched on the edge of the mountain. Kitchen aromas closed the deal, and they pulled into the parking lot.

"Man, those breakfast tacos have limited out." Skeets placated his stomach with a couple of pats. He turned, stretched his back, and saw the sun closing down for the night behind an endless expanse of desert below. Its last gasp sent a shivering blast of orange, red, and purple, which caromed off the flatiron clouds like a fireworks display. "Holy shit. Forget Lake Travis sunsets." After a pause he added, "I wish Gena was here to enjoy this." A cool breeze drifted down the mountainside and washed away the aggravation of the desert highway so the land below took on an inviting softness. Skeets thought for a minute, hummed a tune, then sang a new lyric:

> *The dying sun sets the sky aglow*
> *And brings back the sorrow*
> *That forced me to wander*
> *The deserts of old Mexico*

"Downright beautiful, bro, but not as beautiful as a plate of good hot Mexican food." Jesse locked his bike before he moved toward Cantina Vista's entrance. Cars trickled into the cantina's oversized parking that indicated city customers as well as roadside business.

Skeets motioned toward the attractive entrance to the cantina. "No concrete burros with sombreros at this place."

An elderly man dressed in ancient kakis and the remnants of a military hat sat on a rock near the entrance asked. *"¿Watch you motorcycles, caballeros?"*

Jesse stopped, smiled at the man, *"Our motorcycles are very valuable. You sure they're safe with you?"*

The man stood, and his cap barely reached Jesse's shirt pocket. *"Señor, I am a professional."*

"Thank you, my friend, we need a professional." Jesse handed the man a dollar and turned to Skeets. "We have us a genuine professional to guard our bikes."

"All the same, I'm gonna take my guitar inside." Skeets followed Jesse into the cantina.

The interior of the cantina surprised Skeets. The classic colonial exterior metamorphosed into ultra modern décor with large aquariums that flanked a sushi bar. An Asian chef did his Zorro imitation, as he prepared sushi and artistically displayed them on small wooden trays.

Indirect lighting cast undulations across the walls and ceiling and gave an underwater effect.

Skeets pointed in the direction of the sushi. "It's not a tacos, beans, and rice joint, Compadre"

"Man, I'm so hungry I could chew the ass off a raw tuna. Forget I'm about as far from salt water as I can get." Jesse started into the dining room but a tuxedoed maitre'd cut him off.

The maitre'd looked the two up and down suspiciously and evaluated their blue jeans, Harley-Davidson tee shirts, bandanas, ball caps – and their wallets. He sniffed through an elevated nose and grimaced at the ripeness of the two desert motorcyclists. "Is there something I can do for you?" he said in condescending Spanish-tinged English.

"Not unless you're the cook." Jesse answered in flawless Spanish.

The maitre'd did little to hide his disdain. *"¿Are you dining with us?"*

"You do serve food, right?" Skeets asked.

"Si, señor." The maitre'd gestured around the elegant room. "But we have a dress code."

"Harley riders have a dress code too, and we're wearin' it. So let's quit talkin' and start eating, amigo." Jesse's eyes flashed to emphasize his Spanish.

The maitre'd's expression showed his pleasure at hard-assing these gringos, but before he could speak, a man in a business suit entered from the parking lot and approached them. "Good evening, gentlemen. I'm Fernando, the owner. We don't get many Harley dudes in here. Where you guys headed?"

"How about the table right over there." Skeets pointed to the center of the dining room.

Fernando paused a second and then chuckled at the misunderstanding. "Why, yes. Right, Miguel, please show these gentlemen to their table." Miguel, the maitre'd, slumped a little before he led Skeets and Jesse to the appointed table. Fernando followed.

Jesse slouched into a chair and kicked out another chair with his boot for Skeets to set his guitar. Skeets obliged and set the guitar between them.

"Thanks, pardner." Skeets looked up at Fernando and pointed to Jesse. " I'm Skeets. This here's Jesse. We're scootin' down to a place called Guanajuato."

"You *hombres* got a long trip ahead of you. Business or pleasure?"

"We're on a pilgrimage to pay off a promise." Jesse pointed to the empty chair. "Sit a spell, pardner, and keep us company."

Fernando looked around the room. "We're not too busy." He sat down and snapped his fingers. A waiter scurried to the table for their drink order. "I've always wanted a Harley, but they're very expensive and difficult to buy here in Mexico."

"It's pretty much the same in Texas too. At least the expensive part." Skeets nodded agreement.

"But down here we pay twice as much with all the import fees and bribes to get the dealers to sell us one."

"Wow. I think we'd be ridin' rice rockets for that kind of money." Jesse pointed to the sushi bar to translate "rice rockets" into "Japanese motorcycles."

Fernando slid his chair closer to the table and leaned forward. "It's none of my business, but I looked at your bikes and noticed you don't have an MCVR."

Skeets looked at Jesse and shrugged. "MCVR?"

"When you bring a vehicle into Mexico and you plan to take out again, Mexico Customs attaches a Mexico Customs Vehicle Registration hologram sticker to the windshield, which they remove when you leave the country."

Skeets and Jesse traded glances and wondered where the conversation was going. Fernando spoke first, "Without a sticker, a Harley is worth about twice what you paid for it."

"You mean we could make fifteen grand profit smugglin' a Harley into Mexico." Jesse choked on the Margarita the waiter had delivered.

Fernando looked surprised. "You didn't know this."

"No wonder Redondo stole our bikes." Jesse pounded the table for emphasis.

"Redondo?" Fernando asked. "The coyote up near Laredo?"

"You know *him*?" Jesse asked.

"No, I read about him in today's paper."

"What about him?"

"Killed by a hog in the parking lot of his cantina in Anahuac." Fernando pointed north toward Texas. "Some witnesses said he had talked about a couple of Harley hogs he stole."

Jesse leaped from chair and shouted, "YES, LORD."

Fernando and the rest of the dining room looked shocked by the outburst. "Señor, please." He pulled Jesse down into his chair again. "When I asked which direction you were going, thought you might want to sell your Harleys if you are heading home.

Skeets and Jesse each saw dollar signs in the other's eyes, but said nothing

Fernando looked at each. "I think you could show a sizable profit even though you have older bikes."

"Hey, bro, maybe you could buy your way back into Gena's bed with cash instead of your voyage of redemption. A bus ticket to Austin couldn't be too expensive." Jesse smiled at the conundrum he poised to his buddy. "You know, give up your Harley for *love*."

"Tempting." Skeets smiled. "But we still have to visit Alfonso and Beto's folks. Besides, I don't think there's enough money to turn her around on this one. It'll take a new Skeets to get it done."

"Alfonso and Beto?" Fernando looked confused.

"It's a long story. They saved our lives, and we promised to visit their folks and tell them their boys got to Texas safely and they're okay. So I guess we've got to keep on until we make good on our promise."

Equal parts of confusion, skepticism, and amazement showed on Fernando's face. He stood, shook their hands, and handed them his business card. "Have a good evening, amigos. If you change your mind give me a call. *Vayan con Dios*."

Skeets stood and shook Fernando's hand. "Just out of curiosity, How long will it take to get to Guanajuato?"

"Depends on how you plan to make the trip. You shouldn't ride at night. It's too dangerous. With hard riding, you could be there in about two days, but a leisurely ride would put you there in about three days." Fernando shook Jesse's hand. "Adios."

A defeated Miguel had given up on the two unworthies and retreated to his dais to lick his wounds. The waiter approached the table again and Skeets said, "Hay for the horses and wine for the women. We ride at dawn."

The waiter's face was blank. *"¿Como?"*

Jesse said in Spanish, *"He means bring some sushi and lots of Margaritas."*

"Yeah, amigo, keep the glasses full and bring us a big beef steak with frijoles and rice." Skeets looked at the menu. He turned to Jesse. "They didn't quite get these menus finished – there's no prices."

"Like they say, 'If you have to ask the price, you can't afford it.'"

"That's what's bothering me."

They downed their third Margarita by the time they finished their sushi trays, and the grilled filet mignon arrived. The steaks did not match a good steak in Texas, but hunger can override quality. They said very little while they enjoyed the meal and more Margaritas.

Miguel appeared smiling like he'd just had sex. "Gentlemen, anything else for your pleasure? Cognac? Cigar? We have Cubans."

"Why not, amigo?" Jesse looked at Skeets through tequila eyes. "After what we've been through the last three days, we deserve it, right?"

"If you remember, we just told ol' Fernando there we're not going to sell our bikes, so we just flat lined our financial condition."

"It's only funny money, amigo." Jesse picked out two Cohiba Churchills from the lacquered mahogany box presented by Miguel, as the waiter served two snifters of cognac.

They basked in the glow of tequila and cognac and in the sense of well being a good cigar brings until Miguel offered the check. Jesse picked up the tab and tried focusing on the amount, which seemed like something over fifteen hundred dollars. He looked up at Miguel who choked back a belly laugh. He handed the check over to Skeets. "Here you get this one, and I'll get breakfast."

Skeets looked at the tab. Then held it at arm's length. "Christ Almighty, this says one thousand five hundred fifty-five dollars."

"It's just funny money, bro, not to worry." Jesse turned to Miguel. "How much in good ol' American dollars, amigo."

"It is $155.60 U.S., señor," he said officiously and turned to a group of waiters who stood against the wall. They broke out laughing like jackals and pointed at the gringos.

"Did he say what I thought he said?" Skeets leaned across the table with a tequila whisper, which echoed around the dining room. "Cause it's not very funny money to me."

"Did you bring your Gold Card?" Jesse still didn't get the gravity of the situation.

"Gold Card my ass, I didn't come down here to wash dishes. It's all the money I've got left, bro."

"With the gas and chow I've bought, I'm leaning out a little in the pocketbook myself."

"What do you say we make a break for it?" Skeets drunken whisper again rattled around the room.

Miguel snapped his fingers and a cordon of waiters ringed the table. "Is there a problem, Señor?" Miguel's smile seemed predatory.

"No problem. Do we get to keep the dishes, amigo." Jesse laughed too loudly. The gauntlet showed no response. He slid closer to Skeets, and they pulled out their wallets.

"The check does not include gratuity, señor." Miguel added before anyone asked.

"We're long on gratitude, amigo, but a little short on *dinero.*" Jesse tried to elicit good humor from the stoic Maitre'd.

"Then your stay in Monclova will be a longer one, señores." Miguel seemed almost gleeful at the thought.

In a series of back-and-forths like kids trading baseball cards, the two came up with a hundred and fifty-six dollars. They stood, and Skeets grabbed his guitar while Jesse handed the Maitre'd the money, "Keep the change, Miguel, ol' buddy." They both made haste for the door.

They saw no sign of the professional guard, but at least their bikes were still there.

Wolf had watched two transponder blips on the Wolf Wagon GPS as they stopped and started across the screen all day – first to Sabinas, then slowly toward Monclova. They had been stationary in Monclova for a while, but now moved again. A deep-throated chuckle rolled through the truck cab. "What could those two hombres be up to at this time a night?"

PART TWO

"CAMINOS DE GUANAJUATO"
"Highways of Guanajuato" L. G. Sobrino
(Composer)

Chapter 11

Pedro de Silva knew he didn't look like a criminal. His small stature, oval face, bulging eyes magnified by thick-lensed glasses and the pencil-thin mustache made him a caricature of the movie clown Cantinflas. He didn't consider it flattery when people commented about this. For fifteen years, he had been a clerk at the central post office in Guanajuato, and for ten of those years he had pilfered money and money orders mailed to the families whose members worked as illegal aliens in the United States. He took care not to pinch funds from the same family too often, or at least he tried not to. But lately he had trouble remembering the people from whom he had last stolen. For years, he didn't make any ostentatious display of wealth, but his renovated home and his new car showed signs of prosperity beyond the hope of a postal worker, especially a postal worker with no family to support.

Rumors of theft abounded about both the post office and the telegraph office, but to date, Pedro had never been investigated. He often chuckled to himself at how simple it was to spot letters with cash or money orders in them, even when the sender tried to disguise their presence.

A new customer stood in front of him today, Ariana Gonzalez, a lovely young girl in peasant clothing with the dusty, sandaled feet of a country girl come to town. Her clean and well-groomed long black hair framed her slender body, which bulged slightly with the signs of pregnancy. She had asked with downcast eyes, almost apologetically, for mail for herself and her sister Blanca. After he inquired about the address, de Silva rummaged through the General Delivery mail slots under "G" and saw U.S.A. postmarked letters for both Ariana and Blanca.

He looked around the room to see who might watch him. The money orders in the two envelopes were obvious, and he considered for a moment the beautiful young country girl back at the postal window. He almost weakened enough to give her the letters. But he knew this would not be a repeat heist, and therefore safer, so he returned them to the slot to be harvested later. At the window he assumed a sad face and said, *"I'm sorry, Señorita, but there are no letters for you or your sister today."*

A pall of despair spread over Ariana's face when she heard the news. *"It has been weeks, and I have heard nothing from my husband, Alfonso. ¿Are you sure there is no letter?"*

"I'm absolutely certain." Pedro smiled down at the crestfallen face of the lovely girl. Her sadness made Pedro De Silva shudder in fear of retribution from the Almighty. He could feel the flames of hell lick at his feet, and he knew he must confess and mend his ways before he died. But maybe just a few more thefts so he could live comfortably while he awaited judgment. A sense of dread made him shudder when he thought of confessing to his priest.

Ariana had hoped for money to buy medicine from the *farmacia* for her mother who lay ill with the devil in her stomach. Back at their *casa*, *Mamita* grew weaker each day from dysentery and vomiting, and this morning she burned with a fever.

Ariana had scraped together a little money and had gone to the herbalist in the *Mercado Hidalgo* to buy something to help her mother. After he heard the symptoms, the herbalist rummaged through his various tiny drawers, boxes and sacks until he found powdered stag horn and chamomile powder. He mixed these together and handed the small sack to Ariana with instructions to boil a spoonful of the powder in a cup of water for her mother three times a day. She had only money enough left from the herbalist for one-half kilo of pork, dried beans and corn, six tomatoes, a handful of chilis, and one bunch of cilantro. She loaded these into her *bolsa* and went to wait for the rural bus back to the farm where she, Blanca and *Mamita* lived.

Her worry over her husband consumed her while she waited for the bus. She and Alfonso had married only three months ago. They had a double wedding of brothers and sisters in the small whitewashed church, which served rural parishioners to the east of Guanajuato. The death of Señora González, mother of Alfonso and Beto, two months before, had dampened the joy of the wedding. At the fiesta after the ceremony her new husband and brother-in-law wanted to make plans for the trek to the United States.

Alfonso had pulled younger brother Beto aside. *"We have to make plans."*

Beto looked surprised. *"Plans for what?"*

Alfonso put his arm over his brother's shoulder and pointed toward a man in new blue jeans and gringo cowboy shirt. *"Rodriguez, over there, just got back from Texas where a rancher paid him ten U.S. dollars a day plus a room and frijoles just to take care of his horses. He said he is supposed to go back next month, but he has enough money for a while, and he's not going back. He said we could go and have his job."*

"You want to go to Texas?" Beto's eyes swelled with surprise. *"We just got married a couple of hours ago."*

"Beto, we don't want our kids to grow up as poor as we did."

"We haven't had time to make any kids."

"We have a month before we have to be there. This is a big opportunity for us."

"Papa went to Texas with Señor Gonzalez, and they never came back." Beto pointed in the direction of Texas.

"But remember all the money they sent back to Mama? We can do the same, except we will come back to build our own houses and send our children to school."

"That was Mama's dream, but it didn't work out." Beto shrugged. "We're still poor."

Ariana overheard their conversation, which filled her with dread. Her father and Alfonso's father had both gone north. Money came back for a while and then stopped. They never heard from them again.

As the bus wound its way slowly on the rural roads, Ariana fell deeper into her dread that something had happened to Alfonso and Beto, and tears rolled down her face. What would become of her sick *Mamita*, Blanca, and herself with no money and no father for her child?

The fierce arguments she had with Alfonso over his and Beto's Texas trip still lingered in her mind. "Something bad will happen, just like with our fathers." Tears rolled down her face as she held him and begged him to stay home with her.

He pushed her away. "This is our chance to live a better life. Our chance for our children to grow up with the opportunity we never had. Beto and I will go."

Blanca tended the horses, goats, and to *Mamita* while Ariana went to town. She constantly looked down the two-rut dusty road that twisted away from their homestead for a mile before it reached the highway where the bus traveled.

Blanca sighed as she walked by the adobe brick walls, which had over decades, deteriorated to resemble tall piles of dried mud. Since Alfonso and Beto left for Texas, she and her sisters had to clean the stalls and care for the patron's horses as well as work in the fields. The *patrón's* eight-stall horse barn built from timber and topped with a sheet metal was better constructed than her own thatched roof shed.

Her family's adobe lean-to with a palm-frond roof was built against the crumbling wall. Next to their hut was a structure with alfalfa bales for the horses and a tack room for the saddles, other equipment and grain for the horses. Blanca walked into their hut, two tiny rooms with dirt floors, to check on her mother, who was asleep. She moved to the open air space with the dining room table and kitchen and considered the hammock but went to check one more time for Ariana. She saw her sister trudge toward the compound with her small sack of food. She ran to meet Ariana, elated at the prospect of a letter from Beto, then stopped when she saw her sister's tears. She knew there would be no news or money . . . again.

"Man, we're as lost as two blind dogs in a meat house." Skeets stood by his bike, removed his helmet, and wiped the sweat from the inside headband with his bandana. "I've never been so close to a place I couldn't get to."

"The underground highway can sure enough get you through Guanajuato, but there's no way to get into it." Jesse's bike leaned on the kickstand, and he sat with both legs stretched to one side. He held a piece of paper with lines drawn on it. "Alfonso and Beto's map here shows we have to get to *El Centro* and find this little road to the east."

They had ridden out the three legs of Avenida Hidalgo, the underground highway built sixty years ago in an old riverbed. The city had grown over the highway and had made the most of the subterranean equivalent of an expressway, but they could find no off ramps up into Guanajuato. On their third trip through the city they took yet a different turn and had ended up where they began, on the outskirts of the city. Now they looked down on a picturesque city below them whose early silver mining wealth had manifested itself in an array of grand buildings of classical architecture.

"It looks like a good place to visit, if we can ever get there." Skeets put his helmet on.

Jesse pointed off to their left at a line of trucks that snaked down a mountainside into the city. "Looks like an old highway leading into town."

"It looks crooked, crowded, slow, and painful." Skeets stared in the direction of the highway.

"Sounds like they designed it just for us." Jesse crawled aboard his bike and cranked the engine.

With the clouds of truck exhaust, the trip into town had all the charm of a Nazi gas chamber, as Skeets had predicted. But the old highway from *Ciudad de Dolores Hildalgo* did funnel the two motorcycle riders into their destination at the center of the city. Late afternoon they passed the formal garden and cobblestoned streets of *Plaza de la Paz* with its umbrellaed sidewalk cafes, past the domed *Basílica de Colégiata de Guanajuato,* and into the tree-shaded *Jardín Unión* surrounded by sidewalk restaurants and filled with crowds of locals and students out for their promenade.

The raucous sound of Harley-Davidson Motorcycles turned every head in Guanajuato's central meeting place, the *Jardín Unión* across from the Teatro Juárez and one block from *Universidad de Guanajuato.* By the time Skeets and Jesse parked and had their kickstands down, a small crowd of university students surrounded them. "Hey, Harley dudes, what's up?" a tall, skinny teenager asked.

Skeets had paid little attention to the pedestrians except he tied not to run over them, so the sound of English took him by surprise. By looks the group of gawkers were gringo kids. "We didn't expect to find a nest of *Americanos* this far from the border. What brings you guys here?" Skeets asked.

An attractive brunette with a Texas accent said, "We're university students studying Spanish. Six weeks – six semester hours."

Jesse smiled at the pretty girl. *"¿Bueno, hermosa, dónde puedan viajeros sedientos obtener una cerveza?"*

The girl looked puzzled, then mentally cranked on her Spanish, but finally said, "Smart ass, we've only been here a couple of weeks."

Jesse laughed aloud. "Sorry, pretty lady, where can we all go get a beer and a shot of tequila? We're a little parched after ridin' all day."

Another smiling beauty stood beside the first girl and intoned in an equally deep Texas accent, "You play that thing?" She flipped her blonde hair back and pointed to the guitar strapped on the back of Skeets' bike.

Skeets bowed toward the blonde. "Skeets Hollaran, singer-songwriter at your service."

Both the girls jumped and squealed. "We go to UT in Austin. We've heard you guys at the Dillo Doe."

Skeets turned to Jesse. "I'm afraid the ol' Dillo Doe was once again the victim of fake ID's, wouldn't you say?"

"No. No," the blonde said, "We're twenty-one – well, close to it, anyway – give or take a couple of years."

"The question is, are you old enough to knock a few beers back with two old road-weary troubadours?" Skeets looked around for agreement.

"Only if you sing us a song. C&W music's in short supply down here," one of the two girls said.

"We're professionals and only sing for money." Skeets smiled at the group.

"But – sometimes for love," Jesse added, and the group broke up laughing as he unstrapped Skeets' guitar. "Where's the best place for really serious beer drinking?"

Almost everyone pointed toward the back of *Jardín Unión* at a series of stone arches and outdoor tables under a sign, which announced *Pericos Negros*. Part of the group had wandered away, but the two Texas girls and a handful of others led the way across the Unión. Umbrella tables and shade trees filled the patio except for a makeshift bandstand with an ancient piano and a dance floor. Skeets motioned toward the bandstand, and they pulled tables together.

"A round of brewskis, amigo." Skeets' request failed to register on the waiter's face.

"Una cerveza para todos, por favor." The blonde girl looked around the table and added, "Can the Spanish-speaking *estudiante* get a little love here?" The group dutifully shouted and applauded.

"¿Qué marca de cerveza?" the waiter asked.

"Para todos Dos XX con lima, por favor." Blondie stood with her arms up in victory. "Can you give it up for the Spanish speaking lady?" Louder shouts and table banging this time.

Jesse nudged Skeets, nodded in the direction of the two Texas girls, and said under his breath, "I think we've stumbled into something good here, if we play our cards right."

Skeets looked over the group. "It's a veritable buffet."

Chapter 12

The party raged on for almost three hours. The first hour Skeets and Jesse regaled the group with tales of their adventures on the road, and the last two hours they performed from the bandstand. The brunette and blonde, Jody and Nan (short for Nannette) were industrial strength party animals and kept the group lively. When Skeets and Jesse performed, more students, both Gringo and Mexican, joined in the fun, and the patio filled up with revelers. The waiters broke a sweat hauling all the beer and tequila shots.

Between songs, Skeets looked over the crowd. "I think we're a saleable commodity here, old buddy."

"*Absolutamente del fuego.* Hot, hot, hot. I'd say, but we're running out of songs. It's retreads from here on."

Nan, the blonde, shouted from the crowd, "Do, *If You Really Loved Me, You'd a Married Somebody Else,* again."

"There you have it. They'll tolerate repeats." Skeets did some minor guitar tuning before addressing the audience. "This is a song written by a friend to celebrate my divorce." The two musicians tore into the song and nodded approval when, with Jody and Nan leading, the group sang along on the refrain.

While the applause and laughter died, Skeets and Jesse took a few pulls on their beers. Skeets' beer buzz had not erased his concern over their financial condition. He looked at Jesse through *cerveza* eyes. "Good buddy, you know we're flat broke. I'm not sure we can pay our bar tab, much less get a place to sleep tonight."

"I can guarantee us a place to crash tonight." Jesse nodded in the direction of Jody and Nan. "Brunette or blonde?"

"That Nan looks like a newer model of the blonde that caused all my current Gena miseries and launched us on this voyage of redemption." Skeets shook his head trying to rid the memory. "Scares me to death."

"That settles it. It's Jody the brunette for me." Jesse mimed a finger-thumb pistol shot in her direction.

"Wait a minute. I just said that blondes would be the death of me."

"You get bucked off, you gotta crawl back in the saddle and keep on ridin'." Jesse turned back to the keyboard and slammed into the intro for *Boot Scootin' Boogy*.

Before Skeets started singing, the crowd erupted into a stampede for the dance floor and formed into ranks like the Praetorian Guard. Jody and Nan had given private line dancing instructions earlier in the evening when they played any up-tempo tune. Now the dance floor was full of neophyte line dancers boogying their asses off. Skeets watched the two instructors move through the dancers offering demonstrations for the more terpsichorean challenged.

During the whooping and shouting after the song, Jesse pulled Skeets close. "I think it's time to work on our accommodations for tonight."

Skeets agreed and began putting his guitar back into the case. A rustle of disappointment went through the crowd at the sight of the music ending. After a minute of arms- raised victory salute while the crowd cheered, the two jumped from the bandstand and went to reclaim their seats next to Jody and Nan. When they reached the table, a balding, heavy-set Mexican in a pink *guayabera* shirt greeted them.

"*Buenas noches, amigos.* I'm Miguel, the owner." He held out his hand to the two. "I've enjoyed your music tonight."

Skeets shook the hand. "I'm Skeets and this is Jesse."

"May I buy you a drink?" Miguel motioned for them toward their chairs.

"Thought you'd never ask, pardner." Jesse slouched into a chair beside Jody. "Grab yourself a chair and join us."

With no music, the crowd drifted away, and Miguel took a chair from the adjacent table. "We normally have mariachi bands here, but they never fill the place like you did tonight. This was the best night we've had since the last *Internacional Cervantino Festival.*"

"I recon you've got a bunch of country music-starved gringos down here." Skeets nodded in the girls' direction.

"That's for sure," Nan spoke up as Jody's smile concurred.

"You from Texas?" Miguel directed the question to the four who all nodded enthusiastically.

"Austin, Texas, to be exact." Skeets added.

"I go to San Antonio twice a year to shop with my family, but we've never been to Austin," Miguel said.

"Next time you're that close, come on up and we'll have us a grand ol' time." Jesse squirmed a little in his seat. He was ready to switch his attention to Jody and where they were going to sleep tonight.

"How long you hombres in town for?"

"Hard to say, amigo. We have to find some people and give them some stuff." Skeets arched his eyebrows. "Why?"

"I'd like to hire you to perform here. You guys can bring in a lot of business." Miguel now had both their attention. "I can make it interesting for you."

"How interesting?" Jesse moved forward in anticipation.

"How about your meals and fifty-dollars a night?" Miguel leaned back looking satisfied.

Skeets waited for a reaction. Nan shook her head. "*How interesting?*" he said again.

"Ok, your meals, a place to stay and seventy-five dollars a night. . . cash . . . paid nightly." Miguel squirmed and struck a conspiratorial pose.

"Free drinks?" Skeets interjected.

"Free drinks." Miguel looked a little concerned.

"For our two friends here, *también.*" Jesse nodded at Jody and Nan, who seemed very agreeable to the idea.

"*Para las damas, también.*" Miguel shrugged his surrender.

Skeets glanced at Jesse, and they winked their agreement. He turned to Miguel and held out his hand. "You got a deal, pardner. When do we start?"

"Tomorrow is Thursday. I'll print some circulars and spread them around *la universidad.* How about Friday night about eight o'clock? But you can't move into your room until I kick the mariachis out."

They shook hands, and Miguel excused himself. Jesse looked at Jody and Nan. "Ladies, please excuse having to sit through this high level business conference. However, we find ourselves somewhat economically challenged at the moment, and old Miguel may have saved our asses here."

"Yeah," Jesse chimed in. "We've got to figure out a place to bunk in for a couple of nights."

Jody and Nan looked at each other before Nan said, "We've got room at our place."

Jody added, "We rented a two-room flat that's got a couch in the living room, but somebody would have to sleep on the floor."

"That sounds like paradise to a couple of ol' desert rats used to sleeping under mesquite trees." Jesse winked "I told you so" at Skeets.

Skeets said, "Very kind of you two ladies. We've got bed rolls on our bikes, so sleeping on the floor is no problem, but you've got to promise not to take advantage of us."

"We can't make any rash promises." Jody eyed her roommate.

"Yeah, sometimes us Texans got to stick together, right, Jody?" Nan's laugh had a naughty edge.

The group adjourned and headed for the bikes. Skeets felt a gnawing in his stomach as the four weaved across *Jardín Unión* back to the bikes. He hadn't eaten since breakfast, and the hunger held at bay with beer and the excitement of performing now growled in his entrails like a trapped animal. *Restaurante Truco No. 7* facing the plaza was doing big business with a constant stream of customers entering and leaving. "I'm starving. Anybody else hungry?"

"I'm gettin' a little weak myself. How about you guys?" Jesse gestured toward Nan and Jody who brightened at the idea of food.

"What's that Truco No. 7 like?" Skeets pointed toward the restaurant.

"Great place. Everybody goes there," Nan said.

"Yeah, good food and live music," Jody added.

They settled into the low-lighted and leather-chaired comfort of No. 7, and ordered *fajitas* for four and a first round of beers. A jazz quartet lilted recognizable tunes over a dance floor about half populated. "Pretty cool place here." Skeets looked around the room, then at Nan. "You come here often?"

"A couple of times, but mostly Jody and I just study." Nan cast a knowing look at Jody.

"Yeah, we noticed. You looked like pretty serious students across the street." Jesse gestured in the direction of Pericos Negros with his beer bottle.

"We were just doing lab work on conversational Spanish," Jody said.

"And polishing up our expatriate social skills," Nan added.

When the band struck up a danceable tune, Skeets said to Nan, "Speaking of polishing, how about us polishing our belt buckles out on the dance floor?" All Nan's college "studying" had produced a very competent western swing dancer, and Skeets felt inspired as he initiated the twirls, crossovers, and cross-unders, to dress up his Texas Two-Step. At the end of the song, the crowd exploded into applause as Skeets led Nan into an exaggerated dip, which she accented with a whirl of her blonde hair, ending with her head less than a foot from the floor. He bent over and kissed her lightly on the forehead. She caught his head in her fingers and pulled him down into a sensuous kiss as the crowd went wild.

"Nan?" Skeets said trying to get his breath.

"Yes, Skeets?"

"You're gonna have to stand up by yourself, 'cause I just turned to stone."

Chapter 13

A shaft of sunlight pried open Skeets' eyes as he lay in his bedroll. Confusion ruled for a moment. Then pain pounded into the space behind his eyes and filled the cavity that once held a brain. Nausea traveled down into his stomach. He rolled over on his side and looked around the small room. Jesse snored on an ancient couch over which he had attempted to spread his bedroll. Skeets found one of his boots and lobbed it into Jesse's midsection. "Wakeup, *compadre,* and tell me exactly how much fun we had last night."

Jesse's eyes opened, but he seemed unable to speak for several minutes. Finally, he croaked out a few sounds. "As bad as I feel, I just know we had a good time."

"Why do I think I compromised my journey of atonement?" Skeets sat up and held his head.

"Probably because you're still grinnin' even with a hangover." Jesse sat on the edge of the couch and looked at the empty beds in the next room. "I think our hospitable new friends have left."

"You think we still have motorcycles?"

"I think after the last tequila shot at Truco's, we felt strongly that we needed a motorcycle ride to clear our heads."

"There's a lot of logic there. Especially if we gave our lovely friends a ride." Skeets shook his head in dismay.

"I think it's how we ended up here in the arms of *amor*." Jesse looked around the room.

"God, I'm thirsty." Skeets stood uncertainly and went to the small refrigerator to look for a bottle of water. "I think it's beer for breakfast." Skeets lifted one of the eight beers and three bottles of water in the fridge. "You want your *cerveza* scrambled or over easy?" After he handed Jesse a beer, Skeets saw a note. He read aloud:

Hey, you wild and crazy guys, we have class, but how about we hook up again tonight? You mentioned you have something to do today. So let's eat about six and then you can watch us perform. On a stage this time. Ha. Ha.

Nan

"I'm not sure I can stand any more *performances*." Jesse leaned forward for a better view of the bedroom. "I swear I don't remember how this all worked last night."

"I'm sure I don't want to know. Why can't I get myself under control? I mean, between trying to save our asses down here, all I think about is Gena, and how much I want to go home to the life I had before with her. Then I end up in the sack with another blonde last night. How can I let myself do this?" Skeets slid his butt onto the kitchen counter and sat with his face propped in his hands. "I mean, think about it. This girl lives in Austin, goes to UT, and dances at the Dillo Doe. How stupid can I be?"

"On the surface, she appears to be a bad choice for a dalliance, I will admit. Maybe she'll flunk her Spanish and stay here another six weeks. I doubt your performance last night will be memorable much past that." Jesse snickered.

"I'm somewhat discouraged about finding the new Skeets down here." Skeets dropped his head in his hands and ignored Jesse's comment.

"Well, buck up, old buddy. If we find Alfonso's and Beto's families today, I reckin there's not much holding us here." Jesse leaned back and watched Skeets for a reaction.

After a pause, Skeets lifted his head. "Nothing but poverty. We can barely buy enough gas to make it out of town. I tell you, man, to sell our bikes and fly home is pretty tempting."

"This will all change tomorrow night when we get our seventy-five bucks from Miguel over at *Pericos Negros*." Jesse's voice had a hopeful ring.

"I guess we're stuck here at least 'til we get enough money to go home." Skeets sighed in resignation.

"The sun's over the yardarm, and we haven't even moved in the direction of our destination. Maybe we should get in gear. If I hang around with you, I might get suicidal." Jesse headed for the bathroom.

"I guess so, if we need to be back here by six." Skeets opened the front door onto a balcony, which overlooked a small, attractive patio. "Hey, man, we've still got bikes. Let's hook 'em up and get some breeze on our knees."

The gardener who worked in the patio had watched their bikes all morning and chased away the curious. Jesse slipped him a dollar and asked about the road they needed to find. Surprisingly, the gardener lived on the road and gave Jesse instructions how best to locate it.

They wove their bikes through narrow streets on steep inclines and occasionally missed a turn, until they found *Mercado Hildago*. After two times around the market, they found the road out of the city the gardener described. Thirty minutes later they left Guanajuato behind them, and Alfonso's and Beto's lay somewhere ahead.

They traversed the area of the paved highway back and forth, where Alfonso's and Beto's road should turn. Each time they tried a side road they found nothing. Jesse pulled off the pavement, got out the pencil drawn map again, and shook his head. "This map looks a lot simpler than it is."

Skeets pointed at two ruts, mostly overgrown, on the other side of the highway. "Those ruts go in the right direction. Maybe we should try them."

"Boy, it's a really rural road, but there's no gate, so why not?" Jesse downshifted into first gear, pulled back onto the pavement, and turned into the ruts.

The rough road slowed them, and after about a mile Jesse signaled a turnaround, but Skeets caught sight of an adobe wall and rode past Jesse toward what looked like a corral. As they approached the wall, two young women ran into the corral entrance, apparently attracted by the noise of the Harleys. When they saw the motorcycles, they turned and fled back in the direction they had come. Skeets rode into the walled compound and saw them disappear into a small building against the wall. He turned and stopped about twenty feet in front.

They sat for several minutes on their bikes, but no one appeared. Skeets looked at Jesse. "Maybe you should ask them if this is the home of Alfonso and Beto."

"*¿Señoritas, is this the home of Alfonso and Beto Gonzalez?*" Jesse cupped his hands over his mouth.

They faintly heard the women talk inside the room, but no one came out. "Tell them we bring news from Alfonso and Beto," Skeets said.

"*We bring news from Alphonso and Beto.*" Jesse shouted through his hands.

The door opened a crack and then closed again. After loud language the door burst open, and Ariana strode outside, arms akimbo. "*¿Why do you speak of Alfonso and Beto?*"

Jesse smiled and answered, *"We met Alfonso and Beto in Texas, and they helped us. Actually saved our lives. They wanted you to know they are well. We want to return the clothes and shoes they loaned us."*

"¿Clothes and shoes?" Ariana's eyes grew wide with amazement. She turned abruptly and ran back inside and repeated everything that had transpired with the motorcycle riders. Both women excitedly ran out the door and stood in front of the two riders. Ariana spoke, *"Please excuse us. Your motorcycles frightened us, but, please, I am Ariana and this is Blanca, the wives of Alfonso and Beto. Please, come inside and tell us your news."*

Jesse introduced Skeets and himself. They followed the women into the small, dark room, which was hot and smelled of sickness. An old woman too weak to raise her head lay on a cot. Ariana explained her mother had been ill for days, and then told her these men had met Alfonso and Beto in Texas. She could only smile at the two. *"We should let Mamita rest,"* Blanca said and opened the door for the visitors.

They moved into the open-air living area, and the two women arranged chairs for their visitors. Skeets looked around the dirt-floor room with its thatched roof and then glanced at Jesse, who seemed equally appalled at the living conditions. Jesse asked, "Has your mother seen a doctor?"

"Oh, no. We can't get her to town, and we have no money for medicine or a doctor." Ariana's eyes brimmed with tears that she brushed away with the back of her hand. *"We expected a letter from our husbands with money, but none has come."*

"They had not reached the ranch where they would work when we met them," Jesse explained, *"But they said it was only a day away."*

Blanca could not hold her excitement any longer and blurted out, *"Please tell us how you met our husbands."*

The two wives seemed so hungry for news that Jesse told them the long version. About Redondo who stole their bikes,

Vámonos!

took their pants and underwear, and tied them to a tree. The two women gasped with embarrassment and held their hands in front of their faces when he described their nakedness. They howled with laughter at the story of Alfonso and Beto's reactions when they saw Skeets brought to life and heard the "Voice of God."

While Jesse told the story, Skeets brought in the underwear and huaraches given them by Alfonso and Beto. The two wives received these personal reminders of their husbands like precious jewels, and neither could hold back tears of sadness.

Jesse said "Please excuse us for a minute." They went outside. "I thought we would just deliver our message and be on our way, but I have a bad feeling here. These ladies are really in trouble. I didn't expect all this sadness." Anger flashed in Jesse's eyes as he pointed at the stables. "Those damn horses live better than these people do."

Skeets nodded in agreement. "I don't think we can just ride off into the sunset, do you?"

"We've done what we promised, but I wouldn't feel good if we didn't help them the way Alfonso and Beto helped us." Jesse scuffed his boot in the dirt and glanced up at the wives in the lean-to.

When they returned, Ariana apologized for their tears, and said tomorrow she would go back into town again and see if a letter had come with money.

"*How do you get into town, Señora?*" Jesse asked.

After her answer, Jesse told Skeets, "She'll ride the bus into town tomorrow and see if she got any money from Alfonso, and buy medicine if they did. She says the trip takes her all day."

"Man, this whole deal sucks. I didn't know people lived like this, and her mother looks like she's on her last leg. We've got to do something." Skeets pulled out his wallet and found only two dollars.

"Don't look at me, bro. I'm flat as a tortilla." Jesse patted his wallet.

Blanca got Jesse's attention and offered them food. "No, gracias, Señora. We have to go back to town." Jesse looked at Skeets. "Let's come out here and give Ariana a ride tomorrow morning."

"Maybe old Miguel will let us sing tonight, so we can collect money for their mom's medicine." Skeets looked hopeful.

Jesse asked Blanca her sister to sit together and squatted in front of them. *"We're sorry we can't help you now, but we'll be here tomorrow morning and take Ariana to the post office and for your mother's medicine."*

Ariana looked shocked and put her hand over her mouth. *"Santa Maria presérvenos. Ride on a motorcycle?"*

Chapter 14

By the time Skeets and Jesse parked their bikes, Jody and Nan hung over the balcony railing and offered two cold beers. "Hey, big boys, come on up and see us sometime."

Skeets thought, as he looked up at the two smiling lovelies with short shorts, halter-tops, and beer, God, now trouble starts – again. He removed his helmet and bowed low to the balcony. "I reckon you ladies know the way into a man's heart."

Skeets and Jesse leaped up the stairs, crashed onto the old couch, accepted cold beers from Jody, and immediately drained half the bottles.

Nan asked, "So what exciting thing did you outlaws do today?"

"You mean after our recovery this morning?" Skeets rubbed his forehead behind which a dull ache still pulsed.

"You should've tried getting up at seven." Jody's blood shot eyes told the story. "If we miss a day of this Spanish class, we're a week behind. So we dragged ourselves to class."

"For all the good it did. All I thought about was how bad my head hurt and how much I needed sleep." Nan did the "shame on you" index finger pointing. "You boys are a bad influence on a couple of innocent young girls like us."

"I'm not sure who's bad for who here." Jesse pointed back and forth between the girls and the guys.

"Yeah, you girls should be ashamed of how you took advantage of us last night," Skeets hung his head in mock shame, "after you promised not to."

"Do you feel used?" Nan laughed aloud.

"We do have our reputations, after all."

Jody looked at Nan. "You think they lived up to their reputations last night?"

Nan nodded affirmative. "Might've one upped yourselves a little."

"In last night's condition I can't imagine that." Skeets shook his head in apology.

"Anyway, tonight's another night, so why don't you come to our performance?" Nan stood and took a bow.

"What are you performing?" Jesse asked.

"We're drama students at UT, so we thought while we're here, we'd volunteer for the *Entremeses* the students perform," Nan explained.

"*Entremeses?*" Skeets arched his eyebrows.

"They're outdoor plays performed in the plaza in front of the San Roque Church," Jody chimed in. "They're pretty funky with old-time costumes and lots of actors run around and things happen. It's pretty cool."

"We don't speak Spanish very well, so we just roam around in monk's robes and try to look truly repentant." Nan gave a demonstration of her head-down monk's walk. "Last Sunday night's performance in this same play was so well received, we're performing it again tonight."

"I don't know if we can." Skeets looked at Jesse for backup.

"Yeah, we got something we gotta do tonight," Jesse said.

"Your social calendar's already full in Guanajuato?" Nan stood with her hands on her hips.

"Yeah, we need to raise money tonight for our friends," Jesse explained.

"We need to ask Miguel at *Pericos Negros* if we can sing tonight," Skeets added

"Who needs the money?" Jody anticipated a lengthy story and sat down.

Jesse told them again how the two Mexicans had saved their lives after Redondo stole their bikes and recounted their visit with Alfonso's and Beto's family today. He described the squalor in which the family lived and the mother who looked like she might die.

The two girls wore serious expressions for the first time since they had met.

"I'm sorry to admit it, ladies, but we're flat broke and have no money for their mom's medical care. We need to help these people out somehow, especially after what their husbands did for us." Skeets spoke with a sense of urgency. "Ariana, Alfonso's wife, has checked with the post office several times looking for money from her husband, but so far there's been nothing."

"Yeah, tell us about it," Jody said. "We hear all the time about students whose parents send letters and money, and they never receive it. The Mexican students are pretty cynical about the post office and the telegraph. They think people who work there steal money orders."

"Man, that sucks. I mean this really pisses me off." Jesse's eyes flashed with anger.

Nan had been thoughtful during the conversation. "I love you guys for trying to help your friends. Let's make a plan. Why don't we eat at *Pericos Negros* before the play? You can ask Miguel about doing a benefit concert tonight." She handed Skeets a colored piece of paper from the kitchen. "These flyers papered the university today, so the students know about you singing tomorrow night."

Skeets read the circular aloud:

LIVE

SKEETS AND JESSE

DIRECT FROM AUSTIN TEXAS

Playing Your Favorite Country And Western Music

Nightly beginning at 9:00 p.m.

At

Pericos Negros

"Yeah, lots of students come to the *Entremeses* and then go out and party their asses off," Jody said. "Nan and I can spread the word about the benefit and get them over to Miguel's after the play."

"I reckon old Miguel would pay us for sure if we brought in a bunch of business," Skeets agreed.

"Yeah, and we could pass the hat and collect even more," Jesse added.

"This is great," Skeets said. "We will go back out there tomorrow morning and take Ariana to the post office and the pharmacy. She might have enough money for a doctor."

Miguel didn't show up at their table until the four had finished half their dinner. Skeets pointed at the stage. "No music tonight?"

Miguel shrugged. "The mariachis got mad and quit when I told them tonight was their last night. So no music."

"We could start about ten o'clock." Skeets pointed at his guitar.

Before Miguel could answer, Nan said, "We'll bring the students here to party after the *Entremes*."

The four waited while Miguel looked around the restaurant and measured the night's business. "Would I have to pay seventy-five dollars?"

Jesse explained in Spanish they wanted to have a benefit concert for some poor Mexican friends here in Guanajuato. "Our seventy-five dollars and what the crowd donates will go to help buy medical care for our friends."

"You can't start earlier?" Miguel asked.

"We need them at the *Entremes* to spread the word about the party here tonight." Nan stood up. "We need to get moving."

"Okay, okay. Start at ten o'clock, and you can have the seventy-five dollars." Miguel turned and slouched away.

Because Skeets and Jesse had two of the actors on their bikes, the police officers allowed them to park their bikes behind the barricades, which blocked off the *Plazuela de San Roque* for the night's show. Grandstands erected across the plaza from the *Templo de San Roque* provided seating for most of the audience, and the plaza itself held people who stood or brought their own chairs. Ancient stone steps led up from both sides of the plaza. At a height of about twenty feet above the plaza, the stairs emptied onto a terrace in front of the main entrance of the centuries-old, Baroque church facade. Jody and Nan waved at Skeets and Jesse as they disappeared through a church door on the plaza to put on their costumes.

Skeets and Jesse sat on their bikes since they were so close to the stage, which included the steps and terrace in front of the church. A student approached and said in passable English, "Nice bikes, man. English or Spanish programs tonight?" He held out mimeographed sheets.

"Both, " Jesse replied.

The program said several students in the *Universad de Guanajuato, Departamento del Drama* wrote tonight's play, "The Judgment of Don Ernesto." Apparently they used *The Legend of Calle Del Truco,* one of Guanajuato's many legends, as a basis for the one-act play.

"Some old dude named Don Ernesto gambled away all of his land and all of his money at a gambling house on Truco Street. Then he tried to win it back by gambling his wife." Skeets laughed out loud. "How much can you get for a used wife, man?"

"Yeah," Jesse said. "It looks like the old guy lost his beloved wife then found he had gambled with the devil all night. 'His ghost now roams Truco Street nightly and knocks at the door of the old gambling house and enters once again.'"

"We should watch out for old Don Ernesto if we go back to Truco No. 7." Skeets laughed.

The sun cast long shadows on the *Plazuela San Roque* as darkness crept over the audience. When the church bell tolled eight times, the theater lights came up gradually until a rose glow covered the plaster and stone of *Templo de San Roque* and the surrounding plaza. The actors filed out of the lower door.

"Finally something's happening," Jesse said.

"I wonder which monks are Jody and Nan?" Skeets leaned forward for a better look at the line of actors in brown monks robes with hoods over their heads.

"Probably the two taller, truly remorseful penitents."

As the play progressed, the two neophyte theatergoers became completely engrossed in the plot. Jesse said in a husky whisper, "Ol' Don Ernesto's a real piece of shit, man."

"Shhhhhh." Skeets and those around them all replied.

Toward the end of the play, the lights lowered, and a lone figure entered the stage, Don Ernesto wore a long black coat and broad-brimmed hat pulled low over his forehead. His staggered gait told how the weight of his foul misdeeds now burdened him. "It's ol' Don Ernesto the asshole," Jesse offered again.

"Shhhhhh."

Don Ernesto reaches center stage; a blinding shaft of light floods down on him from the heavens. An ear shattering blast from herald trumpets rends the air, and there is a rumble from a sheet metal thunder machine while a CO2 fire extinguisher gushes out a cloud near the top of the church. Through the cloud descends the Angel MICHAEL who brandishes his sword.

Don Ernesto drops to his knees trembling. "PROSTRATE YOURSELF BEFORE GOD, SINNER." The Voice of the Ages echoes around the plaza. "I AM MICHAEL, THE SWORD OF GOD, COME TO PRESCRIBE YOUR PENANCE. CONFESS, SINNER."

Don Ernesto prostrates himself on the ground, shaking, but says nothing.

Michael hovers about ten feet above Don Ernesto. "CONFESS, BEFORE I SMITE YOU WITH MY SWORD AND SEND YOU TO BURN IN HELL FOR ALL ETERNITY."

Don Ernesto slowly rises to his knees and bows his head to his chest. "Father, forgive me for I have sinned. My family is now destitute as I lost all my land and money gambling with the Devil."

"AND?"

Don Ernesto pauses a moment. "And with my foolish pride I gambled away my wife to win back my possessions."

"YOU FOOLISH EVIL MAN. YOU ARE UNWORTHY TO ENTER THE KINGDOM OF GOD." Michael rises toward heaven, plucks two coals of fire from the firmament, and returns to stand before Don Ernesto. "YOU ARE DOOMED TO ROAM THE STREETS AS A GHOSTLY SHADOW, AND YOUR EYES WILL BURN AS COALS OF FIRE." Michael slams a pair of bug-eyes painted to look like coals of fire into Don Ernesto's eyes. The trumpets and another explosion drown

out Ernesto's screams. Michael ascends back to heaven through the cloud of smoke.

The stage lights lower and Don Ernesto rises from his knees and staggers around the stage with the coals burning in his eyes. "I AM DAMNED." He collapses to the stage.

The audience erupted with applause and shouting. "Holy Shit. Ol' Michael's meaner'n a peach orchard boar." Skeets turned to Jesse and saw him still wide-eyed with awe.

"Man, I think I'll go to church on Sunday."

Chapter 15

Skeets looked around Pericos Negros at the hundred or so patrons still partying after midnight, mostly gringo students, but a significant contingent of Mexican students had joined the festivities. Nan and Jody had continued their line dance instructions and interspersed Texas Two Step lessons for the Mexican revelers.

"Listen up, all you shit kickers out there." Skeets held up his arms to quiet the crowd. "How many of you out there performed in the *Entremes* tonight?" Shouting, applause. "Listen, you guys did a great job. You scared the bejesus out of Jesse and me. Jesse says he's even going to church next Sunday." A rustle of laughter. Skeets held up one of the fliers, which announced their performance at *Pericos Negros*. "Most of you know we weren't supposed to play here until tomorrow night, but Miguel, *el gerente del Pericos Negros,* let us have this benefit concert tonight. Mexican friends of ours here in Guanajuato need help. They can't afford medical care for their mother. Miguel, Jesse, and I will donate our pay for tonight. Why don't you guys throw in a bunch of *dinero* to help? Give it up for a good cause."

Applause rippled through the crowd. Nan and Jody, who opted for western outfits after the *Entremes*, took off their cowboy hats and passed through the crowd, smiled, rubbed against the guys without their own women, and generally cajoled the revelers to help fill the hats. A tequila and beer mood prevailed, so their hats filled quickly with the help of Nan and Jody's enthusiasm.

Skeets and Jesse took a break during the donation drive. They saw Miguel seat a beautiful pair of twin ladies along with a man who could be their father. His good grooming and expensive clothes reeked of money. The twins had shoulder length jet-black hair and classic Spanish features. They wore spaghetti-strap, tight fitted blouses and mini skirts, which showed their natural endowments. Tall to begin with, they stood out like beacons in their high heels.

Their short, heavy-set escort wore a mustache. He had a full head of professionally styled black hair. His pride in the twins seemed more trophy hunter than father. The twins showed him only the amount of interest congeniality demanded, while they scanned the crowd as if looking for an escape route.

Miguel bowed and scraped very solicitously. His waiters jerked the chairs from under two customers and shuttled them off to another table. Miguel seated two caricatures of Hollywood wise guys on either side of the trio. Clown suits with red noses would be less conspicuous than these guys' polyester suits and ties. Miguel snapped his fingers at two waiters who received their instructions and hurtled to the kitchen and bar.

Jesse stared so intently at the twins one of them winked an acknowledgment. He turned to Skeets. "Hey, man, did you see those twins?"

"I'd be the only guy in here who didn't." Skeets fine tuned his guitar and watched the twins and their sugar daddy.

"I think one of them likes me. Think about it, dude, a two-on-one with beautiful twins. That's always been a fantasy of mine."

"Your two-on-one would be those two goons beside them beatin' the livin' shit out of *you* – so forget it." Skeets walked to the microphone, and Jesse turned to the piano and tore into the introduction of "Milk Cow Boogie." The crowd leaped onto the dance floor and line danced.

Half way through the song, Skeets saw Nan pass the hat at the twins' table, and the sugar daddy waved her away with a nasty expression.

Skeets and Jesse wound down the music an hour later. After Skeets put his guitar away, the two jumped from the stage and joined Nan and Jody at the table where they counted the money.

The crowd filtered out into the night, and the twins stood to leave. Both smiled over their shoulders at Jesse as their entourage escorted them out.

Miguel stood at the money-counting table and paid the seventy-five dollars for Skeets and Jesse. "How much did you take in?"

"It looks like $200 US." Nan looked up from her counting. "Two-seventy five with Skeets' and Jesse's money."

"A lot of money. For whom?" Miguel looked longingly at the cash.

"For the family of the guys who saved our lives up in Texas. We owe those guys plenty." Jesse explained. "Another twenty five makes it an even three-hundred bucks, Amigo."

Miguel hesitated but finally shrugged and dropped the money on the table.

"Who were the twins over there?" Jesse pointed in the direction of the table.

Miguel looked startled by the question. He became irritated when he saw Jesse's interest. "They are the property of Carlos Algo, Señor."

"The property?"

"Bought and paid for, Señor." Miguel's eyes flashed in irritation as he made a gesture of counting out money.

"Who's this Carlos Algo guy, anyway?"

Jody looked up from the table where Skeets stacked and folded the money. "The local drug lord." She gave him a knowing look.

Miguel looked directly at Jesse. "A very dangerous man, Señor. You would do well to forget the twins." He turned and hurried away while he glanced in every direction like he thought even talking about Carlos Algo was dangerous.

Skeets stuffed the last of the money in his jeans. "Looks like your big fantasy is still on hold, good buddy"

Jody grabbed Nan and pulled her close. "A two-on-one with twins, I'll bet."

Jesse almost blushed. "Well . . ."

Nan put her arm around Jody. "How much alike do we look?"

The alarm clock placed on the floor between their two bedrolls did its job. Jesse dragged himself to the kitchen stove and boiled water for coffee. Halfway through his first, he stared into his cup like a man convinced Nescafé instant coffee was not the best way to start a day. "Those post office people stealin' money really pisses me off."

"Maybe it's just an urban legend."

"I think we should find out." Jesse paced the floor. "Ariana goes to the post office by herself, and they could be jerking her around."

Skeets slouched down on the couch and. "Why do I think another Jesse scheme is coming?"

"Think about it, man. We should go into the post office. You know, check out whoever's stealing from her. Better still, why not Harley up and scare the crap out of this guy?"

"A show of force?"

"Exactly." Jesse dug into his Harley-Davidson bag for the right clothes. He pulled black jeans, a black long-sleeved shirt, and a black leather vest from his bag. Skeets did the same.

Downstairs at their bikes, they put on black leather gloves and their black helmets with the smoked visors. The patio gardener expected another tip for watching their bikes, but moved out of sight instead. "He looks like he just saw Darth Vader." Skeets laughed. They cranked up their bikes and headed for a bank to change the dollars into pesos for Ariana and Blanca.

Three blocks down the street, they parked their bikes, but still wore their helmets as they entered the bank. The building looked a hundred years old. Marble columns and carved stone filigree conveyed the message that this bank is here to stay. Their boot heels rang on the marble floor and resonated off the domed ceiling.

The security guards, slouched in chairs leaning against the wall, rocked forward and checked their weapons. Skeets saw the guards' interest, and the whites of the tellers' eyes. He tapped Jesse's arm and motioned to take off his helmet. Skeets removed his with an exaggerated movement and took the money from his pocket and brandished it where all could see. "I don't want them thinkin' we're making a withdrawal."

"Good thinking, amigo, I saw one of those guys who wears a size five hat load cartridges into his pistol." Jesse moved with great caution toward the teller window.

"We only want one-hundred peso notes. I don't want an asshole taking advantage of Ariana while he changed a big bill." Skeets handed the money to Jesse.

The distraught teller counted the bills three times before he gingerly slid them under the ornate wrought iron teller-cage bars. Jesse counted them again, and they took three slow steps backward before they turned and strode from the bank.

"I guess next time we'll wear our banker clothes." Skeets laughed as he cranked up his bike, and the two roared out on their errand of mercy.

"¿Three thousand pesos?" Ariana held up her hands and backed away from the pile of money like a basket of snakes.

"I reckon she's never seen three thousand pesos at one time." Jesse shrugged at her reluctance.

"¿Where did you get this money?"

The money lay on the table in the living area of the lean-to. Skeets placed a bowl on it so the wind would not blew the pesos away. "Explain where the money came from."

Jesse motioned for the two wives to sit down, pulled a chair up in front of them, and explained in Spanish how many people had given money for their mother's medical care. Tears welled in their eyes at the thought of people helping them. *"Now we'll take Ariana to the post office, to El Mercado, and for your mother's medicine."*

"Ah, no, Señor, I've never ridden a motorcycle." Ariana looked terrified at the idea.

"It's just like riding a horse. You sit down and hold on." Jesse swung his leg over the bike and held out his hand for her to climb onto the back seat. With encouragement from Skeets and Blanca, Ariana finally tucked her skirt under her legs, climbed aboard, and held onto Jesse like the jaws of death. She soon leaned with Jesse on turns and finally relaxed her grip. The excitement of the ride released alternating shrieks and laughter.

The small square in front of the post office had little automobile traffic. Pedestrians crisscrossed as they went about their business. Midmorning coffee drinkers filled the outdoor restaurants.

The two Harleys growled into the square and people stopped and stared at the loud machines. Every eye was on them by the time they parked at the post office. Ariana swelled with pride at her newfound status. Jesse raised his visor. "I've told Ariana to stay between us all the time. Wear your helmet visor down. Let's put the fear of God in the bad guys."

"Yeah, that or maybe another size five hat will just blow our ass off." Skeets shouldered-up on Ariana's right side, and the three marched through the front door.

Chapter 16

The post office itself did not help Pedro de Silva's mental angst. It truly was a grubby old place, ill cared for and depressing in the extreme. An air of neglect hung over it. The bile green paint was cracking and peeling, and the air was musty from mold. The pile of mail sacks containing something, but who knew what, had lain in the corner, untouched for months. The plain brown cotton pants and shirts of the workers were an insult to de Silva who felt they were professionals and should be in coats and ties. All of this fueled his larceny, which he rationalized with the thought that if no one cares what happens, then I'll do what I like.

With that mantra, Pedro de Silva had systematically stolen his neighbors' mail for years. Lately, though, their condemning stares had begun searing his soul, and he could no longer look into the eyes of those who approached his General Delivery window, as he said, *"I'm sorry, no letter today."*

He now walked blocks out of his way to avoid the reproachful façade of *Templo de San Roque,* his parish church. He seldom used his brand new Ford Explorer, stolen in Texas, transported by a smuggler, and purchased with cash filched from his neighbors. He rued the renovation of his house that set it apart from all the others on his street. The guilt of his evil deeds constricted his heart until a dull ache tortured him daily, leaving him exhausted, panting in the dark of his bed with nightmares of hellfire and damnation.

Today was Friday. He counted the hours until he could return to Truco No. 7 to drown his guilt, postponing his return to the terrors of his bed – when he again saw the lovely young girl who had visited his window two days ago for the first time. Today she walked between two black specters escorting her to his window. In panic he looked around for someone to spell him. Finding no one, he reached to close the window just as two gloved fists slammed onto his counter. He recoiled and stood speechless, waiting.

Her sweet voice filtered up to him. *"Do you have letters for Ariana and Blanca Gonzalez?"*

He stood rooted, praying that new letters had arrived after the ones stolen two days before.

"¿Is there a problem, señor?" Her sweet voice floated up to him. The two "spacemen" stood staring at him with unseen faces.

¡*"No. There is no problem."* His eyes flitted from one black specter to the other, trying to assess what evil force he was pitted against. Turning, he walked stiffly to the letter slots and searched through the "G's" twice. There were no letters addressed to anyone named Gonzalez, an absolute first in his memory. He muttered a curse and stood too long before returning to the window. *"I'm sorry but there are no letters."* The news that no letters had arrived seemed not to register on the three who stood motionless staring at his blanched face. He shifted uncomfortably from one foot to the other.

A deep voice in perfect Spanish rumbled from the specter on the girl's left. *"Beware, sinner – your days are numbered."* The three did an about-face and walked in step from the post office.

De Silva stood pale and paralyzed until the specters left the building. A rumble from heaven receding into the distance brought him back to consciousness. Trembling, he closed his window, hurrying to the restroom.

They stopped at the mercado, Jesse still laughing after they parking the bikes. "Did you see the look on that guy's face? I swear to God he'd a chewed up paper and shit a letter from Alfonso if he could've."

"He's one creepy looking dude that's for sure. He's got more feathers in his teeth than a chicken killin' dog." Skeets helped Ariana from Jesse's bike.

"We need to check this guy out, right?" said Jesse

Ariana pulled on Jesse's sleeve, "I'll be back soon." She rushed into the market.

"Why don't you wait here while Ariana shops? I'll go look for a doctor." Jesse swung his leg over his bike.

Jesse saw the impenetrable throng of those seeking medical attention at the hospital. The room reeked of unbathed bodies and the noise level was deafening. Nurses ran in every direction with the waiting patients calling after them for attention. Jesse cornered a nurse for a moment who laughed at the idea of someone treating Señora Ortiz at her home in the country. *"This woman's going to die if we don't get her help."* The look on Jesse's face softened the nurse's posture.

"There is a private medical clinic two streets down. Maybe they can help you," she offered before hurrying down the crowded hall.

The medical clinic was not crowded, and the facilities were immaculate. A strange aromatic blend of medicine and money pervaded the place. The counter attendant was telling Jesse they had no way of attending to Señora Ortiz in her home when a young man in a white coat passed by. Seeing

Jesse's Harley clothes, he stopped, looked out the front door, and a big grin split his face.

"Your Harley?" he asked in English.

"You guessed it."

"I'm Doctor Ruiz. What seems to be the problem?" He smiled and held out his hand.

Jesse shook his hand. "We have a friend who's very sick about thirty kilometers out of town, and we need to get a doctor to her."

"What are her symptoms?"

"She's had dysentery and been vomiting for days, and she looks very bad." Jesse made a loop of his thumb and forefinger to show how thin and frail her arms were.

"She's dehydrated, I'm sure. You don't have a way to get her into town?"

"My buddy and I only have our Harleys." Jesse pointed at his bike.

"I've always wanted a Harley-Davidson Motorcycle, but I've never even ridden one." Dr. Ruiz's expression was envious.

"How'd you like to ride one today?" Jesse again motioned toward the bike.

Dr. Ruiz turned to the receptionist. "I need three sacks of saline glucose and three sacks of liquid Cipro, an IV setup, and alcohol swipes. Oh, and some Cipro tablets and four bottles of sterile drinking water." He turned to Jesse. "I've got to pack my bag. I'll be back in five minutes."

When Jesse arrived back at the mercado with Dr. Ruiz in his second seat, Skeets was helping Ariana onto his bike while wrestling with an ambitious sack of groceries. Introductions went round, and the two Harleys rumbled out of Guanajuato, each with a "CARE" package.

After only a few minutes in the mother's bedroom, accompanied by Blanca, Dr. Ruiz came out and announced, "That room's an oven. We've got to get her where she can breathe. Let's move her out here in the breeze way; at least she can get some cool air and be away form the stench in that room."

Skeets went into the bedroom and gently lifted her from the bed while the others moved the bed into the open-air living area. Ariana and Blanca quickly changed the bedclothes, and Skeets laid the mother back on the bed.

Jesse asked, *"Do you have some netting to keep the flies off your mother?"*

Blanca rushed back into the other bedroom and returned with mosquito netting, which Skeets and Jesse installed over the bed. Dr. Ruiz set up the IV with both the saline/glucose and the Cipro antibiotic and then showed the daughters how to change the sacks when they emptied.

A pot of beans and another of rice simmered on the stove, and mesquite coals glowed in the grill. Ariana dropped to her knees on the dirt floor and began grinding corn in a stone *metate*.

"What's she doing?" Skeets asked, pointing down at Ariana

"Grinding corn for tortillas. Looks like we're invited to lunch. It smells pretty good." Dr. Ruiz took the mother's vital signs again. "I need to stay here for a while to see if she starts responding, anyway. We'll need to get an ambulance if she doesn't."

"You ever driven a motorcycle?" Skeets pointed to his bike.

"Some 250 cc Japanese bikes, but never a Harley." Ruiz walked to the Harley, gave it an admiring look, and kicked the tires.

"Well, it's about time, don't you think?" Skeets showed the doctor the various controls. "It's all the same except it makes a bigger noise when you fall."

"Hop on." Jesse encouraged the doctor. "Just remember to turn your head the direction you want the bike to go."

Jesse got on his bike and gave a demonstration of how to turn the bike by making tight radius turns in the corral. "It's simple. Just keep turning your head and the bike turns with you. If it starts to fall, give it more gas."

Ruiz sat on Skeets' bike, eased out the clutch, and rolled forward a few feet before applying the brake. Soon he was making long radius turns and riding in and out of the compound with Jesse following at a distance on his bike.

A loud clanging of a dinner bell came from the kitchen of the lean-to, and Blanca waved her apron for them to return for lunch.

"My, God, what a sense of power that Harley gives you," Ruiz said while he checked Señora Ortiz again. He put his stethoscope back into his bag "This lady's a real trooper. Her vitals are already improving."

Ariana and Blanca displayed visible pride in their culinary offering. The feast they had prepared covered almost every inch of the rudimentary dining table. A huge platter in the center had a pile of beef fajitas surrounded by grilled onions, poblano peppers, red and green bell peppers and grilled scallions. Bowls of fresh-made guacamole and *pico de gallo* sat in baskets of tostados fried from freshly made, stone-ground tortillas. Crumbled goat cheese covered a platter of shaved lettuce and diced vine-ripened tomatoes. Hand-shredded grilled pork tenderloin was topped with a green sauce of onion, cilantro and *tomatillos*. Bowls of *frijoles a la charra* and *arroz mexicana* sat on either end of the table. The aromas wafting up from the table made even Skeets and Jesse want to bless the food.

Blanca stood over the comal griddle, cooking tortillas to order while Ariana served the food and poured glasses of fresh squeezed orange juice and bottled water.

"*There is no restaurant in Guanajuato with better food.*" Dr Ruiz busied himself with a beef fajita taco made from a griddle-fresh tortilla and all of the condiments available.

"We've eaten a fair amount of Mexican food on our way down here, and I can't remember any better." Jesse hoisted his second taco.

"Even the beans and rice are excellent." Dr. Ruiz said to Skeets and waved the aromas to his nose before taking another spoonful.

"I would comment except I'm too busy eating."

As the meal wound down, Dr. Ruiz made a small plate of beans and rice for Ms. Ortiz. "*I think your mother can hold down a little food now.*" He moved to her bed and gave her small bits of mashed food on the tip of a spoon. He called Ariana and Blanca to the bed and explained again how to change the IV and antibiotic sacks. He pulled out the Cipro pills. "*Give your mother three per day when the IV runs out.*" He showed them how to remove the IV needle and to sterilize and bandage the puncture. "*Oh, and only give her this sterilized water to drink.*"

He walked over to Skeets and Jesse. "As much as I've enjoyed this, I really have to get back to the clinic."

"Doc, you're a real guy for coming out here today. I think you've made three ladies very happy." Skeets held out his hand to the doctor. "*Muchisimoas gracias, amigo.*"

"I got a great meal and a Harley ride. Thank you." Dr. Ruiz finished packing his black bag and shook Jesse's hand.

"How much do we owe you, Doc?" Jesse asked.

"How about paying for the supplies. Say twenty-five dollars U.S.?" The doctor shrugged at his guess.

"Here's fifty. Apply the rest to someone else who needs help." Jesse handed him five one-hundred peso notes from the funds given to the ladies.

Before Dr. Ruiz could climb onto Jesse's bike, the two wives rushed up to him, talking at the same time, trying to thank him. *"Easy, Ladies, I should be thanking you for that wonderful meal. Your mother should be well in a few days."*

The women moved to Skeets and Jesse, shaking their hands and thanking them for their kindnesses and for the money.

"We'll be living and singing at Pericos Negros in Guanajuato for a week or two. We have to move into our new rooms this afternoon, but we'll be out here Sunday to check on you," Jesse explained to the wives, who laughed and waved as the Harleys snarled and throbbed out of the corral.

Skeets and Jesse summarized the day's activities. Nan and Jody howled at the post office scene. Getting Dr. Ruiz to make a house call to the sick mother seemed a miracle, and Jody and Nan clapped their hands with pleasure at the wives' appreciation of the money.

"We might be criticized for kicking two such angels of mercy like you out of our apartment." Nan lifted her beer and motioned around the room. "You really don't have to leave you know. It's been sort of cozy here."

"You've put the spice in our enchiladas, you know," Jody added with a flourish.

"You ladies certainly upheld the hospitality tradition of the great state of Texas, but we've been a bother long enough." Skeets cinched up his bedroll and Harley bag.

"Besides we'll be seeing you at the old Negros, right?" Jesse hoisted his gear in preparation to leave, then paused. "Why don't you two come over and check out our new digs with us?"

"We thought you'd never ask, " the two said in unison.

Jesse and Skeets had a bit of a problem loading everything and everybody on the bikes, but they finally were underway and within minutes were at the Pericos Negros asking Miguel where they were going to bunk. Miguel told them to ride around back and meet him at the bottom of some stairs leading to a rooftop apartment.

As he unlocked the apartment door, Miguel motioned around the room. "It's not great, but there are worse places to bed down in Guanajuato. When you open the windows, there's a nice breeze to keep you cool."

Skeets and Jesse looked around and gave an approving nod. "We'll do fine here, amigo." The room was not fancy, but it had two beds on one wall and a bathroom in the opposite corner. A few touristy pictures hung on the walls, and a mirror hung above a small dresser. The kitchen, a sink with a small refrigerator next to it, was open to the room.

Will our bikes be safe behind the restaurant?" Jesse motioned downstairs.

"We have two guards twenty-four hours a day. Give them a couple of dollars every now and then, and they'll probably even wash them for you." Miguel handed the key to Skeets, turned to leave, and then stopped. "How did your mission of mercy go this morning?"

"We found a doctor for the mother, and the money is going to make a big difference to these people," Skeets explained.

"Yeah, and the lunch they fed us was the best we've had in Mexico." Jesse rubbed his stomach in appreciation.

"That good? Maybe I should try it some day. I always need good cooks." Miguel laughed and turned again to leave.

Nan and Jody flopped down on each of the two beds for a mattress test. "Shows promise, wouldn't you say, Jody?" Nan struck a sultry pose on her bed.

"These girls just won't leave us alone." Jesse held his hands up in a defensive pose.

Skeets heaved his Harley bag onto the bed with Nan. "Why don't you make yourself useful and unpack while I shower off this Mexican road dust. Then we'll see what mysteries the evening holds.

Chapter 17

The evening had a pleasant, cool breeze, so Skeets, Jesse, and the two girls ate their early dinner on the *Negros* patio. The sun shone over the top of the arches and cast elaborate shadow patterns on the flagstone. Trees in terra cotta urns rustled in the breeze to the subtle beat of soft background music.

"So you girls are footloose and fancy free? No significant other back in Austin?" Jesse addressed the question to both Jody and Nan as the waiter brought the meals. They looked at each other and laughed.

"Well, you know, I like a lot of guys, but there's no one I can't live without. You know? I mean, maybe one day." Jody wrinkled her nose seeking comprehension if not understanding.

All eyes turned to Nan, who took a bite and held the fork in front of her for a time. "I really liked one guy last year, but he got too complicated. He got serious and even talked about marriage. I've got a few more things on my bucket list before I think about settling down."

Skeets ate his enchiladas and listened. He thought back to when he and Gena had first dated. Each time they met, or even the thought of her, had sent a thrill rippling through his stomach. When he watched her sleeping, her genuine goodness had made him feel like apologizing for the scoundrel he was. God, he thought, if there was any way to get her back . . . He put down his fork and wiped his eyes with his napkin.

They walked through *Jardín Unión* for a little fresh air. Dozens of couples promenaded on the tree-lined sidewalks arm-in-arm. The four stopped for a drink at Truco No. 7 before Skeets' and Jesse's gig. Jesse stood and stared toward the bar before he slid into the comfortable leather seats with the others. "Look, the post office creep's at the end of bar."

"It's him alright." Skeets watched the man for a moment. "He must have been here a while 'cause his head keeps banging on the bar." The postal clerk slouched over his drink and occasionally nodded off, only to catch himself after his head bounced off his glass. He wore his work clothes with the addition of a felt fedora covering his bald head.

"You know, Nan and I went for a letter once with a friend, and I remember him. He had the jitters and the concerned look of a man with hemorrhoids. You know?" Jody said.

"Yeah, he seemed really nervous and edgy." Nan thought for a moment. "Actually, we see him every time we come. Always on the same stool."

"Excuse me a minute." Jesse got up, went to the other end of the bar from the postman and called the bartender over. *"¿How well do you know the guy at the end of the bar?"*

"¿Old de Silva?" The bartender nodded in de Silva's direction and grinned. *"Nobody knows him very well. Pedro de Silva's a loner. Comes in here just about every night and gets completely shit faced."*

"¿He works in the post office? ¿How can he afford to come in here every night?" Jesse watched closely at the bartender's reaction.

"You should see the brand new Ford Explorer he drives. He got so messed up one night I drove him home in his car, and his house is way out of his league also. He must have a rich uncle or something." The barkeep shrugged.

"Thanks, amigo." Jesse threw a couple of dollars on the bar and turned to leave, then returned. *"¿Where did you say he lived?"*

"I didn't." He glanced down at the two dollars on the bar. Jesse picked them up and threw down a fifty-peso bill in their place. *"Up on Calle Aldama near Templo de San Roque. Look for the nicest house. You can't miss it."* Jesse turned to leave again, then stopped when the barkeep offered more information. *"I think he's really religious, or something. When he gets drunk, he gets out his rosary and starts mumbling Hail Marys."* The bartender finished polishing a glass and poured de Silva another drink

Jesse slid back into the chair next to Jody. "The sombitch's name is Pedro de Silva, and he's definitely stealing. He runs up a big bar bill in here every night. The bartender says he drives an expensive car and lives in an expensive house. He needs a good old fashioned ass kicking."

"Great idea. We spend the rest of our lives in a Mexican jail for assault and battery of a public employee." Skeets shook his head in disgust.

"Every night he gets out his beads when he's *borracho* and mumbles Hail Marys, like he's a religious freak or something. He's crooked, man." Jesse fumed. "It's not right, bro."

"Maybe Mexico should take care of its own criminals." Skeets swirled his glass and took a pull on his drink. "Besides, anything we do will get us in trouble with the law."

Nan smiled and elbowed Jody. "If he's a religious penitent like you say, maybe there is something."

Jody caught Nan's drift and laughed aloud. "You know? Nan and I might have to do a little finagling, but you've probably noticed we're pretty persuasive. You know?"

"That's God's own truth," Jesse and Skeets said almost in unison.

The Friday night crowd at *Pericos Negros* was bigger than Skeets had expected. The bash rocked until three in the morning. Miguel grinned like a lottery winner, when he joined Skeets, Jesse, and the girls at closing to pay their entertainment fee.

"How many weeks can you guys perform?" Miguel arched his eyebrows hopefully.

Skeets and Jesse looked at each other. "I reckon we'll move along when the time is right."

Miguel waited but got no other answer.

Skeet's psyche showed a few frayed edges after the past week's excitement and the late night performances. "Ladies, I need a little sleep tonight. In fact, I might sleep until a fire alarm wakes me."

"I'm a little beat myself," Jesse said with less conviction than Skeets as he looked at Jody's inviting expression. They offered the girls a taxi, but they declined, as they wanted to walk because they might find another party.

The breeze promised by Miguel kept the rooftop apartment cool, and the two weary travelers' raucous snoring caused periodic explosions of pigeons fleeing from their rooftop roosts.

Their apartment door burst open shortly after noon. Nan and Jody ran in and pounced on the two moribund musicians. "Wake up. Wake up. We've got places to go and things to do," they shouted.

"There's no place better'n where I am right now." Skeet pulled the pillow over his head

"We're having lunch with friends of ours. You know? So get a move on." Jody pounded on Jesse's back.

"Skeets?" The muffled voice came from Jesse's pillow.

"Yes, Jesse?"

"Who are these people, and what do they want?"

"We want you to get your dead asses out of bed, cause we have an appointment at Truco in about thirty minutes." Nan grabbed Skeets pillow and joined in the back pounding.

"Truco can't be open this early." Skeets rolled over and pinned Nan down. "Come to think of it, there is something better than sleeping."

Nan bucked him off. "No time for messing around, big boy. Get a move on."

Nan and Jody towed a bedraggled Skeets and Jesse through the door of Truco No. 7, looked around, and then waved at a table of five student types. They arrived tableside and Nan announced, "Meet Skeets and Jesse, those two adorable C&W singers at Pericos Negros."

A muscular, handsome Mexican guy held out his hand. "I'm Rafael." He continued introducing the others at the table. "Man, we danced our asses off at Pericos after the *Entremes* the other night. You guys are good."

Before Skeets and Jesse could acknowledge the compliments, Nan butted in and pointed around the table. "These're the stars of the *Entremes*."

Skeets and Jess rocked back in surprise. "Wow. You guys were great. You scared the living shit out of me. I still look over my shoulder at night for the creepy dude with the burning eyeballs." Jesse demonstrated his backward glance.

A broad smile spread over Rafael's face. "Nan and Jody told us how much you enjoyed the play the other night. We want to talk about the play."

A Saturday afternoon nap and an earlier night than usual after *Pericos Negros* had left Skeets restored. He sat on his bike with engine idling. "It's a good day for Harleyin', pardner." Sunday had dawned cool and glorious, with no clouds. The church bells tolled and sent the faithful home for their Sunday meals and siestas. The breeze wafted down the mountains and carried the scent of cedar, huisache, and agarita blossoms. Very little traffic plied the streets as Guanajuato had powered down for Sunday.

"A night off and not bustin' our buns sounds great." Jesse strapped on his helmet and started his bike. "*Despacio, amigo. Let's take our time.*"

They rode leisurely through the empty streets of the quaint city and appreciated the architecture, picturesque gardens, and landscaping, all of which made Guanajuato the colonial classic so many enjoyed. They gained speed as they exited the city but continued toward the Gonzalez sisters' home at an unhurried pace. Skeets, in the lead, passed the turnoff at the road leading into the compound and continued about a mile down the road. A small stream passed under the road. Skeets slowed, made a u-turn, and stopped on the ancient bridge. He raised his visor to look upstream at the lush grass and flowers bordering the water and the single rut trail beside the stream. He turned to Jesse. "Beautiful stuff, man. Let's ride up there."

"Naw, let's go see Ariana and Blanca." Jesse gunned his engine and rode back toward the compound. They saw Ariana at work in the stables as they rode into the compound and Blanca cooking in the lean-to. Their mother was setting up in bed with what looked like a bowl of soup.

When they entered the living area, Jesse gestured in surprise. "*Good afternoon, Señora Ortiz. You look much better. Soon we must go dancing.*" He demonstrated a Mexican polka step.

The señora glanced away coyly at the idea of dancing. "*Thank you, señor, I feel much better. You must have my daughter's wonderful soup.*" She gestured toward Blanca with her bowl.

"*We're very familiar with your daughters' cooking,*" Jesse and Skeets shook Blanca's hand. She blushed at the attention like the bride she was. Ariana continued working in the horse stalls, and Blanca saw Skeets look in her direction.

"The patron usually comes for horse riding on Sunday and Ariana cleans the stalls before his arrival. We must take care of the horses since Alfonso and Beto left." Blanca again ground corn in the *metate* for tortillas

"My God, these ladies work hard." Skeets walked toward the horse stalls. Ariana was leading the last horse out of its stall when Skeets walked up. The horse shied slightly at the sight of Skeets. "Whoa, big fellow." Skeets patted his withers and calmed him as Ariana tied him up. *"Buenas tardes, Ariana."*

Skeets looked at the large horse stalls, well constructed and even insulated against the heat, and shook his head at the difference between where the horses and the people lived.

"Buenas tardes, señor." Ariana seemed a little embarrassed. She straightened her hair and brushed straw from her peasant dress, but made no eye contact with Skeets. Their greeting left little else to say that either would understand. An awkward silence followed, and Ariana went back into the stall. Skeets rolled the wheelbarrow with straw and manure into the empty stall. *"No. No. Señor, no es posible."* Skeets picked up the pitchfork, and Ariana grabbed it. *"Por favor, Señor."*

He prevailed and began forking the manure into the wheelbarrow.

"Well, *amigo*, if your singing doesn't work out, you can always drop back and shovel shit." Jesse leaned diagonally in the doorway of the stall with a stalk of straw in his mouth.

"Señor Jesse, please tell Señor Skeets he should not work in the stalls. He is a guest in our house." She seemed a little frantic over Skeets' assistance.

"Señorita, Skeets is doing what he does best. I think he wants to show you how good he is at cleaning stalls. We should just watch him work." Jesse laughed and motioned her over.

Ariana looked puzzled by this strange behavior but moved beside Jesse.

Skeets looked up from his straw and manure detail. "Feel free, Bro. Leap in here and help anytime."

"Actually, Ariana said she wonders how good a white guy can clean a stall. Since I'm Hispanic, I'm afraid I can't join in the fun. But you should pick up the pace a little so you won't embarrass your race." Jesse asked Ariana. "*¿Do you think Skeets should clean the stall?*"

"*No, no. I should clean the stall.*" Ariana motioned all around the stall and shook her head dramatically.

"There you have it, ol' buddy. I just asked her if you were doing a good job, and you heard her answer."

Skeets hung his sweaty shirt on a bridle rack and spit on both hands. "She wants some shit shoveled, then move 'cause the shit's gonna fly." He pushed the wheelbarrow out the stall door headed full speed for the compost pile.

Jesse and Ariana stepped aside as Skeets barreled past. "Way to go, *hombre*. Show her what a gringo can do." Outside they watched him trot behind his wheelbarrow.

Diablo, an unusually tall, handsome horse, knew he had a truly badass black coat. He stuck his head out his stall door and put the evil eye on everything happening around the stalls. Today confused him. First, the woman led him out of the stall. Ok, this is great, he thought, even though the fat-ass with those two look-alike foxy ladies might crawl up on his back. Fat-ass tries to be impressive in the saddle. What a laugh. He can't get in the saddle without a stool, and, God, what a lardo. He weighs a ton and smells evil – but not exactly like a mountain lion, but just as evil. Like a guy who might hurt a horse.

Then the woman put him away again in the claustrophobic stall. I need a good run and a good sweat, to get the kinks out, he thought. Now I'm back in prison again. This really sucks.

He gazed out at all those big fields of grain and corn and thought, this pisses me off, standing here day after day with nothing to do. Actually wanting old fat-ass to crawl up on my back is sick. I need professional help. Something's gotta change.'

At least he had clean straw, and the evil smelling stuff went away. God, I hate that stuff, he thought. It plops down on the straw from somewhere behind and stinks up the place. I can't even lie down with the stuff around. A magnificent animal like myself deserves more respect. He stood, head out of the stall door and wondered if unseen forces plotted against him.

A car pulled up in front of the stables, and Jesse and Ariana saw a black Mercedes with two people in the front seat. Carlos Algo's twins stepped from the car, hair in buns, feet in riding boots, legs in jodhpurs, and breasts straining at their equestrian shirts. They carried riding helmets and quirts, and they stood for a moment as if wondering why Jesse was leaning against their horse stall.

Diablo thought, now we're talking, the Foxy Ladies are here, and maybe I'll get a little action after all.

"Buenas tardes, señoritas." Jesse tipped his bill cap. *"At last we meet."*

"¿You are the piano player from Pericos Negros, right?" One of the twins asked.

Jesse removed his hat and made a deep bow. *"Jesse Suarez, at your service."*

The second twin asked Ariana. *"¿Why is Señor Suarez here?"*

"Señor Jesse and Señor Skeets brought us news of Alfonso and Beto from Texas." Ariana looked at the ground while she spoke.

"*¿Alfonso and Beto are in Texas? Who takes care of the horses?*" The first twin motioned toward the horses, irritated by the news their hired hands had left.

"*Blanca and I take care of them.*" Just then, Skeets trotted up - disheveled, sweating, and pushing the smelly manure wheelbarrow.

The twins looked at Jesse and the first twin pointed at Skeets. "*¿Isn't this the singer?*"

"*Actually, he only sings part-time. Mostly he cleans stalls.*"

Jesse told Skeets. "They asked if you were doing a good job cleaning the stalls."

"Please, have them come on in and do a better job, if they like." Skeets slammed the pitchfork into the ground.

The second twin pointed at the horse tied outside the stable. "*¿Who will saddle our horses for us if Alfonso and Beto are gone?*"

"*The stable boy.*" Jesse pointed at Skeets.

Ariana had already bridled a second horse, brought her out of the stall, and led the two horses toward the tack room in the lean-to.

Diablo watched the two mares walk away, whinnied, and shook his head. If I could just get out of this stall, I could spend quality time with those two beauties.

Jesse pointed at the two horses. "Hey, good buddy, would you help Ariana saddle up the horses for these two lovely ladies?"

The two twins looked at each other and laughed. "*¿Do you ride, piano man?*"

"*Many ladies have complimented my riding.*" Jesse's face split into a toothy grin.

"*¿Maybe you will ride with us, hombre?*" The first twin raised a knowing eyebrow at the second. She took a bridle, went into a stall, and led out Diablo, who cast a mean eye on all present.

Jesse surveyed the evil-looking animal and wondered about the throttle, clutch, and brakes. I ride a Harley. How much harder can a horse be, he thought. *"An impressive animal you have there, but of course, not the quality I'm accustomed to back in Texas."*

Diablo couldn't believe what he'd just heard. "Not of the quality?"

Jesse patted Diablo's neck, and barely escaped with his hand when the horse turned and nipped at him. The twins snickered and led the black horse for saddling.

Skeets and Ariana had finished with the second horse when the twins and Jesse arrived with the third. "Which of these ladies can ride two horses at once," Skeets said.

"Actually, I've been invited to ride along with these two lovelies." Jesse gestured at the horse that still held a wicked eye on him.

"Since when did you develop equestrian skills?"

"How hard can it be, man? I'd ride a Brahma bull for a shot at these twins." Jesse smiled in their direction. *"I just asked the stable boy to saddle up this noble mount."*

Skeets helped Ariana saddle the horse. "I can't wait. Seeing this is worth the shit shoveling."

The twins stood by their horses and waited. Finally, one asked Skeets, *"¿Will you help us up?"*

Skeets looked at Jesse for a translation. "Help them up on their horses. I'd appreciate a little help myself 'cause this bastard's taller'n a giraffe. This leather strap on its back doesn't look like any saddle I've ever seen."

Skeets had already helped the twins up. "All sophisticated equestrians of your caliber ride on English saddles."

"I think the whole thing will disappear into the crack of my ass. What do I hold on with?"

"With your life." Skeets vaulted Jesse up enthusiastically, and he almost rolled over the horse headfirst. He lay across the horse on his stomach and flopped around helplessly.

Diablo looked at Jesse with disgust. "I can't believe this. It's just not my day."

Jesse saw the twins laugh at him. He reached down and picked up the opposite-side stirrup and inspected it. "*Right, this stirrup's ok.*" He struggled to sit upright and once vertical, feet in stirrups; he motioned grandly for the twins to lead off. They obliged and spurred their horses into a slow, long lope and circled the compound counterclockwise.

Jesse's horse, uninspired by the twin's leadership, stood straddle-legged, like a statue. Jesse wiggled the reins and clucked at the horse.

Diablo considered Jesse with his mean-eyed stare. "Are you kidding me?"

"This wild-eyed bastard needs a starter button." Jesse now used a hunching motion without success.

"Bro, you're supposed to ride a horse, not hump it." Skeets laughed so hard he could barely talk. Ariana and Blanca held their hands over their mouths muffling laughter. The twins flashed by on their third circumnavigation of the corral, still steady on a lope.

"The stall is better than a day with this clown on my back." Diablo thought and commenced backing toward his stall, clockwise.

"Hey, bro, I think I've found reverse gear." Jesse motioned down at the horse with his free hand. Skeets slapped his thighs as tears of laughter streamed down his face.

Each time the twins loped passed his backsliding-bastard of a horse; Jesse smiled, doffed his hat, and said something like, "*¿Lovely day for riding, don't you think, ladies?*"

The twins reversed their direction, and one rode up on each side of the backward-bound beast, and swatted the contentious animal on the ass with their quirts. Now, Diablo understood this language. No translation required. He laid his ears back and leaped forward as if he just blasted out of the starting gate, 'Running for the Roses.'

Jesse grabbed the mane with both hands and somehow stayed on as the horse galloped full throttle out of the compound and turned left through a field leading toward the small stream he and Skeets had seen earlier. The twins looked astonished and spurred their horses into hot pursuit. Skeets, Ariana, and Blanca ran after them until Jesse disappeared over the next hill with the twins gaining on him. Skeets heard Jesse's expletives, "Evil-eyed son-of-a-bitch," "Vile mother-fucker," and "Canned dog food," until they faded into the distance.

Skeets ran back for his bike and gave chase across the field, but the terrain became too rough. He turned back toward the road and trailed a rooster tail of dirt as he rode toward the pavement. He rode in the direction of the horses past the stream, but could not see the riders. Finally, he returned to the corral and waited for them. Blanca fixed him a bowl of *caldo* and heated fresh made tortillas on the *comal*.

Time passed slowly because of the language barrier. Skeets checked his watch and wondered what he should do. Almost two hours later the three horses appeared over the hill. One of the twins led Jesse's horse. Jesse rode behind the second twin. They seemed in very good humor and in no hurry.

When they reached the tack room and dismounted, Jesse smiled broadly. "It takes a while to get the hang of this horse ridin' thing."

The twins' shirttails hung out of their jodhpurs. Their hair, no longer in a bun, hung tousled around their shoulders, speckled with bits of grass. Jesse's shirt had a few more buttons open and his hair needed brushing. After a long look at Jesse, Skeets said, "Tell me you didn't leave me here for two hours while you screwed the drug dealer's twins."

"I think they felt sorry for me. After they caught up with me and stopped the miserable beast, we sat down on the grass by the beautiful stream we saw earlier. One thing led to another, and pretty soon we ended up naked. Fantastic, man, I can die happy."

"I don't know about 'happy,' but there's a good chance you could die."

Jesse said the twins. *"The stable boy expressed his concern for your safety."*

"He's very kind, but tell him the horses need a good cool down and currying," one of the twins said as she dismounted.

The second looked at her watch. *"Vámonos. We're late."* They ran for their car while they stuffed in their shirttails. One of them looked back and shouted, *"¡Hasta el Miércoles."*

"What did she say?" Skeets looked at Jesse.

"They just expressed their gratitude."

"It sounded like *'Miércoles'.*" Skeets frowned. "Wednesday?" He paused for a minute. *"'Miércoles.'* Tell me you haven't planned another dalliance with the twins on Wednesday."

"I'd consider myself downright impolite if I didn't. I mean international relations might suffer otherwise"

"Forget international relations. I doubt Carlos Algo wants to share the twins' *sexual* relations. I mean, he looks like a guy who kills people just to keep in practice."

Chapter 18

Pedro de Silva stood in his post office General Delivery window just before his noon break. Tuesday morning few people, whose itinerancy or separation from postal routes required a visit, showed up at his window. The previous day he had sorted the weekend pileup of general delivery mail and felt good because he had not stolen a single letter. The absence of any likely cash or money order letters caused his hiatus from larceny, but he thought, a righteous day is a righteous day, regardless.

Monday's reprieve from postal poaching helped his self-esteem crawl to a level where he felt comfortable at home, and, after only two drinks, he ventured into bed, though still fearful of nightmares. The nightmares did not come, and he awoke rested and in a particularly good state of mind.

Now, just before his noon break, the two black specters returned and approached his window in lock step. Two gloved fists gaveled his terror to order: *"Beware, sinner de Sila, your time has come."* The two wraiths stood motionless and stared at de Silva whose brown skin, now a light shade of taupe, quivered while they turned on their heels and strode from the post office. Pedro de Silva, visibly shaken, stood motionless until he could no longer see them and then headed toward *el baño* with the urgency of a visiting tourist.

De Silva yearned for Truco No. 7 as he counted the afternoon minutes until he could wash away the visage of the specters still plaguing him hours later. Fear and loathing replaced his pleasant day. Would he never get relief from his guilt?

Pedro de Silva checked his Rolex – one o'clock. He had not hurried his drinking, but his head banged the bar like it was three o'clock in the morning. The bartender's look said, don't even ask for another drink. Pedro called for his check, paid, and drew himself up to leave Truco. He reached the front door by holding onto a succession of chair backs and finally the front door handle. As he left, the bartender made a cell phone call. De Silva stepped through the door onto Truco Street and drew in a deep breath of the night air. He looked both directions before he walked up toward his car, balancing himself with one arm against the walls of the buildings along the sidewalk.

He stopped to get his breath from climbing the steep street and thought he heard something. He turned, but saw nothing. Trudging on once again, he felt someone behind him and stopped again. When he turned this time, his heart almost stopped. A figure in a long black coat and black flat-brimmed hat with coals of fire for eyes stood behind him within his reach. De Silva visibly shook and his teeth chattered involuntarily. "Don Ernesto?" he mumbled. The vision nodded affirmation.

Everyone knew the legend of Truco Street, but few had seen Don Ernesto's ghost. When de Silva saw the spirit face to face, a rivulet of piss ran out of his pants leg and down the hill. Don Ernesto raised one arm slowly and with a colorless hand pointed at de Silva. A dry tortured voice like the echoes of hell moaned, "¡*Confess. Repent. Or be damned.*" The ghost took a step toward de Silva, and the postman turned and fled in an alcoholic stumble toward his car. He looked back when he reached the Ford. The street was empty. He was confused for a moment, and then shook his head trying to clear it. After several stabs with the key, he unlocked the car and drove toward his house. His heart still pounded his ribs when he reached the wrought iron gate in front of his house. He looked all around before leaving the car. After he unlocked and shoved the gate inward, he turned toward the car. Four figures in hooded monks robes were behind him. Their faces, barely visible behind the folds of the hoods, looked old and white, with dark wrinkles of death.

De Silva quivered again and felt weak in the knees. *"Who . . . who are you?"* he managed a stammer. *"What do you want?"*

The four were silent and only stared at him. A voice again echoed from the depths of hell. *"You've been summoned. Your time has come."*

"Summoned?" De Silva's' eyes glazed and his knees wobbled and gave way as he sank to the ground. He mumbled a barely intelligible *"Santa Maria . . ."* then passed out, prostrate.

The four hooded figures each grabbed an arm or leg and put him in the back of the Explorer, got into the vehicle, and drove away toward the *Templo de San Roque.*

Pedro de Silva awoke lying on the stage in front of the entrance of *Templo de San Roque.* His head remained on the stage while his eyes moved slowly around his field of view. He saw the *Plazuela San Roque.* The clouds covered the moon and left the small plaza dark, vacant, and foreboding. His brain, still alcohol fogged, tried to reconstruct the previous events. Then he remembered Don Ernesto's warning on Truco Street and shuddered as if a cold wind passed over him. He lay in the quiet darkness of the plaza remembering another disturbing visage, when out of the gloom appeared the four ghostly monks. They stared at him but did not move or speak. Only watched him. He raised himself with one arm and rolled over into a kneeling position and faced them. He clasped his hands in supplication, "Please, please don't take me until I've confessed." He sobbed uncontrollably, "I beg you."

A blinding shaft of heavenly light flooded over him. Herald trumpets rent the air, and a rumble of thunder and a cloud of smoke issued above the cathedral. Pablo de Silva fell backwards thunderstruck and gazed up as the Angel Michael descended toward him, sword in hand. *"PROSTRATE YOURSELF BEFORE GOD, SINNER."* The voice rang with the sound of eternity. *"I AM MICHAEL, THE SWORD OF GOD, COME TO ADMINISTER YOUR PENANCE. CONFESS, SINNER."*

De Silva attempted rolling over face down as instructed, but he had little muscular control, and he shook violently. Finally, he was prostrate just as he shit himself.

"CONFESS, BEFORE I SMITE YOU WITH MY SWORD AND SEND YOU STRAIGHT TO HELL FOR ALL ETERNITY."

With great effort, de Silva rose to his knees and bowed his head, chin to chest and sobbed, *"Fa . . . Fath . . . Father, for . . for . . . forgive me. I...I...have sinned.*

"CONFESS, SINNER."

"I have stolen money from poor people." His body racked with the shortness of breath from sobbing.

"HOW MANY TIMES HAVE YOU STOLEN?"

"Many hundreds of times."

"WHY DID YOU STEAL FROM THE POOR?"

A long pause preceded the answer. *"Because I was greedy and wanted a better life."*

"YOU FEEL A LIFE OF SIN IS A BETTER LIFE?"

He sobbed during another pause. *"I have lived in torment knowing what I did was wrong, but I couldn't stop. My greed was too great."*

"PEDRO DE SILVA, YOUR SIN IS HORRIBLE AND YOUR PUNISHMENT MUST BE SEVERE. . . ."

"Father, I beg you for another chance." De Silva fell forward on his elbows – face in hands.

AND WHAT WILL YOU DO WITH THIS CHANCE?

"I will empty my bank accounts, sell all my possessions, and return the money to the poor." His head now rested on the stage and his hands covered his neck as protection from Michael's sword.

VILE SINNER, THIS IS NOT PUNISHMENT – ONLY RECOMPENSE FOR YOUR SINS.

"What else would you have me do?" He fell on his side and rolled into a fetal position.

SINNER DE SILVA, PUT ONE FOURTH OF THE MONEY IN THE TEMPLO DE SAN ROQUE POOR BOX. THEN YOU MUST VISIT ALL THOSE YOU STOLE FROM, CONFESS YOUR SIN, AND RETURN THEIR PORTION OF THE REMAINDER. FROM THIS DAY FORWARD PUT ONE-FOURTH OF ALL YOU MAKE INTO THE POOR BOX BEFORE YOUR WEEKLY CONFESSION.

De Silva's groan echoed across the Plazuela.

FAIL IN THIS, AND I WILL RETURN AND DRIVE A SWORD OF FIRE THROUGH YOUR HEART. YOU WILL BURN IN HELL FOR ETERNITY.

The trumpets and another explosion drowned out Pedro de Silva's scream of anguish. Michael ascended back to heaven through the cloud of smoke, the four monks faded into the gloom of the plaza, as Pedro de Silva fainted.

Those who first ventured out into the *Plazuela San Roque* the next morning gathered in groups and asked the others what they had heard the previous night. A dead man lay crumpled on the stage. Finally, someone approached close enough and saw the postal worker, de Silva.

The noise of the plaza woke de Silva, and both he and the onlookers were terrified. Finally the dead man jumped up, and fled in the direction of his home.

Chapter 19

I've heard of scaring the crap out of somebody, but to see it happen is something special." Jesse laughed until tears came. The other actors of the *Entremes* group and the bartender at Truco No. 7 howled along with him.

The actor who played Don Ernesto stood at the bar and picked up his feet alternately. "Man, the guy pissed so much I couldn't stay dry."

"It was pretty rough hanging right above him." Rafael fanned the air in front of his face. "His penance should have included 'bathe, three times with lye soap while you say your rosary'."

"You think he will give the poor all his money and quit stealing?" Nan asked the group.

"We'll check him out, but I doubt he wants another night like tonight, and we have the video of his performance," Raphael said

"The *Federales* might be interested," Jesse laughed again at the prospect.

"Yeah, they'll want a percentage of what he steals." Rafael frowned and shook his head in disgust.

Jesse looked at an unusually quiet Skeets who only smiled at the boisterous laughter around him. He moved onto the empty bar seat vacated by Nan. "Hey, dude, we pulled it off, but you don't seem very happy."

"No, I think we did a good thing tonight, and I enjoyed it." Skeets looked blankly at his beer bottle.

"But?" Jesse leaned down to make eye contact.

"But I keep thinking about home. I just can't get Gena out of my mind. I miss her a bunch."

"More important, does she miss *you*?" Jesse laughed and slapped Skeets on the back. Skeets' expression told Jesse home was not just a passing thought. "Well, man, if you're homesick, then let's finish out the week and boogie."

Skeets seemed to perk up at the thought. "Yeah, that's a plan. Bartender, another round for my friends here."

Nan made her way back to the bar and Jesse nodded in her direction. "I could really use a little quality time with Jody tonight, if you'll be my wing man."

"Maybe if I drink enough I can play like Nan is Gena."

"That's the old Skeets I know and love." Jesse hugged Skeets around the neck and moved over to Jody.

"What's with all the male bonding thing?" Nan crawled up on her barstool and pointed at Jesse.

"Aw, we were just planning our future." Skeets rolled his beer bottle between his hands before he took another swig.

"Why do I get the feeling you're a guy who wants to be somewhere else?"

"It's late. Why don't I walk you home?"

"Uh, oh. This sounds serious. A late night stroll in Guanajuato." Her eyes sparkled, but her smile was hesitant. "You're about to tell me the fun is over, right?"

"Truthfully, I'd just like a normal conversation with a lovely, intelligent lady." Skeets looked down at the bar and slowly shook his head.

"A lovely, intelligent lady . . . like the one you left behind?" Nan lifted his chin to look in his eyes.

"We've never talked about why Jesse and I came down here, but I guess you figured me out."

Nan slid off the bar stool and took his hand. "Actually, I'd like a normal conversation with a handsome, heartsick cowboy."

Outside, in the Jardín Unión, breezes from the mountains brought the scent of agarita blossoms and cedar trees and cooled the day's heat. Trees in the *Jardín* rustled as they walked past, and only an occasional car on Avenida Sopena disturbed the quiet. The usual bustle of restaurant and bar patrons had faded as the establishments darkened for the night.

They sat on a park bench and held hands. "So who is this lovely, intelligent lady you left behind?" Nan faced him with a knee up on the bench seat.

"Left *me* behind is better said." Skeets looked down at his boots and with one toe flicked a weathered cigarette butt out onto the walkway.

"Another man, or 'you done her wrong'?"

"I'd call it stupidity. I tried too hard proving I was not good enough for her, and I finally convinced her." He glanced up and puckered his mouth ironically. "I hoped I could come down here and work myself into a better person. Someone worthy of Gena."

"Gena?"

"Yeah, Gena Koster. She goes to UT in Austin."

"Well, we have something in common." A giggle bubbled up in Nan.

Skeets looked up startled when he remembered the opportunity for disaster a chance meeting of the two females might engender. "See – that's what I mean. Why can't I be faithful to a wonderful woman? Here I am sitting beside a beautiful girl I've slept with for a week or so – it's hopeless."

"I'll grant you have some work to do on the monogamy thing, but why do you think you're such a bad person?" She slid over beside him.

Skeets thought for a moment. "I only think about what's happening now. I don't think about how things affect other people. I just do what makes me happy."

Nan took one of his hands and turned his head toward her. "You're absolutely wrong. Everybody you meet likes you. You show respect for other people. You've certainly been kind and thoughtful to Jody and me. You've gone out of your way to help people. What about the women out the ranch? You saved their mother's life and gave them money to live on. Tonight you helped rid Guanajuato of *'Bandido Postal Numero Uno.'* I think you're pretty near a hero."

After a long pause he looked down and said, "I only wish you were right."

Nan was still awake. She got out of her bed, took off her "Hook 'em Horns" T-shirt, and slid under the sheets of Jody's bed with Skeets. His heavy breathing continued until she kissed him on the forehead. He opened his eyes and blinked awake. She kissed each of his eyes. "Shhhhh . . . Close your eyes." She moved very slowly as she caressed his body and finally his masculinity. Imperceptibly she joined him and offered up lovemaking so gentle and sweet she knew she had transported him back to happier times. After they both convulsed and relaxed, she whispered, "Go home to your Gena, hero."

A chopping sound woke Skeets, and he lay in bed and wondered what made the noise. He finally sat up, swung his legs onto the floor, and slid on his shorts. The smell of coffee drifted into the bedroom, and he moved in that direction.

A note lay beside the simmering kettle. He put a spoon of Nescafe in a cup, poured in water, and read the note.

Skeets,

Sorry there is nothing to eat, but have a cup of coffee on me. Had a class this morning. Last night was special. Glad you made me part of your life. If you ever need "a normal conversation with a lovely, intelligent lady," call me back in Austin.

555-736-5880.

Nan

He opened the front door and walked out on the balcony. The gardener was chopping up a major limb that had fallen from a tree. The gardener stopped, took out a rag from his back pocket, wiped the sweat from his forehead, and looked up at Skeets who wore only his underwear. Skeets toasted the gardener with his coffee, and looked around for his bike; then remembered his motorcycle was back at Pericos Negros. Inside, he finished his coffee and decided he would ride out and say goodbye to Ariana, Blanca and Senora Ortiz that morning.

Skeets did not wake Jesse when he came into their apartment atop Pericos Negros. Instead, he stripped, took a shower, and dressed in clean clothes before he nudged Jesse awake. "Wake up, bro, let's ride out and say goodbye to Ariana and Blanca."

Jesse rolled over, but kept his eyes closed. "Didn't get much sleep last night, good buddy. Jody made unusual demands on my body."

"Where is she?"

"I guess she went to class."

"You look a little frayed around the edges, that's for sure." Skeets sat on the edge of the other bed. "To tell you the truth I don't feel that great myself, but we can't just disappear on them. Besides, I need to tell them they should get their letters from Alfonso and Beto from now on and even get past money de Silva stole from them."

"Don't forget you told them you'd sing them a song the next time we came out." Jesse mumbled. "You'd better brush up on your Spanish."

"That's right. There won't be much talking without you there." Skeets frowned and rubbed his forehead."

"Feeling as bad as I do, I'd still come with you, but I can't disappoint the twins this afternoon."

"Good God. *Miércoles*? You're gonna screw the drug dealer's twins again today? Up here?" Skeets shook his head in disbelief. "You have a weird death wish?"

"A man's gotta do what a man's gotta do." Jesse stood up and started for the shower.

"That does it. I'm outta here. I'll take care of our social obligations while you handle our breeding program." Skeets grabbed his guitar and headed for the door.

Chapter 20

Skeets enjoyed the uneventful ride to the ranch. A cloudless sky reinforced the summer drought that now started to brown out the grass and flowers. As he rode into the ranch compound, he could smell Blanca's lunch prepared for another visitor who sat under the lean-to. Señora Ortiz stood up and looked completely healthy. Her two daughters gleefully rushed out and greeted Skeets as he unstrapped his guitar. They introduced Señor Rodriguez when Skeets reached the living area.

The women all jabbered in Spanish, and Skeets held up his hands in surrender until Señor Rodriguez interpreted for them. Once the greetings and questions slowed, Rodriguez said, "You have been a great help for these ladies. "

"We owed Alfonso and Beto a lot for their help up in Texas." Skeets motioned north in the direction of the two husbands.

"They are on the ranch where I worked last year," Rodriguez said. "Ariana and Blanca worry because they've heard nothing from them."

"A man at the post office stole letters and money, but I think that's over." Skeets leaned his guitar against a chair.

Blanca and Ariana shouted, shook their fists in the air, and did a frustrated version of The Mexican Hat Dance after the translation. Rodriguez finally quieted them, and they continued preparing lunch.

Rodriguez said, "That explains why my wife never got all the money I sent. We had lots of undelivered letters."

"You might get most of the money back in a week or two."

Rodriguez translated for Ariana and Blanca. All three asked, *"How?"*

"At the 'General Delivery' window, speak with Pedro de Silva in a voice only he can hear. Say, 'The Angel Gabriel told me you must return the money you stole from me.'" Skeets laughed as he gave the instructions.

Ariana and Blanca looked puzzled after the translation. Finally, Ariana asked, *"Is he the man we saw at the post office?"*

"That's him, but talk with him so no one else hears what you say. If you know of people who have missed letters and money, they should do exactly the same, and they will get their money back." Skeets held his finger over his lips showing the need for secrecy.

"But why would he do this?" Rodriguez asked.

"He has repented" Skeets chuckled again as he thought of de Silva's night of confession. "He must give all the money back before anyone at the post office learns of his crime and puts him in jail."

Rodriguez nodded. "I see. In jail there is no reason to give back the money, right?"

Skeets looked pleased at Rodriguez's comprehension. "That's right. In jail he has no *way* to give back the money."

Blanca had prepared *caldo de calabasita con pollo*. The rich broth and squash picked from their garden covered large chunks of chicken in the soup bowls Ariana set on the table.

The aroma of *cilantro* and *comino* hung in the air along with tortillas on the *comal* griddle.

Rodriguez could barely eat with the translations Skeets required. The wives and their mother laughed and retold the story of how Skeets cleaned the stalls and of Jesse's riding adventure. Ariana told of her first motorcycle ride and about entering the post office with the two *"hombres negros."* Rodriguez laughed while tears cascaded down his cheeks, and he commented on the exciting life the ladies lived.

As the meal wound down, they clamored for a song from Skeets. He got out his guitar and tuned it. "I don't know any songs of Mexico, so I'll sing *my* songs." Rodriguez translated, and the three women nodded approvingly.

As Skeets sang the songs he so frequently had sung in the bars of Austin, many times with Gena in the audience, sadness came over him and performing became difficult. After each song, the women and Rodriguez applauded heartily, but in the end, Skeets felt an emptiness only Gena could fill.

The afternoon had slipped by and before he left, Skeets hugged the women and thanked them for all their hospitality. All three shed thankful tears for what Skeets and Jesse had done for them.

Rodriguez followed him out, and they shook hands. He gave Skeets a piece of paper. "When you are back in Texas, here's the phone number of the ranch where Alfonso and Beto should be. Maybe you could give them a call and tell them about your visit with Ariana and Blanca. It gets lonely up there . . . I know."

On the ride back to Pericos Negros, Skeets felt a bedspring of excitement wiggle up through him at the thought of home and Gena. Why wait four more days? Why not leave tomorrow? The possibility made him smile all the way into Guanajuato.

As Skeets approached the Pericos Negros driveway he saw a black Mercedes parked in a "No Parking Zone" in front of the restaurant. His pulse rate jumped when he saw Carlos Algo and his two goons crawl out. Skeets had never wished Harleys made less noise before, but now the roar stopped the three, who watched him turn into the driveway.

At the back of the building, he panicked at the sight of Jesse's bike with the twins' Mercedes parked beside it. He slid to a stop, leaped off the bike, and took the stairs three at a time. When he threw open the apartment door, Jesse and the twins lounged naked in the afterglow of what appeared, from the condition of the two beds, a significant fornication.

The twins recoiled in fright and screamed as they fumbled for something to cover themselves – a leftover reflex of long lost modesty. Jesse's Harley bag slammed into his chest before he could register a complaint. "Get your ass dressed and pack what you can. Carlos Algo is downstairs with his goons," Skeets hissed through clinched teeth.

"Christ Almighty." Jesse jumped into his jeans and left his underwear on the floor, stuffed his feet into his boots, and pulled on a T-shirt. The Twins learned about Algo and screamed like cornered beasts as they scrambled for their clothes. Skeets rushed around the room and gathered clothes and stuffed them into his duffel bag at a speed of contestants in a TV supermarket-shopping game. The twins caromed off each other as they hopped around on one foot stabbing the other at their underwear. They banged into Jesse and Skeets who unceremoniously shoved them back onto the beds. They rebounded from the beds and again slammed together with a thud, still naked.

Downstairs Miguel greeted Carlos and the boys in his most solicitous manner in the Pericos patio. *"Buenas tardes, amigos. Can I get you something?"*

Carlos and the two bodyguards looked past Miguel and surveyed the patio. He turned to see what Algo looked at. Finally, Carlos said, "Where are Sonia and Selena?

Miguel continued to look around the patio at the few remaining lunch diners. *"I just arrived myself, but I know they are not inside."* As Miguel's mind raced through all the possibilities, he remembered Jesse's hungry look when he asked about the twins on the night of the benefit concert. He sagged when he thought of the gringos upstairs. Surely no. It can't be, he thought, as a massacre loomed in his mind. He said hopefully, *"I guess they've already left."*

Carlos could not answer before shouts and screams rained down from above. He pointed up. *"What's up there?"*

Miguel shook visibly. *"Just a storeroom and a small apartment where the caretaker lives."* He gulped twice and added, *"His parrot makes a lot of noise."*

"Where are the stairs?"

"Stairs?"

"How do you get up there, idiot?" Carlos' voice boomed across the patio. Miguel said nothing but pointed toward the rear of the restaurant. Carlos hollered at the goons. *"Go check it out."*

The two stiffs moved quickly through the dining room, slammed the kitchen door into the face of a waiter carrying a tray of food, and knocked him flat. Dishes and food clattered and rolled in every direction. The cooks looked surprised when the two crashed through the kitchen door shouting, *"Where is the back door?"*

One of the cooks pointed behind him with a spatula, and the two ran around the service counter and out the back door. The parking lot had only a few cars, but at the base of the stairs sat two motorcycles and the twins' Mercedes. The second hoodlum turned and ran back through the kitchen and dining room and shouted out the door, *"Their car is back here, Jefe."*

Miguel slumped into a chair, held his head, and mumbling, *"¡Great Jesus, Joseph and Mary, I'm a dead man."*

Goon Number One was halfway up the stairs when Skeets appeared at the top with his duffel, which he hurled down at the adversary. The bag slammed into the goon's chest and tumbled him backwards down the stairs like a Slinky. Bag and desperado landed in a heap on the ground and left the potential assailant dazed. Skeets followed in hot pursuit, grabbed his bag, and wedged it between his seat and the guitar. Jesse heaved his own bag over the railing, and it crashed beside his bike. Skeets crammed it onto the sissy-bar rack and "X-ed" two bungee straps over the top.

The thug revived from his tumbling exhibition as Jesse cleared off the stairs, but as he got on hands and knees, he exposed his posterior. Jesse buried his boot toe squarely in his ass and sent the outlaw skidding forward with his face in the gravel. The restaurant backdoor flew open as Carlos Algo and Goon Number Two ran into the parking lot. The motorcycles fired on the first try, and Skeets and Jesse lunged forward toward the driveway, rear wheels spinning. Algo saw his henchman get up from the gravel with face bleeding, pull his revolver, and squeeze off a shot, which thumped into Skeets Harley bag. The bikes cleared out of sight around the corner before Algo or Hood Number Two could fire. *¡"Andale. Vámonos, hombres. I'm gonna catch those bastards and shoot them down like rabid dogs."* The drug dealer ran back through the restaurant with the other two.

Skeets and Jesse had vaulted onto Aveneda Cantarranas and headed north before Algo could get the Mercedes moving. The two bikes swerved left onto Truco Street near Obregon before the next bullets from the chase car whined past. Skeets did a foot down, sliding right turn north onto Obregon and headed for Plaza de la Paz and Aveneda Juarez. Pedestrians and pushcart vendors flung themselves from the motorcycles' path as tents and produce flew in every direction. The screeching turn of Algo's Mercedes echoed through the plaza as two more gunshots whizzed past Skeets and Jesse. A shopkeeper's window splintered into flying shards. People ran in every direction and hid behind anything available, even restaurant umbrella tables.

To escape Algo's line of fire, Skeets and Jesse dropped down onto *Tunel Miguel Hildalgo*, and again headed north in the general direction of home. The tunnel looped back around and kept them out of sight of their pursuers but now headed them south. They raced, zigzagging between cars, until they went under *Plaza de Los Angeles* where the tunnel forked, and they took *Tunel de Los Angeles,* which funneled them further south. The motorcyclers could three-lane between cars and put distance between them and Algo's *pistolerio*-laden Mercedes. A wrong turn onto a tunnel exit ramp dumped them out onto *Carretera Panorámica* and headed up into the mountains south of Guanajuato. The Mercedes now gained on them.

Skeets imagined a fusillade of gunfire, so he turned right onto what looked like a good road, which quickly changed into the entrance to the Super Highway 57 South toward Salamanca. Light faded as the sun set behind the Sierras, but they weaved through traffic at a speed of one hundred miles per hour anyway. Identifying Algo's headlights in the rearview mirrors was impossible, so Skeets kept the throttle cranked and hoped they could outrun them. The road forked about half an hour later – the right to Irapuato and the left to Salamanca. Skeets had no time to flip a coin. He closed his eyes in hope, signaled a right turn for Jesse, and headed toward an unknown town.

After they passed through Irapuato, he turned onto a highway marked 'Cueramarco' thinking, surely, nobody goes to Cueramarco. About ten miles later his bike coughed, sputtered and the engine died. He switched to his alternate tank. Now their biggest problem became finding gas before they ran out altogether. A small side road had a sign, 'Tolencita,' with an arrow pointing the way. A tiny vacant roadside produce stand stood by the turnoff. Skeets slowed, stopped, and motioned Jesse alongside. "I just went on auxiliary."

"I've been on auxiliary since the last town. How far is the next Pemex?"

"How would I know? Unless *you* know where we are – we´re lost. This Tolencita place can't be far. Let's turn here and gas up." Skeets pointed in the direction of the town.

"Anything to keep from walking." Jesse dropped his visor and shifted into gear. Skeets, turned right and led off into deepening darkness.

Dusk had faded into night, and a new moon gave little light through the patchy clouds. The high desert temperature dropped with the sun, and a chill made Skeets want a jacket. The rough road had a straight downhill slope that lulled him into carelessness while his speed crept up unnoticed. "Jesus Christ." Skeets shouted into his helmet when the road disappeared into an unmarked tight right turn. He flagged a "slow down" for Jesse and skidded his back wheel and sent up a howling screech and billowing smoke, as he braked for the turn. He leaned the bike, dragging his tailpipe on the pavement and sparks cascaded skyward. He gritted his teeth and prayed the tires held their traction. When he tried to right the bike, he screamed. "Holy shit." A major *topes* speed bump guarding a low water crossing appeared from nowhere, dead ahead. He executed a drastic swerve left and headed toward the bar ditch and barbed wire fence on the other side of the road. The bike, now completely out of control, hit the speed bump and launched skyward over the fence that trailed down into the dry stream. In one of those "your whole life passes in front of you" moments, he felt like Steve McQueen in "The Great Escape." He bit his tongue and blood gushed when the Harley landed, fishtailing toward a mesquite and huisache grove. With difficulty, he turned into the huisache thicket and barely missed the bigger mesquite trees with their heavy limbs and three-inch thorns. The limber huisache bows whipped him like a cat-o-nine-tails and their tiny thorns ripped his shirt and jeans and bloodied his arms and legs. An errant, overhanging mesquite tree limb tore his helmet off and the bike wedged between two other trees, pivoted over the front wheel, and body-slammed him into the ground. The motor snuffled for a moment and died.

Jesse had run up on Skeets and barely missed him as Skeets swerved for the *topes*. He managed the swerve, but like Skeets, found himself airborne and following him into the same thicket. He could not miss the clump of mesquite trees and barely brushed a monster specimen as he ducked under its limbs. He dodged, veered sharply, and wove through the trees, which flailed him with their thorny lower branches. Almost at the far edge of the thicket, a heavy limb smacked him in the chest and knocked him from the bike as if he had hit the end of a tether. The bike ran several more yards and fell while the back tire spun until the motor quit. He lay half conscious, gasping with the breath knocked out of him. Beyond his motorcycle stood a house with a concrete burro in front. His last thought before he passed out was, great, another concrete burro place. The burro turned and looked at him.

PART THREE

"EL RANCHO GRANDE"
"The Big Ranch" Emilio D. Uranga and J. del Moral (Composers)

Chapter 21

For most of her life, Josefina had felt the job of a Mexican burro held potential, if not, indeed, upward mobility. She hoped with enough courage, hard work, and application of her considerable intelligence that one day she would take her rightful place alongside, if not ahead of, horses. She often thought the only animals on earth dumber than horses were people, and both groups had attitudes. She felt this shared stupidity and attitude provided the fertile ground in which to plant the seeds of opportunity.

God, it really burns me, she thought, to watch them prance around together as if they owned the whole world. And after riding, the people would give the horses a nice rubdown, put them up in luxury suites with straw beds, water them with fresh, clear water, and feed them huge portions of grain.

Josefina, on the other hand, pulled a plow all day, and they penned her up outside with a mud hole for drinking water, hay to eat, one scrubby mesquite for shade from the sun, and Flaco, the horniest old jackass on earth, who followed her around and constantly looked for a quickie. She had patiently persevered for years with a good attitude while she waited for her big break. Currently, however, she suffered from midlife crisis as, to date, she had little hard evidence supporting her previous feelings about job enrichment. Years of complete cooperation, of hard work, of walking faster than any other burro, of no complaints, and of careful personal hygiene, went unnoticed by People in the House. Never an "Attagirl," or a rub behind the ears, or extra portion of corn, which she loved, or even a kind word.

Some time ago, the Pretty Lady started hauling the People in the House and the produce to *el mercado* each Saturday morning in a machine. Josefina stayed on the ranch, no longer needed to pull the produce cart. She considered this a professional setback because of the difficulty demonstrating burro superiority with no other lesser burros around for comparison. Time had passed slowly for her on the farm with only Flaco and his lascivious grin for company.

Imbedded in Josefina's optimism was the knowledge that when one door closes, another opens. People in the House had built a small produce stand out on the highway to Guadalajara because the recent rains produced a bumper crop of corn and vegetables. Each day the Young Boys hitched her up, and she pulled the cart loaded with vegetables and corn fifteen miles out to sell at the roadside produce stand. The boys took turns walking and riding Flaco. Josefina's blistering pace pulling the cart left old Flaco behind. She smiled a special burro smile at each whack the Young Boys laid on Flaco's butt to make him catch up.

Josefina knew the People on the Road could not resist her considerable charm and often patted her and rubbed her ears. A few even gave her nibbles of the produce they purchased. She particularly enjoyed People who wanted their picture with her, as this big time exposure would look good on her résumé.

Now she wallowed in a malaise of personal crisis because the produce stand trips, over time, became less frequent as the Pretty Lady took more corn and produce into town each day.

She thought the gods had interfered with her march toward personal success and satisfaction. Josefina slept fitfully these nights and often stood in the darkness, looked up at the stars, and wondered just what force out there was messing with her. Her emotional crisis often crept into her dreams, but this night she slept pleasantly dreamless, until a roar awakened her. Machines and People hurtled through the trees toward her. An attack, she thought. I must warn the People in the House. She commenced a level of braying at such volume and with such deep emotional content that the People in the House, clad in their nightclothes, ran out in the yard within seconds. Josefina, pleased with her contribution, continued braying at a volume that could wilt crops.

Jorge Ramos stood outside with his family – momentarily paralyzed at the sight of men and machines lying about his property. His wife waved her arms and screamed religious epithets, invoking the saints, while his daughter and sons rushed to help the mangled men. Ramos finally sprang into action, cursing El Jefe, the Police Chief of Tolencita, who had years ago inflicted so much pain and emotional torture on him the trauma blocked his reflexes.

Chapter 22

The Ramos family huddled in their dining room and wondered what they should do. They could not get the two injured men to the *Clinica de Tolencita*, which lacked an ambulance. Angelita finally said, *"I will go into town and bring the doctor."* She had checked each of the men and knew that one remained briefly conscious, an incentive for getting real medical help quickly. No medical doctor lived in the backward little town. Only a medical student. The superstitious townspeople mistrusted medical doctors and preferred traditional healers and herbalists instead.

As she raced through the streets of the sleepy little town, a policeman stopped her and asked why she drove so fast. "There has been a motorcycle accident on the highway at our ranch, and I am going for the doctor."

"Who got hurt?" the policeman inquired.

"Two Americano men are in very bad condition, and they need a doctor quickly." She raced away while the policeman scratched his head.

Back home, Angelita and the doctor cut Jesse's torn and tattered clothes off so he could perform an examination. He slept through the entire procedure.

"He might be in a coma." The doctor moved a chair beside the bed for the examination.

"His eyes opened just before I left, but he went back to sleep." Angelita's voice carried more than a casual weight of concern.

The doctor took his pressure cuff and stethoscope from his bag and took his blood pressure. *"His blood pressure is low, but unless it goes lower there won't be a problem."* The otoscope light startled Jesse when the doctor examined his right eye and he made a vain attempt to sit up. *"Easy, señor, don't move."* The doctor held a slight pressure on Jesse's chest, and he winced in pain.

"I'm sorry, amigo, but you must lie still while we check for broken bones." The doctor gestured at Jesse. *"We have no x-ray, so I will have to check for pain."*

"You won't have to look far." Jesse took in a ragged, painful breath.

"¿Breathing hurts?"

Jesse nodded, then, as if he remembered something long forgotten, asked, *"¿Where's my friend, Skeets? ¿Is he okay?"*

"He's alive but still unconscious. You guys took a really nasty spill." The doctor listened with his stethoscope on Jesse's chest. *"Take deep breaths."*

Jesse tried, but pain halted him in mid breath. *"My chest really hurts."*

"Try again. You may have a broken collar bone or cracked ribs." He nodded at Jesse's halting breathing. *"Your lungs seem clear."* He picked up Jesse's arm and pushed his shoulder slightly toward his neck. Jesse grimaced, but said nothing. *"Your collar bone isn't broken, or you would have screamed."* He cupped his hands, first on one side of Jesse's chest, then the other and applied pressure. He watched Jesse's reaction. *"I*

don't think you have any rib fractures. Possibly there are deep bruises in your chest muscles, and damage to the cartilage between the ribs. ¿Do you remember what happened?"

Jesse thought for a moment. *"It's all a little fuzzy right now."*

The doctor took out a penlight and looked into Jesse's eyes. *"Follow this light with your eyes as I move it."* The penlight moved slowly, left and right, then up and down. He looked at Angelita. *"He has a severe brain concussion, without doubt."*

The examination continued as the doctor moved each of Jesse's arm and leg joints and checked his bones. *"There don't seem to be any broken bones, dislocated joints, or torn cartilages. It's amazing, really.* He turned and addressed Angelita, *"He must not sit up for several days. After that, he needs bed rest for several more days. Then I will have another look at him."*

Angelita and the doctor bandaged Jesse's flesh ripped up by mesquite thorns and other abrasions, then gathered his bag for Skeets' examination. They stopped in the doorway when Jesse spoke.

"I'm sorry about this, doctor. I don't know who you are but thanks for your help."

Skeets' examination yielded less information because he remained unconscious. He did not respond while the doctor punched and prodded. The doctor examined Skeets' skull at length and looked for fractures, which might cause his unconsciousness.

"He certainly has a very serious concussion also and possibly internal injuries, but there is no sign of internal bleeding at this time. He must lie horizontal at least four days for the concussion's swelling to reduce. Both of them will have great pain for a long time, so give them these pain pills, as they need them. I've given them tetanus shots and an antibiotic. All we can do here is wait and see what happens. If he doesn't

revive by this afternoon, we must get him to the hospital in *Irapuato.*" The doctor gathered his equipment and closed his bag.

As Angelita and the doctor left the house, she saw that Quito and Bosco had scoured the mesquite grove and found two duffel bags, two helmets, and a guitar in a banged up case, which they had piled on the veranda. Now the two teenagers tried to push a motorcycle toward the house. *"These things are really heavy,"* Quito complained.

"I've ridden before. Let me help." The doctor moved the gearshift into neutral and turned off the ignition switches on both bikes. Together, the four of them rolled the battered-up bikes out of sight behind the house. Because of a flat tire Skeets' bike was harder to push.

Angelita heard a police siren approach from the direction of Tolencita, and shortly after, El Jefe's car turned into the Ramos house road. He stepped from the car and surveyed the scene. El Jefe stood slightly over six feet in his black cowboy boots. He wore starched khakis with a razor crease while his military style shirt remained wrinkle free. He pinned his police badge to his left shirt pocket. Around his waist, he wore a broad, black cartridge belt with a holstered chrome plated revolver weighty enough that a Sam Brown shoulder strap diagonally across his chest was required. He looked trim and fit with a handsome mustached face partially hidden by dark aviator-style sunglasses, which remained in place along with his gold filigree-brimmed police officer's hat. *"What's happened here? My officer reported a motorcycle accident. Where are the men and the motorcycles?"*

Quito and Bosco said in unison, *"We moved the motorcycles behind the house."*

"I've treated the men, and they are resting in the house," the doctor said.

"Why don't you move them to the hospital in Irapuato?" Jefe pointed in the direction of the city.

"They have serious concussions, and we cannot move them at this time." The doctor crossed his arms and assumed a position of muted defiance.

El Jefe turned to Angelita, *"You're not keeping them here are you?"*

"Yes, they will stay until they are well." Angeltia stood defiant.

"That's not a good idea. You know nothing about these men. I will have them moved." Jefe started toward his car.

"You will do not such thing. What happens in this house is none of your business." Angelita's face paled with anger. .

"I will come back tomorrow and we will see about that." He got in his car and roared away.

After she dropped off the doctor, Angelita drove to Casa de Masa, her cantina, which faced La Plaza opposite the cathedral, the oldest surviving building in town. The church's white stone spire stood guard above the small, single story town. Cylindrically shaped acacia trees bordered La Plaza like sentries, while oak trees spread their limbs and offered shade for those who rested on the park benches. Shrubbery, grass, and flowers, planted and cared for by the townspeople, lined cobblestone walkways. A large cast-iron gazebo erected by Agapito Tolen, the town's founder, was the hub of the plaza and therefore of the town itself. Life in Tolencita revolved around La Plaza.

The town still slept in the predawn light of the cool morning. Angelita stood in the cantina's entrance for a moment with the key in her hand and looked back at the plaza and the old restlessness swelled inside. She put the key in her pocket and walked across into the plaza and wandered through the walkways until she stopped at a particular bench where she stood for a time.

Angelita remembered growing up on the family farm in the full belief that God is good and life is sweet – before El Jefe stole Tolencita's soul.

She remembered vividly the first time she became aware of El Jefe. She sat in the plaza and watched her brothers play with the other boys. Her father tended the business of selling his corn, and her mother shopped in *el mercado*. Time spent in the plaza at age sixteen was a good thing, particularly for beautiful girls. The matchmakers observed the girls in the park and looked for possible marriages.

"Buenas tardes, senorita hermosa." The voice came from behind her park bench. Her blushing backward glance, her first sight of him, astounded her. Tall, slender, and masculine with a straight-toothed, pleasant smile, he stood resplendent in his uniform with the *pistola* glimmering in the sunlight. Tolencita could not produce such a vision. He had come from out there, and he liked her.

Footsteps moved around the bench. She glanced up and saw him stand a decent distance in front of her. He let his eyes wander over her unhurriedly. His head fell backward into a loud laugh, and her brothers looked up from across the square. He turned on his heel, and vanished.

The next week dragged on as she struggled with the new feelings El Jefe had stirred in her. Indecent feelings like none she had felt before. She longed for the relief of Saturday.

"¿Would you like a soda, Angelita?" Again the voice behind her park bench. He had used her name without an introduction. He broke all the rules. She dropped her head, too embarrassed to speak, even if propriety allowed it. Boys her own age could not take such privileges, she thought, but, after all, an older man might. Didn't *compadres* offer their god-daughters cold sodas? What could be the harm?"

Her mother saved her when she brushed passed Jefe and dragged her into their town house. Señora Ramos reviewed the rules of proper behavior at length with her daughter.

Angelita next saw him across the road from the farmhouse, parked in a huisache thicket. She could barely make out "Policia" on the side of his automobile for the brush. He was definitely interested. She lingered for a time outside.

Time and pain had dulled the memory of when she first sat in Jefe's *Policia* car near La Plaza. She only knew her dreams had filled with visions of her cathedral wedding to this handsome and powerful man.

"Vamonos." He laughed as he reached across her and pulled the car door closed.

"No, hombre." she said excitedly. *"It's not proper."* The car started moving. *"Stop, please, take me back before someone sees us."* She turned and looked at the plaza as it faded in the distance.

"You're with El Jefe," he laughed. *"No one will see us."*

"If you love me, you will take me back." Her eyes brimmed with tears.

"Love you? Who loves you? You are desirable. I love that, nothing more." He spoke no more, but drove out of town and pulled off the main road into a mesquite thicket. At first she struggled, until he hit her. Again. And again. The insect sounds in the mesquite were the only noises except for his animal grunts and her quiet weeping.

When he heard of Angelita's defile, Sr.Ramos went to the police station to kill Jefe. About midnight, a friend brought Ramos into the family's town house. One eye was missing, he bled from his mouth, and he had two broken arms. The bottoms of his feet looked like ground meat. He could not speak. Señora Ramos quickly loaded him on the burro cart along with Angelita, and the Ramos family returned to the country.

Word of the atrocity spread through Tolencita the next day. El Jefe denied everything when the townspeople confronted him in the plaza. He took out his pistol, polished it, and advised them to go home. He arrested and jailed the mayor, a friend of Angelita's father, when he persisted in questioning Jefe. Each day Jefe beat him so the Tolencitans could hear him scream. Two weeks later, no one remembered the Ramos episode. No one but the Ramos family.

Angelita prayed and helped care for her father as he lingered near death for weeks. He improved physically, but not emotionally. Body well, he still had long bouts of brooding, which always ended in tears -- the tears of desperation over his failure to avenge Angelita and the family's honor. Eventually his wife's and Angelita's caring compassion brought him back. They would maintain their farm; rebuild their emotions and their lives. Angelita, no longer marriageable, would have to make her own way. El Jefe now had complete control of Tolencita, and they could only wait.

The next year, fate again intervened in the Ramos' lives. He had already planted the crops, and the blessed rain came. The harvest of corn far exceeded what the family could use or sell. The next year the rain continued so Ramos expanded the vegetable garden, and each day the sons loaded the burro cart with fresh corn and produce and traveled to their stand on the highway to Guadalajara.

When the rain continued the third year, Ramos finally had the idea, which would provide for his daughter. They would turn their house on La Plaza into a restaurant – a cantina. The restaurant profit from the corn and vegetables would be greater than in el mercado or on the roadside. Then after he died, Angelita would have "Casa de Masa" and the boys the farm.

Jefe normally expected a large mordida for starting a business and subsequent weekly payments. But he caused less trouble than they thought he might. Had he developed a conscience about his transgressions against their family? In truth, what he took by force, he now wanted lovingly bestowed on him. He caused outrage in the family when he asked to call on Angelita. Everyone but the brutalized nineteen year-old.

She saw this as an opportunity to extract her revenge. El Jefe's destruction lay between the loins of one of his victims.

Casa de Masa succeeded from the start. The food, made from family recipes and fresh produce, soon became renowned locally. The cerveza was cold and the tequila generous. The family prospered, and Ramos bought a used Volkswagen beetle for Angelita who lived on the farm and drove into town each day with her provisions. But the car brought an abiding restlessness. She longed for escape.

Angelita returned to her restaurant and wrote a note to her bartender saying she would not return until the afternoon, and a note asking the cook to prepare a pot of *Caldo de Pollo* for her family's evening meal. She smiled thinking of the healing power of chicken soup.

Chapter 23

When Angelita parked at the farmhouse, Quito and Bosco ran toward her and shouted that the second man had awakened.

"He wants out of bed." Quito jerked open the car door. She ran into the house, straight into Bosco's bedroom where her mother struggled with a belligerent Skeets. Angelita knew he was still dazed from his glazed eyes.

"*No, Señor. You must not move. You have a head injury.*" Angelita put her hands on his shoulders and gently pushed him back down.

"No *ablo Espanoe*," Skeets said, his voice groggy. "'res my frien – ¿*mi amigo?*"

Angelita attempted translating this strange English language in her head. She smiled and answered slowly, "*Your friend is in the next room. He also has a concussion of the head and must not move.*" She first gestured toward the next room, then to her head. Skeets shrugged without comprehending, his eyes fluttered, and he slipped back into unconsciousness. She stood over him for a time before returning to Jesse's room.

Jesse lay with his eyes closed, shielding them from the light, which made his head hurt more. He took shallow and irregular breaths limiting the pain in his chest. He heard someone move in his room, opened his eyes, and saw the face of an angel again. *"¿Are you an angel?"* he asked in Spanish this time.

"I'm not an angel, but you can call me 'Angelita.'" The beautiful face smiled down at him as she straightened his sheet. *"¿What is your name?"*

He didn't answer immediately, but rather admired the lovely lady before him. She was mid-to-late twenties, a good height, with a beautiful, olive complexion, and long raven black hair. She seemed well put together even though her peasant blouse and full skirt hid her body well. Finally, he answered, *"I'm Jesse Suarez from Austin, Texas. We must have wrecked our motorcycles. ¿How is my friend Skeets – Skeets Hollaran?"*

"He has regained consciousness but has difficulty speaking. The doctor says both of you must lie still for several days because of head concussions." She wrinkled her brow in concern and pointed toward Skeet's room.

Jesse looked around the small room using his eyes only. *"If one room's big enough, maybe you could move us into the same room. I could translate for him then."* He paused, and added, *"You could have one room back."*

They first took the chest of drawers and chairs from Bosco's room where Jesse rested. The room looked bare with only the bed, Jose Canseco's Major League Baseball Poster on the wall, and Bosco's baseball bat leaning in the corner. Then the five Ramoses, with difficulty, moved Skeets' bed into Jesse's room. Skeets' mind seemed a bit clearer, and he managed a smile when he saw Jesse.

"ooks ike our uck's pumb ru ou." Skeets' thick, sore tongue barely moved after he bit it in the crash.

"No, if it'd run plumb out, we'd be underground." Jesse lifted his arm at the elbow and pointed downward.

"I gess ere's somein to at."

"A doctor's been here and examined us as best he could. We're really banged up, but still in pretty good shape except for brain concussions. We have to lie horizontal for a few days until the swelling goes down. We don't want permanent brain damage." Jesse wiggled his forefinger, nixing the prospect.

"We thidn't star wi much. We can't saan any brai amage." Skeets watched Jesse for a response, but he just stared at the ceiling.

"You're not talking too good, bro. I can barely understand you. You sure you're okay?" Jesse rolled his head toward Skeet.

"Ith ma ongue. I bi ih whan I anded." Skeets opened his mouth and pointed inside.

"Great luck." Jesse chortled.

"Grea uck?"

"Yeah, 'grea uck,' 'cause now I won't be listening to you all the time." Jesse laughed but grabbed his chest in pain

" 'ery fahee. Ervs u riii, ass ol." Skeets made the best obscene gesture possible with a bandaged hand.

Angelita arrived at dinnertime with a huge pot of *caldo de pollo*. She brought two large bowls of the healing chicken soup and several *bolillo* rolls for the two men. Since neither could sit up, Angelita's mother fed Skeets spoonful at the time while Angelita spoon-fed Jesse. The room had filled with the rich aroma of chicken broth. The soup had chunks of carrot, onion, celery, and chicken. Black pepper and *cilantro* floated in the broth adding sumptuous flavor and aroma.

They had eaten half of the soup when an authoritarian knock on the door sounded through the farmhouse. Quito and Bosco who had loitered outside the bedroom door while the two gringos ate, now ran and opened the front door to see El Jefe. Speechless the two boys ran back and reported his arrival. Jefe stepped into the house without an invitation and followed the two boys toward the bedrooms.

Señor Ramos came into the living room and shouted, *"Why are you in my house?"*

"Shut up old man. I'm on police business." El Jefe waved him off with a condescending gesture and continued toward the bedrooms.

The mother spilled some soup when she leaped up at the sound of El Jefe's name. Angelita got up from the bedside just as El Jefe shoved the two boys aside and stepped into the bedroom. She shouted, *"What are you doing here?"*

El Jefe jerked back, startled by the aggression in Angelita's voice. *"I must find out who these two are."*

"¿Why is it any of your business? You're just being nosy." She threw her head back, and jutted her jaw in defiance.

"When there's been an accident, I must make a report." Jefe took out a small notebook and officiously took out his pen. He asked Skeets in English, "What's your name?"

"Skeets Holloran," Jesse replied. "He bit his tongue in the accident and has trouble talking."

El Jefe marked in his notebook. "And you? Your name?"

"Jesse Suarez."

"From where?" Jefe held his pen poised above the notebook.

"Austin, Texas."

El Jefe gave a little anti-gringo smirk. "What happened?"

"The turn in your road and the *topes* are both unmarked. We saw them too late in the dark. They bounced our motorcycles over a fence into a grove of mesquite trees. Close this house, I think."

"Where are your motorcycles?" El Jefe motioned outside the house.

"I don't know." Jesse looked in the direction of Angelita.

El Jefe asked Angelita, *"¿The motorcycles?"*

"Behind the house. They were badly damaged in the accident." She pointed toward the rear of the farmhouse.

"¿How bad were they damaged?" Jesse looked at Angelita.

"They will need repairs."

El Jefe spied the Harley-Davidson duffel bags piled in the corner. "Are they Harleys?"

"Yeah." Jesse lay back watched El Jefe who looked impressed by the news.

"¿How long will you be here?" El Jefe asked in Spanish so Angelita could understand.

Jesse tried to answer, but Angelita interrupted. *"Until they are well."*

El Jefe glared at her for a few beats and then at Jesse. "See me before you leave." Jesse did not respond. Jefe looked at Angelita. *"Let's talk."* Angelita followed him out of the room and out onto the veranda. *"I don't like the idea of these two men here in your house. I should arrange to have them moved."*

"This is our house, and they can stay as long as they need. Besides, the doctor said not to move them." Fire flashed in Angelita's eyes as she spoke.

"¿Why are you interested in these two gringos? They mean nothing to you." He motioned toward the two patients and shrugged.

" ¿Are you jealous?" Her laugh carried no mirth.

El Jefe moved forward as if to hit her, thought better when she stood her ground, then strode from the porch. *"I'll see you in town."*

She stood on the veranda as the police car's taillights receded toward the highway, and the old hatred welled in her. *"One day. Oh God, soon very soon."*

Lobo had tracked the dots across the Loran screen each day. There had been no movement since they rode from Guanajuato almost to the small town of Tolencita, where they had stayed for four days. One of the dots had disappeared from the screen four days ago, which meant the battery was down or the transponder had been damaged. The dots had settled in Guanajuato for almost two weeks with only short trips of about

30 clicks east and back. At the time he had thought they must have found those two Mexican boys' family, but why so long in Guanajuato? Now the question was, why did they head for one of the cartel's distribution centers? And why stationary there for four days? The deep voice growled into the truck cab, "Those two hombres are up to something."

Chapter 24

The dizziness had subsided shortly after Skeets and Jesse sat up for the first time. Skeets had noticed something different about Jesse after the four days during which Angelita and her mother fed them. Jesse's interest in Angelita grew disproportionately to anything in Skeets' experience. He couldn't understand their conversations, but he knew Jesse. At least he thought he knew Jesse, because the new Jesse's whole countenance buoyed when she entered the room. Jesse's compromised condition could be the reason, he thought, but still he had never known anyone who enjoyed convalescence more.

Jesse told Skeets how Angelita was captivated by his descriptions and stories of life in Austin. She had confessed her total travel experience was one Guadalajara school trip and several trips into Irapuato when she needed restaurant equipment or supplies.

Skeets tongue had mended some, and he said painfully, "So you're gettin' a major case of the sweet ass, bro?"

"What makes you say that?" Jesse became defensive.

"I've never seen a man want to touch a woman so much and still not do it." Skeets made a squeezing motion with his fingers. "I mean, you two just yammer on and on. I can understand all your talk without translation."

"It's all just small talk. These people have taken us in like family. The least we can do is be friendly." Jesse flicked invisible lint from his bed sheet.

"It's truly amazing how they've treated us. We crash into their lives all banged up, and they nurse us back to health and ask nothing of us." Skeets looked at the ceiling. "I guess we need to make plans, though."

"Yeah, we can't stay here forever, right? Step one is repair our bikes. Otherwise it's a long walk home."

Quito and Bosco came into the room on one of their many visits inquiring if the two needed anything. Jesse asked where the things from their pants pockets were. Bosco left the room and returned with two sacks, which contained the contents of their pockets, including deflated wallets.

"We left our Pericos Negros wages back in Guanajuato." Jesse held his wallet open for Skeets. "I don't think we can pay for fixing our bikes."

"I just hope we have enough for the Ramos family for all they've done, forget about the bikes." Skeets shook his head sadly. "We're in a bit of a pickle here, good buddy."

"It's not like the old Skeets I know to worry about a little thing like being broke, busted up, and afoot in a foreign country."

"The old Skeets can't remember why this trip sounded like such a great idea in the first place. I had a good life with a wonderful woman before I ended up in God knows where, Mexico, flat of my back, penniless, and with no way home." Despair crowded into Skeets face. "I need my old life back."

Jesse took in Skeets' concern, then shouted, *"Hey, amigos."* Quito and Bosco came back into the room. " *¿Could you find our bags for us? ¿And can we have a bath?"*

The two boys looked at each other uncertainly. Finally, Quito said, *"I thought you couldn't get up for several more days."*

"That's for ordinary men, not for supermen like us." Jesse almost pounded his chest, but caught himself in time. The two boys laughed at Jesse's clowning, then dragged the two duffel bags into the room and pulled out clothes.

The dizziness had faded, but the muscle and joint soreness had maxed out. The wreck had involved muscles Skeets didn't know he had. He sat on the edge of the bed, stood, then walked gingerly, and eventually bathed and shaved. Jesse followed close behind Skeets. Quito and Bosco supported them as they walked through the house. Señora Ramos followed and ordered them back into bed before a calamity befell.

They walked around the Harleys for a time and assessed the damage. The front fender of Skeets' bike had crumpled and blown out the front tire. The handlebars were bent, the gas tank dented, the clutch and the hand brake were fritzed, and the rear fender bent inward against the back tire. The tires on Jesse's bike seemed okay, but everything else looked bent, twisted, or scraped.

"You think the restaurant guy back in Monclova would buy them now?" Skeets tried kicking the front tire with little success and much pain.

"They're really ugly, but at least the frames look sound, and the engines and gear boxes are intact. It could be worse." Jesse's sore hand could not work the clutch lever on the handlebar.

Skeets walked around his bike again with Quito's help. "If we can get a new tire for my front wheel, we might get them going again."

"Maybe we should wait a couple days before we tackle any repairs. I'm feelin' a little weak-kneed about now." Jesse turned back toward the house with his arm around Bosco.

Jesse and Skeets napped, but as a surprise for Angelita, Jesse sat up still clothed when she returned from the restaurant with dinner. They weathered the scolding from Angelita and her mother about getting up too soon and persevered until granted permission for dinner at the table.

The ladies brought a platter of squash blossoms stuffed with a filling of goat's cheese, herbs, and mild peppers, lightly fried in thin batter and a *cazuela* brimming with egg white battered and fried poblano peppers stuffed with shredded pork, sauted onions, almonds, raisins, and bits of candied citrus fruit in a sauce of tomatoes, meat broth, garlic, onions, cilantro and *comino*. Bowls of whole pinto beans and Mexican rice rounded out the feast. The room filled with the aroma of *chilies rellenós* and *frijoles al charra*. The diners' interest focused more on the table than on heaven during the blessing.

The Ramoses talked among themselves about the day's events while the food passed around the table. Jesse sensed a strong resentment when Angelita told of another visit at Casa de Masa by El Jefe. He once again voiced his disapproval of the two guests in their home and demanded they be moved elsewhere. Senor Ramos seldom spoke, but he became visibly distraught when they talked about El Jefe. Jesse tried breaking the tension. *"We really don't won't trouble for you. Skeets and I can move out if there's a room we can rent. Once we fix our bikes we'll be on our way."*

After a short pause a clamor rose from the two women and the two boys that Skeets and Jesse must stay until fully rehabilitated–even longer. Only Señor Ramos did not comment until he finally raised his head with ferocity glowing in his eyes. His voice quivered. *"We must destroy this evil."*

The table fell quiet for a time until Jesse translated. The two were somewhat speechless. Finally, Señora Ramos said, *"Our family has been grievously wronged by El Jefe. He almost beat my husband to death many years ago, and he is still a despot to the Tolencitans."*

"Yeah, one day our father will kill him." Bosco spoke casually.

"Be quiet, you stupid boy." The mother cuffed her son on the head. *"Never say that again."*

After a long pause Angelita tried explaining. *"Everyone in Tolencita is terrified of El Jefe and his men."*

Skeets and Jesse looked at each other and ate while they wondered what to say.

Finally, Skeets changed the subject. "Sr. Ramos, you have a really nice place. We saw your farm for the first time today."

Ramos beamed at the complement after Jesse interpreted for Skeets. *"It has been in our family since the revolution."* He never spoke much and surprised and delighted the family when he told the history of the farm. Grandfather Ramos fought beside Pancho Villa and mustered out with one hundred acres, a home, and the money for animals and implements. The place had a spring-fed pond built by the original landowner, Señor Tolen, Tolencita's namesake. The pond covered about one-fourth of the land and assured good crops in all but the driest years. They planted corn and vegetables. The grandfather had prospered until they could afford a house on the plaza of the little town. *"I learned farming from my father who learned from his father. Now I teach my sons."*

The sun slipped below the mesquite trees, and the high desert air cooled the evening and summoned the family onto the veranda. Quito and Bosco sat on the edge of the porch while the others sat in large comfortable lounge chairs woven from willow boughs and covered with leather.

Skeets looked around the yard and saw where their bikes had plowed through the grove of trees. "When I look there and then see us here, I think we are pretty lucky."

"I hear you on that, bro." Jesse leaned back and drew in a breath of air, heavy with the scent of rural life. "It's really peaceful here. Like the world stands still."

In the distance the sound of a car on the road from Tolencita broke the tranquility. The car stopped at the entrance into the Ramos' house. In the growing dusk they could barely make out the word "Policia" on the car door.

Chapter 25

Skeets suggested he and Jesse borrow Angelita's car and search Irapauto for a *vulcanizador* to fix or replace the deflated Harley-Davidson tire. But Jesse, very transparently, said a more efficient approach might be for Skeets to work on the bikes while he and Angelita went into town.

The combination of the Harley tool kits, Ramos' tools, and a lot of hard work had produced progress on the repairs. With the help of their benefactor and his sons, the bikes sat on wooden "horses" under a shade tree for protection from a scorching sun in cloudless skies. Parts removed for repair and refitting piled up in a bucket of kerosene.

"Okay, let's see now. You go into town with the beautiful Angelita, have a nice lunch, look for a tire, and I'll just work out here in the hot sun and fix the bikes. Is that what I hear?" Skeets wiped his brow on a bandana and pointed at the bikes with a wrench.

"A lot of small stuff requires only one man. You can work on those while I, because I speak fluent Spanish, can negotiate with the locals about your tire." Jesse indicated the handlebars and controls needing repair.

"Your idea smells a lot like shoveling shit in horse stalls, bro. I've been there, remember?"

"Angelita offered to drive for me, so I thought I should accept her generosity." Jesse didn't look at Skeets and worked on the bike's front wheel.

"I guess I shouldn't stand in the way of true love, right?"

"True love?"

"Yeah, bro, if Angelita's father could drive, I think *I'd* ride with him instead of you, right?" Skeets grabbed the front wheel as Jesse loosened the axle bolts and pulled it out of the bike's front fork.

The Ramos dinner table had two empty seats and sparse conversation. The family used little Spanish out of respect for Skeets, since he could not participate in their conversation. Bosco, the youngest Ramos, had paid more attention in English classes and spoke more fluently than the others in his family. He used his own version of "Spanglish" as he translated, so Skeets smiled and nodded often to set the family at ease. He knew their concern about Angelita and Jesse – uneasiness he shared. Irapuato was close, and the couple had left midmorning after Angelita opened her restaurant.

Dinner wound down and darkness settled over the farm before they heard the Volkswagen chug up the entrance road. The whole group moved onto the veranda to witness the arrival. Each had questions about the late return. Skeets wondered if he had again been left to baby-sit the natives while Jesse went off for a connubial dalliance. The thought irritated him enough he had already decided to address the problem at length. Then he saw the two act like love-struck teenagers. He smiled at Jesse, oblivious of his glow in Angelita's presence. Jesse, the guy who seldom bothered calling any girl he bedded, was in love. Skeets felt sadness open inside him as he thought of the early days with Gena – the gut-burning tug when they were apart and the elation when they again saw each other. He stood and looked out into the night and thought, I must get back home soon.

Jesse dove into the Volkswagen and resurfaced with a Harley-Davidson wheel and inflated tire. "Check it out, bro." He held the tire aloft in a victory stance. "We went all the way to Salamanca, but we found one. The tire's used, but it's, by God, a tire."

Skeets worked reforming his back fender. Jesse held the bike as Skeets tugged on it. He felt something odd where the fender ran under the seat. They had removed the sissy-bar rack, so when Jesse bent down to look under the seat he saw a small cylindrical gadget stuck on the fender.

Jesse said, "I don't remember one of these on Harleys. What is this thing?"

Skeets looked and thought for a minute. "The thing's definitely an aftermarket addition. Who put it there and why?"

"What can this thing do, stuck out here on the fender? I mean, whoever put it there didn't do a very good job. It's off center." Jesse grabbed the apparatus and tried to shake it loose.

Skeets twisted the cover and it unscrewed. When the cover came free, electronic components filled the inside. "It's a kind of electronic device."

"It's a bug, man. Somebody's bugged your bike." Jesse gestured accusingly.

"Why would anybody put a bug next to an eighty-three cubic inch Harley engine? They don't need a bug, man. They can hear our bikes half a mile away without a bug." Skeets turned the cover over and saw writing on the inside. He couldn't read the tiny letters, so he handed Jesse the cover. "See if you can read this."

Jesse held it up to the sunlight. "Texas Instruments – Transponder model – I can't read the model number. What the hell's a transponder?"

"They use them on airplanes to show their locations, but I don't see why they would put one on a Harley." Skeets scratched his head puzzled.

"Aftermarket, dude. Somebody put this thing on here to know where we are. Jesus, man, somebody out there knows right where we are. Redondo's people? Carlos Algo? Who, man? This is creepy." Jesse made agitated circles with his arms. He picked up a hammer and put a screwdriver at the base of the transponder. With one blow the transponder popped off the fender. He picked it off the ground. "Adios, motherfucker." He threw the transponder into Josefina's pen where it landed in a pile of hay.

The next day brought the decisive moment. They had reassembled the bikes with only minor modifications necessitated by lack of spare parts. No longer things of beauty, Skeets and Jesse hoped the Harleys would make the trip back home. Jesse got very quiet each time Skeets brought up going home. Skeets knew Angelita had thrown a pretty tight noose on Jesse, and he didn't want to leave her. Finally, Skeets brought up the subject. "You don't seem very interested in returning home."

"Yeah, man. There're such nice people I really hate leaving. They've been great to us, you know, and we still haven't paid them for all their help." Nighttime approached and the two had just finished the bike assembly. The air cooled rapidly while the sounds of nighttime insects played an obbligato behind the unfolding scene. A minor domestic disturbance erupted from Josefina and Flaco's pen. Angelita and her mother prepared dinner inside while Ramos and sons still worked in the fields. Jesse looked up at a sky painted with the dying embers of sunset. "It's a really nice evening out. Maybe I'll walk with Angelita after dinner."

"Let's be honest here. With no Angelita, you'd swing your leg over the bike at first light tomorrow and head home." Skeets stood, arms akimbo and stared down Jesse.

Jesse looked at the ground and scraped his boot toe in the dirt. "Man, I don't know what the deal is. I've never felt this way about anybody before. The idea of riding off and leaving her really sucks." He looked up at Skeets. "I'll bet it'll be a downer for her too."

The dinner bell interrupted their conversation. The Ramos men walked up just as the bell rang. Jesse looked at the three, "*You guys are just in time.*"

The family gathered on the veranda after dinner and enjoyed the night air, which had not yet cooled the house. They sat in the darkness and watched a starscape so bright the twinkling lights seemed suspended in the trees. Jesse secretly held Angelita's hand and wondered how he should ask her out for a walk.

Angelita's mother pointed inside the house. "Do you gentlemen really play the guitar and sing?"

Skeets hesitated before he said, "I guess working on the bikes has loosened the stiffness in my fingers enough to play" Before Jesse could translate; Bosco jumped up and brought Skeets' guitar case.

Jesse said, "I reckon we could sing for our supper."

Skeets checked out the guitar for damage from the accident. Tuning the guitar reminded him how much he'd missed playing. The two sang several songs for their small but appreciative audience.

Jesse stood up and said, "Come on, man, I need to do this." Skeets stood reluctantly and followed Jesse down the steps and to stand in front of Angelita. "You know '*Besame Mucho*?"

"Are you kidding?"

"I don't mean the words, just the music."

"I've heard it, but I don't know the chords."

"Okay. Set your capo for key of 'b-flat,' and use D, G, E and A chords and just strum. I'll do the rest." Jesse looked up at Angelita on the veranda. He counted off the tempo, and Skeets strummed.

"Bésame, bésame mucho, como si fuera esta noche la última vez
Kiss me. Kiss me often as if tonight were the last time to kiss.

Bésame, bésame mucho que tengo miedo perderte, perderte después.
Kiss me. Kiss me often for I'm afraid I will lose you, will lose you then.

Quiero tenerte muy cerca, mirarme en tus ojó, verte junto a mé.
I want to hold you close, look into your eyes, know you are here beside me.

Pienso que tal vez mañana yo ya estaré lejos, muy lejos de aqui
Think that perhaps tomorrow I will be far, very far from here.

Bésame, bésame mucho, como si fuera esta noche la última vez
Kiss me, kiss me deeply, as if this night were the very last time.

Bésame, bésame mucho que tengo miedo perderte, perderte después"
Kiss me, kiss me deeply often for I'm afraid I will lose you, will lose you then.
(Consuelo Velázquez, Composer)

Skeets knew the moment was magic. Jesse sang in a smooth baritone while he serenaded Angelita with the classic Mexican love song. Even with no understanding of the lyrics, Skeets' eyes brimmed at the thought of serenading Gena – to once again hold her, and never let her go.

The quiet filled the veranda for a long period before Señora Ramos squeezed her husband's hand and motioned with her head toward their bedroom. Quito and Bosco followed them into the house without being asked.

Skeets cleared his throat. "Yeah, listen, I'm a little tired, sooo . . . I'm hittin' the sack."

Skeets overslept, but when he awoke, Jesse still slept the sleep of the dead. He heard voices and activity in the kitchen and dining room. Angelita normally had left for the restaurant by this time, but this morning she sang softly as she worked in the kitchen with her mother. Skeets got out of bed, dressed, and joined them.

"*Buenos días, Skeets. ¿Como está usted?*" Angelita washed her hands after she sliced and prepared a large fruit tray. She smiled happily when she greeted Skeets.

"*¿Bien, gracias, y usted?*" Skeets poured a cup of coffee. Señora Ramos looked up with a broad knowing grin while she prepared *chilaquiles*. The aroma of the tortillas frying and the onions and garlic simmering in readiness for the salsa, eggs and cheese made his stomach growl with hunger.

"*¿Donde esta Jesse?*" Angelita's voice tinkled with merriment.

"Jesse? He's still asleep." Skeets laid his head over and closed his eyes to translate.

"*Señor Jesse is very tired.*" Angelita's mother cut her eyes toward Angelita and nodded again knowingly. Both women laughed.

Skeets felt an air of anticipation hang over the breakfast table while everyone wondered what events the day held. He waited for Jesse's lead before venturing into when they might leave for home. Jesse finished his plate of chilaquiles and refried beans then said, "I explained to Angelita last night we must repay them for their hospitality, but we had no money. She said they would not accept money from guests in their home. I told her we couldn't interrupt their lives and have them bear the expense of our convalescence. Finally, she agreed to let us sing in Casa de Masa for a few days as a gesture of friendship. She thought her patrons would really enjoy us, and she could borrow an electric keyboard from the doctor."

By the happy looks of anticipation on the family's face, Skeets knew Angelita had already told them about the prospect of their music at Casa de Masa. He must agree, especially since they owed the family so much. "Great idea, bro. We'll rock the place to the ground."

Every face at the table turned toward Jesse for a translation. Jesse's broad smile lit the room, "¡Si." The table erupted in cheers.

Quito and Bosco had already loaded the Volkswagen with produce, so Angelita rushed off for Casa de Masa where she would make preparations for her new entertainers. The men went out for a bike test run. Ramos filled the gas tanks from his gasoline drum in the storage shed. They hoped the batteries still carried enough charge to crank the engines. On what sounded like the battery's last gasp, Skeets' engine caught and coughed into life. Jesse's battery only clicked the starter solenoid. Skeets and the two boys pushed Jesse's bike, but it refused any show of life until the fourth try when the engine growled a loud complaint at being disturbed.

Angelita said that Tolencitans filled La Plaza on Saturdays, so Skeets and Jesse decided to play for both lunch and dinner. At about noon they cranked up the bikes while the Ramos men stood silently by. Skeets and Jesse looked at each other, then at Quito and Bosco. Finally they waved the boys aboard. When their father nodded his approval, they leaped in the air and ran for the bikes.

The revamped bikes performed well and Skeets and Jesse felt the freedom only straddling a Harley could give. As they entered the small town of Tolencita their noise turned every head unaccustomed to "rolling thunder." They noticed the cleanliness of the town and how well dressed the Tolencitans were. No beggars lined the streets and the people went about purposefully, but with little joy in their faces. They took a victory lap around La Plaza so Quito and Bosco could wave and show off for their friends who looked on with envy.

They parked in front of Casa de Masa beside El Jefe's *Policia* car. The two boys jumped off and ran bragging to their friends. Jesse looked at Skeets and then at the police car, and his lips turned downward.

"I know how you feel, bro," said Skeets "But sometimes we must face our demons. So let's go face this asshole."

PART FOUR

"EL REY"
"The King," José Alfredo Jiménez, Composer

Chapter 26

El Jefe had spent another uncomfortable night, alone. Vexed, frustrated, and barely in control, he watched Casa de Masa from across La Plaza until the lights went out. For over a week Angelita had gone home early. He'd had little affection since the two gringos arrived at the Ramos' home. As the cantina windows darkened, he started the pickup and drove home. He hoped she might visit, but he remembered only the midnight gong of the church bells.

He rose early, dressed, and drove to Angeltia's cantina for his complimentary breakfast, and found only Gustavo, the cook, and Chaquita, the barmaid serving. No Angelita. He drank his coffee slowly and stalled. Finally, he ordered a second *torta de huevo* and deliberately chewed every bite. Still no Angelita.

When he menaced Gustavo and Chiquita about Angelita's whereabouts, he received a shrug in return. "*We don't know, Jefe.*"

Angelita walked in just as El Jefe stormed out of the restaurant. She carried a box of tomatoes, peppers, and onions. "*Jefe, would you bring in the rest of the produce?*"

"Bring in the rest of the produce? Where the hell have you been?" He made a menacing gesture.

"Picking vegetables." She set the box down and pointed to it. *"There are more out in the car."*

"I haven't seen you in a week. You come in late and leave early. You quit coming to my house." Angry, he sat down at the bar. *"It's those two gringos."*

"They need care, and I help my family with them as much as I can. Is this a problem for you?"

"I've told you to get rid of them. When will they leave?" He made a backhanded gesture toward the north.

"They'll be here awhile, and they will sing here at Casa de Masa." Angelita tied on an apron behind the bar while enjoying El Jefe's annoyance. *"Come in for lunch, and you can hear them."*

"Singers? Come in for lunch?" Jefe sputtered. *"I want them out of town. Today. Now."* He pounded the counter while his voice boomed out into La Plaza. Angelita shrugged, picked up her box of produce, and went into the kitchen. Jefe stomped out the front door and burned rubber as his car caromed away from the restaurant.

At police headquarters, three blocks from La Plaza, he entered, and brushed past his policemen without comment. His office door slammed behind him. He slumped in his chair and thought, 'how did I let myself fall in love with her?' How stupid can I be for letting a woman have any control over me? He pulled his hat over his eyes and put his feet on his desk. He drifted and dozed while flickers of insecurity from his youth flashed through his mind.

He remembered his unwed mother who raised him in the barrio of Guadalajara, and sent him begging from gringo tourists at age six. He had quickly picked up elementary English and his communication ability with the Norteños became useful when he was too old to beg. He "guarded" tourist vehicles at age fifteen, and by eighteen he hustled as a tour guide.

When twenty years of age, he spent time in a Mexican prison for theft, and learned real power rested in the grasp of the true criminals, the *Policia*. Nothing was better than being a criminal *and* a law enforcement officer. While in prison, he courted the favor of the *Federales*, and at age twenty-five he wore their uniform.

El Jefe still smarted after his transfer from the good life in Guadalajara where he worked in the city's branch of Mexico's *Federales*. He felt his transfer to "this shit hole" was a downer, but he quickly learned Tolencita was ripe for the picking. He first recognized the possibilities in the small town from the townspeople's respect. He sensed the faint smell of fear in their flickering glances, which avoided any confrontation. These sheep needed shearing.

He learned Tolencita existed and prospered in the northern Jalisco desert within sight of the Sierra Madres because a spring gushed up forming a stream, which flowed northward only to die in the desert. A Spanish immigrant, Juan Ignacio Tolen, used early residents - most with pure Indian heritage - and built a series of holding ponds and captured this water for use in rudimentary crop irrigation, primarily corn. Indian lore said, "A good life requires only water, corn, and cactus." The town's founder used "cactus" in two forms, pulque and peyote. With these two incentives he accomplished major civil works with few Indian labor problems.

A stubborn man, Tolen would not allow modern roads to dissect the enormous rancho he assembled with his land grants and the proceeds of his agricultural prowess. Thus, thirty miles of bad road, even today, left Tolencita isolated from modern Mexico and essentially free of tourists. The Revolution saw the Tolen Ranchero divided and deeded to the peasants, and his hacienda made into public buildings. This remained the only apocalyptic event in memory until the arrival of El Jefe.

The culture flowed unctuously greased by a collage of religious beliefs formed by Indian lore, superstitions, legends, and Catholicism. The outsized cathedral, built with the labor of Indians, reflected Tolencitans' desire for immortality, but lacked the finesse and beauty required for tourists. The Church's attempts to educate the people had failed so dismally, that little educational effort remained. The people of Tolencita remained essentially self-sufficient, aloof, and suspicious of the rest of the world.

The fiefdom of Tolencita needed a king: "El Rey," or "El Jefe," as the case may be. When he arrived ten years ago as the official representative of the government of Mexico, El Jefe quickly wrested control from the elected officials of Tolencita and ran the city now with an iron fist. His political power exceeded any of the city government officials' because he and his policemen had the only guns in town. *Federales* across Mexico envied El Jefe's "mordida" scam by which he extracted a heavy tribute from Tolencitans in all forms of payment. He levied his licenses, fees, and taxes randomly, on an ascending scale. His supporters paid little, but those who for any reason resisted anything he desired, paid dearly.

As his power increased, a following appreciated his contributions toward their lives. El Jefe made outsiders very uncomfortable so few visited the town. He provided health and family benefits because of the high cost in personal discomfort and fines from drinking too many *cervezas* or *tequilas*. El Jefe wanted a quiet town. There was no crime. Crime didn't pay. He forbad the use of cactus in any form except tequila, because Indians on pulque and peyote sometimes visited their ancestors and brought foolish notions about freedom back from antiquity.

Even the local padre basked in El Jefe's accomplishments, especially compulsory church attendance. The padre often reminded Tolencitans, "If one minds his own business and pays his 'taxes,' El Jefe would give them few worries." But parishioners always added, "Unless you have an attractive daughter."

El Jefe improved Tolencita over time. The *Policia* headquarters expanded and included a large jail. The police force grew in number, and they enforced firearms regulations vigorously. He built an enormous police shortwave radio broadcast tower, his lifeline to civilization. Police stations within the tower's reach grew accustomed to his regular broadcasts of anecdotes about his sexual peccadilloes and his *mordida* program.

He improved the road into the town, and a bus arrived weekly on its circuitous route to and from Guadalajara. This road had its requisite number of *topes,* speed bumps installed in the area of farmhouses for the foolhardy, who attempted excessive speed.

El Jefe knew the locals said, "Mind your manners, pay your taxes, hide your daughters, and life is good in Tolencita." But he knew from the heaviness in their faces few, if any, believed this. He trusted no one.

He still stung from a lifetime of racial slurs and disrespect from the gringo tourists. His aggravated hatred for those who visited and demeaned him in his own country still smoldered. Hatred gritted his straight-toothed, mustachioed, smiling good looks. One day *everything* would go his way.

Now the town was all his. Everyone in Tolencita feared him, with good reason. When this didn't satisfy him, he made the townspeople give up their self-esteem and satisfied his ego as he flaunted his advances at the citizens' daughters. Anyone who crossed him disappeared. He took pride in the number of widows and unmarried daughters in Tolencita who reared his fatherless children.

A knock on his office door awakened him from his reverie. A jail guard announced a call from Carlos Algo in Guanajuato. *"¿Buenos dias, Carlos, how are you?"*

"Okay. Listen, Monday I will send two men over for a pick up. ¿Any problem?" Algo showed he was a consummate asshole even on the phone.

"They're a little late this week, but they're most welcome." El Jefe spoke with the confident knowledge this week's delivery waited safely in solitary confinement in Cell *Numero 5*, the cell for which only he had a key.

"Expect them around noon. These two stupid pigs would rather eat than shoot policemen. They like the restaurant there." Algo's voice still showed no humor. *"We're late because you gave us the wrong package last week. I went to San Miguel de Allende last week and beat the shit out of that asshole before he gave me the rest of my delivery. Will this happen again?"*

"Don't worry, Carlos, there are no problems." El Jefe thought one day soon he'd show Algo just what happens to an asshole that disrespects him. He unlocked Cell 5, and opened this week's shipment and made sure the last package was still there. Opening the suitcases after they arrived always made a mess. The loose ground coffee added for the benefit of drug-sniffing dogs always spilled everywhere. The code numbers changed each week, so he never knew to whom the packages belonged, but he knew the last package resting in a scattering of coffee grounds was Algo's.

El Jefe's old boss in Guadalajara had called the year before and told him suitcases would arrive on the next weekly bus from Guadalajara. "Store the suitcases in a safe place and open them only when certain visitors came to collect packages inside." El Jefe was cautioned, "Never open a package. Just hand the packages to those who came with a matching code number. The unmarked package in each suitcase is for your efforts."

Jefe's ego was a little hurt when they gave him no choice about his old boss's orders, or even a decent explanation. When he opened his unmarked package in the first suitcase, he saw the stack of one thousand peso notes and promptly forgot any previous misgivings. Suitcases came, packages went, and empty suitcases returned to Guadalajara on the next bus. Now, three large suitcases arrived per week. He ran a small clearinghouse for the Guadalajara drug cartel on the side, augmenting the *mordida* he collected from the Tolencitans. Life was good, and his men had plenty of free coffee to drink.

Noon approached along with the arrival of the two gringos who Angelita said would sing for the Saturday noon crowd in Casa de Masa. El Jefe left instructions for the on-duty policemen to stay awake in case he needed backup and headed for the cantina.

Chapter 27

The main doors to Casa de Masa were tied back to the outside wall, and a pair of barroom swinging doors hung in the doorway. Skeets and Jesse peered over the doors before they entered the cantina. They saw El Jefe seated at the bar and a handful of other patrons at the tables, but no Angelita.

They pushed their way into the room, Skeets first, carrying his guitar. The doors flopped back and forth after Jesse passed through. Skeets stopped again to let his eyes adjust to the dimness. The room had tasteful decorations that included a mural on the wall beside the bar depicting Indians planting corn and harvesting *pulque*. The bar itself could seat a dozen customers and had a simple back bar made from mesquite lumber hand-hewn to look antique. A mirror ran the length of the back bar where the available bottles of liquor, mostly tequila, stood. About a dozen tables sat neatly arranged around the clean and orderly room. Delicious aromas of grilled meat, beans cooking, and the piquancy of chilies and spices wafted through an open door at one end of the room. Jesse smiled when he saw the electric keyboard set up in front of the mural.

Skeets' eyes locked onto El Jefe's, but before a word was spoken, Angelita came through the kitchen door with two plates of food for a table of customers. Her face lit up, and she smiled broadly, *"Buenas tardes*, Jesse y Skeets. *Bienvenidos a Casa de Masa."* She gestured around the room with the two plates, before she delivered them to the table. *"Mi casa es su casa."*

Skeets could tell Jesse wanted to give Angelita a big hug but had to settle for a handshake and an escort to the "bandstand." *"This is quite a nice place you have here."* Jesse gestured around the room.

"Thank you. It's quite small but adequate for Tolencita." Angelita reached and gave Jesse's hand a squeeze of endearment.

El Jefe watched the two gringos' entrance from across the room with unfeigned interest. He saw the affectionate gesture by Angelita and could hardly remain seated as jealousy crept up his spine. He cleared his throat to get Angelita's eye. She frowned at him and continued to show her entertainers where to set up. Finally, El Jefe rose and walked to the three. *"Hombres*, I thought you would go home by now." He showed no humor.

"I reckon we had a little mending up to do and a few motorcycles repairs." Skeets unpacked his guitar.

"So when do you plan to leave?" El Jefe shuffled from foot to foot, like he expected them to leave instantly.

"Depends on Angelita. We're indentured to her for all the Ramos family did for us." Jesse adjusted the keyboard height and plugged in the electrical cord. El Jefe tried to respond, but Jesse noodled an intro to one of Skeets' songs at a volume startling the police chief and silencing him. The room reverberated as the customers ducked their heads and several people peered over the swinging doors to see what caused the commotion.

El Jefe pointed at Jesse and tried again to speak as a series of ten-finger arpeggios rocked out of the electric piano's speaker. The chief tried to talk but looked look like a ventriloquist. The sound rattled around the room and sent shockwaves out the door, where the next several pedestrians pushed through into the cantina.

"Keep going, bro. You're drawing a crowd." Skeets finished tuning his guitar and pointed to the people at the door.

Jesse waved to the crowd at the door. *"Come on in, amigos, and have fun."* Then he loosed twelve bars of a blues tune that shook the bottles on the back bar. El Jefe, now apoplectic, lunged between the two musicians, grabbed the keyboard electrical cord, and ripped it out of the wall socket.

Jesse righted himself. "Easy, dude, it's a borrowed instrument, here."

El Jefe wheeled on the two. "There won't be any music here today, *hombres*. You don't have an Entertainer's License."

"An Entertainer's License? What the hell is that?" Skeets held his guitar by the neck, more like a club than a musical instrument. Angelita stepped between the two and shoved El Jefe through the kitchen door.

Their voices rose in a jumbled, strident argument that ended in a slap of someone's face. Angelita screamed, *"Get out of my cantina, and don't come back."*

The chief stomped out of the kitchen and shook his fist at the two musicians. "You two will hear from me again." He strode through the dining room and shoved his way past the people gathered at the door. *"¡Get out of my way, you stupid idiots."* His tires squealed at a volume equaling Jesse's piano as he drove away.

Angelita came out of the kitchen and held her reddening cheek while she dried her eyes. *"Will God never deliver me from this miserable bastard?"*

"He's definitely not a music lover," Skeets said before he saw how distressed Angelita was. "How does he get off hitting you?"

Jesse's jaw jutted in defiance.. *"Something's not right here. I don't care if he is the police, he can't hit you. I'll kick his ass."* He headed toward the door.

Angelita knew the imminent danger in Jesse's bravado and grabbed his arm. *"It's nothing, really. He just gets excited. He won't come back. Look, you came to play, and you will play."*

The two looked at each other and wondered what they should do. "We don't want to cause you or your family any trouble. I think we should just head on back toward the farm." Jesse searched her eyes for her real feelings about El Jefe. He knew there was something he had not been told.

"¡No. You will play." She turned and jammed the electric piano cord back into the socket. A crowd had filtered into the cantina and rubbernecked at the excitement. She waved at them, commanding, *"¡Sit down. Enjoy the entertainment."* Most obeyed her command and moved around the bar and the tables, while a few sidled toward the door like they'd had enough thrills for one day.

Skeets and Jesse interspersed the few mariachi songs Jesse knew with Skeets' songs and the other tunes in their repertoire. The crowd swelled and people danced in the street and even in La Plaza where the music drifted from Casa de Masa. With the brisk sales, Angelita, Chiquita, the bar maid, and Gustavo, the cook, barely kept up. Angelita immediately pressed her brothers into service in the kitchen when they came in from La Plaza.

Skeets and Jesse played until about midnight with very few breaks, when Angelita said, *"If you don't stop playing, these people will never leave."*

The evening exhausted everyone, and, as the patrons filtered out of the cantina, Skeets and Jesse joined the staff for a beer at the bar. Gustavo said, *"The people haven't had a good time like this in years. Just like a fiesta."*

They sat quietly, discussed the day's events, and stalled before cleaning up the cantina. No one mentioned the scene with El Jefe, but the pall of uncertainty, and the issue of exactly what Angelita's relationship with El Jefe was, hung heavy over Skeets and Jesse. Angelita wanted them to leave the clean up for her and the staff, but they refused. Jesse put the chairs on the tables while Skeets swept the floor. Then one mopped while the other returned the chairs onto the clean floor. With the bar and kitchen clean, the group sat at the bar for one last beer. Bosco and Quito went outside to sit on the bikes, but ran back and shouted excitedly, *"El Jefe's outside."*

Angelita, her face a mask of anger and concern, grabbed Jesse's arm. *"The son-of-a-bitch is not going to hit you again."* Jesse pushed her back even as she begged him not to go outside. Skeets followed Jesse while Angelita frantically tried to stop them.

A *Policia* pickup truck and El Jefe's car book-ended the two Harleys. El Jefe sat on Skeets' bike, and another policeman sat on Jesse's. Two other policemen leaned against the pickup truck. All had the humorless smile of malcontents.

Skeets stopped a step away from his bike. "Listen, we're ready to head out."

El Jefe's smile broadened as he worked the clutch and throttle. "I never rode no Harley-Davidson. Maybe sometime soon I will."

"Well, not tonight, dude. We've had a hard day and we're headed for the barn." Skeets motioned for El Jefe to get off his bike.

"These bikes are really nice. A little banged up, but everything's still here, except for one thing." El Jefe chuckled to himself with pride as he folded his arms across his chest.

"I give up. What's missing?" Skeets looked at the ground and shifted to his other foot with his hands on his hips.

"You've got Texas license plates, and no Mexico Customs Vehicle Registration sticker." El Jefe reached and tapped on the windshield at the spot where the MCVR sticker should be. The three policemen laughed and nodded a confirmation. "These are smuggled motorcycles. They're contraband, and you two are smugglers." Jefe swung his leg over the bike and stepped up on the curb.

Angelita couldn't understand the conversation, but she knew there would be trouble. She moved to confront the chief. *"Jefe, please let these men alone. They leave for Texas in the morning."* She tried to speak from strength, but she feared things were already out of control.

"They won't go anywhere tomorrow, because these smugglers will be in jail." He turned to the other three policemen who had gathered in anticipation of a problem even though they didn't understand the conversation. *"Handcuff these two. They're under arrest for smuggling."*

Angelita screamed, *"No. No. You can't do this."* She lunged at the police chief.

El Jefe swung a backhand and caught Angelita on the cheekbone with a crack that sent her sprawling on the sidewalk. Jesse leaped forward and punched his fist into the man's stomach. He folded over at the waist. With a double-fist, he clubbed El Jefe behind the head and dropped him on his knees. As he backed up to kick the chief in the face, something exploded in his head, and his knees buckled.

The policeman raised his baton to hit Jesse again when Skeets caught him beside the head with an arm's length swing of his guitar case. The policeman's hat briefly hung in the air where his head had been as he crumpled sideways onto the walk. Angelita tried to stand again while Quito, Bosco, Gustavo, and Chiquita stood spellbound. Skeets raised the guitar for another shot, but another policemen pinned his arms behind, and the third landed his baton on the side of Skeet's knee. He crumpled up like a piece of paper. As Skeets lay on the ground and groaned, the baton slammed into his head, and things went black.

El Jefe struggled to his feet and kicked Jesse in the stomach. *"¡Pick this son-of–a-bitch up."* he shouted at his other two men. They left Skeets and grabbed Jesse under the arms and lifted, but he could not stand. *"Give me your baton."* Jefe drew the baton back and buried it in Jesse's ribs. He screamed and writhed in pain. *"Cuff these pinche cabrónes and throw them in the truck."*

Chapter 28

Tolencita's two newest inmates awoke to the church bell tolling early mass. Semi-darkness was the only comfort afforded the two occupants of the jail cell. The air, hot and oppressive, hung like a veil of stench. Two cots, made of rough lumber crudely nailed and strung with rope, rested across the cell from a barred hole-in-the-wall window at the ceiling. Mattresses and bed clothing did not make the amenity package. A thunder-mug that held the remnants of the last occupant sat nearby, and a delegation of flies buzzed around it discussing how best to approach their work.

Skeets and Jesse lay on the rope-cots and took inventory of their condition. Finally, Skeets swung his feet over the side and sat up – head down and stared into his crotch. He looked up and saw his guitar case leaning in one corner. His head throbbed when he moved, and his right knee locked up in pain. He felt dried blood crusted on his face even before he touched it.

Skeets looked at Jesse lying prone on the cot, possibly unconscious. "Jesse?"

"Skeets?" Jesse rolled his head until he saw Skeets from the corner of his eye.

"Yeah."

"You feel as bad as I do?" Jesse raised himself on one elbow and looked around the cell. "It feels like I have a cracked rib, and they must have used my head as a bowling ball."

"I've got a few cricky places myself." Skeets gingerly felt the knot on his head.

Jesse sat up with difficulty, groaning. "I don't remember much after I hit that son-of-a-bitch, but I don't think they checked us into the Four Seasons Tolencita."

"Actually, the accommodations are several cuts below a Motel 8." Skeets shifted his weight, but the pain in his bruised and swollen knee stopped him. He settled back on the edge of the bed. "We might be in a world-a-hurt if El Jefe makes something of the smuggling charge—and don't forget assaulting an officer of the law. I understand federal prisons make this place look first class."

"Problem is, we might not get into a federal prison." Jessie tried standing but gave up. "Angelita told me a little bit about this El Jefe guy, and none of it's good. A lot of people he didn't like just disappeared out of this jail."

"As in, 'forever'?" Skeets' voice elevated with surprise.

"As in out there in the desert somewhere." Jesse groaned as he felt his ribs. "I can't figure why he has this personality conflict with us. What have we done to him?"

"Maybe Angelita hasn't mentioned it, but I think he's got the sweetass for her, and he thinks maybe you're playing ol' *Sancho* with his woman."

"Apparently, there's a whole lot about El Jefe she's not told me." Jesse shook his head in resignation. He looked up and caught Skeet's eye. "Good buddy, considering our current plight, would you accept my apology for insisting we hang around here instead of just Harleyin' our asses on home?"

"Never apologize for commitment to a higher goal, bro. Consider this part of my new self-help, personal improvement program." Skeets' smile lacked assurance.

"If I was the worrying kind, I might start right about now, cause this Jefe guy plays for keeps." Jesse managed to stand and drag himself toward the clay shitpot. His head and ribs translated into pain lines in his face.

"If you're plannin' what I think your plannin' on the pot, I'm sick with worry."

"Actually, I think we might be fast approachin' the praying phase of our lives." Jesse groaned audibly dropping his jeans and lowering himself.

"I've heard people do that. Praying would be something of a switch for us." Skeets watched Jesse struggle. "Son, even knowing what you're about to do, I swear I'd help. But I've almost wet myself cause I still can't move my knee without screaming. I just ain't gonna give those bastards the pleasure."

The sunrays no longer slanted through the window. The church bells confirmed noontime, and, almost on cue, two policemen from the night before unlocked the cell and called for Jesse.

"I'm having a little trouble getting around. What do you want?" Jesse didn't move from the edge of the cot.

"El Jefe wants to see you."

"Tell El Jefe he can come in here if he wants to see me." Jesse tried sounding confident but failed.

"Easy, old buddy, these assholes mean business." Skeets turned toward the guards, but one had drawn his pistol.

The other walked to Jesse with baton in hand and hit him on the back of the neck. *"Get up you piece of shit."* Jesse sat stunned for a moment then lunged at the guard who pummeled him with the nightstick.

Skeets could not take Jesse's screams. "Stop it. Goddamn it, you're gonna kill him." He stepped toward the guard and the second policeman cold cocked him with his pistol.

Vámonos!

"Alto, hombre, enough for now." Skeets looked around and saw Jefe in the cell door. *"We don't want to have all our fun the first day."* The guard backed off and left Jesse a crumpled, bleeding heap on the floor. El Jefe looked at Skeets. "Are you enjoying your stay with us?"

"You miserable cocksucker, why did you do that? You almost killed him." Skeets clinched his fists and the veins stood out in his neck.

"The killing comes later, but first we must play a few games." El Jefe translated for the guards as they laughed their agreement.

Skeets got Jesse up and onto his cot before he regained consciousness and treated his wounds. A pot of stale water, supposedly for drinking, had a couple of dead flies floating in it. Skeets dipped his bandana and washed the cuts as best he could. The worst cut, just above his right ear still oozed blood, so Skeets tied the bandana around Jesse's head as a bandage.

The sun's rays had almost traced their full course across the cell before Jesse finally came to. "Oh, God, I hurt. I think I'm hurt bad."

"Hang in there, buddy. They roughed you up pretty good, but we'll find a way out of this mess. Sometime in the future we'll look back and laugh about this." Skeet placed his guitar wipe-rag across Jesse's forehead after dipping it in the water jug.

"What future?" Jesse voice croaked from his dry throat.

"Now, amigo, we need a skosh better attitude if we're gonna rise above our condition." Skeets' words rang hollow in his throat.

"Attitude, my ass. A sawed-off shotgun rolled in a burrito is about the only thing that'll help my attitude in here." Jesse tried a painful gesture with no success.

"Partner, we're gonna end up a couple a piles of coyote shit somewhere in the desert unless we come up with a plan.

Right? We've got to keep trying." Skeets shivered a little at the prospect.

"Somehow I thought my life would end up more than just cactus fertilizer." Jesse barely mumbled.

"For damn straight we gotta get help." Skeets felt weak and moved back to his cot.

The light in the window faded, and the cooler night air flooded through the unglazed cell window when they heard footsteps in the hall. A guard led Bosco, who held a tray of food and two bottles of water. The guard unlocked the cell door. *"Andale, muchacho."* He shoved him into the cell and locked the door. The tray held two plates of fajitas, beans, rice, guacamole, and tortillas, but no knives or forks.

Bosco's eyes brimmed with tears of fear as he spoke. *"Señor Jesse, are you all right?"*

"I've been better, amigo. How is Angelita?" Jesse looked at Bosco.

"El Jefe took her away somewhere after a big argument. She screamed and cried. We didn't know what we could do, so Quito and I made these plates for you. The cantina always feeds the prisoners."

Jesse stiffened at the news of Angelita and tried sitting up. "The rotten bastard. I'll kill him. I swear to God."

"Easy, man, I don't think you should be sittin' up."

Jesse kept struggling, so Skeets helped him up.

Bosco made a fajita taco, which Jesse took and hungrily chewed through the pain. About halfway through the taco Jesse put it on the tray and lay back on the cot. "I'm hungry, but chewing hurts too much. He must have knocked out a tooth." Jesse's voice trailed off as he slid back into unconsciousness.

Skeets said, "Hang on, bro. Translate something for Bosco." He had finished most of the food on his plate and slid the rest onto Jesse's plate. With the napkin, he cleaned the plate and dipped his finger into the guacamole. He wrote the name, "Gena," on the plate. With several guacamole dips he finished the number: "505-342-6600." He shook Jesse gently awake. "Hey, man, tell Bosco he must call Gena's cell phone in Austin. Tell her we're in a lot of trouble and in jail in Tolencita, near Guadalajara. Tell her our lives are in danger and we urgently need help."

Jesse translated for Skeets and Bosco's eyes widened. *"I don't speak English good enough for all that, Señor."*

"He says he can't tell her that in English." Jesse drifted away again.

"Come on, man, he's gotta call. He must call and do the best he can. Maybe she'll be with someone who speaks Spanish. Just call, Godammit." Skeets' frantic voice scared Bosco, who recoiled with eyes brimming.

Chapter 29

PK, Gena Koster's tomcat, checked his parts and gave them a friendly little lick. The swelling had receded soon after The Tall Evil Smelling One had disappeared. But since the disappearance, PK now, mostly from gratitude for his balls still remaining attached after the vicious attack by The Tall Evil Smelling One, checked them regularly and gave them a little love. At the time of the attack and for several days after, he had felt differently, but now it seemed a small price to pay for all the attention and tasty treats heaped on him by The Sweet Smelling One. Not since he had been uprooted from the pleasures afforded by all his lovely neighbors up and down the alley and summarily deposited in this strange Big Box had The Sweet Smelling One shown so much affection and kindness toward him. He could sleep the night through, cuddled up against her, since the disappearance of The Tall Evil Smelling One. Whoever out there among the stars that jerked him around before, had eased off. Now if they would just come up with a pussycat – any pussycat – his would be the ideal life.

These had been the longest three weeks of Gena Koster's life. How could she miss a cheating, lying bastard like Skeets Hollaran? The idea made her think less of herself. Made her sit for long periods absorbed in self-doubt, rubbing on PK, who luxuriated in her lap. Time had blunted the sting of Skeets' betrayal somewhat, but remained a detracting irritant for everything left in her life. He called into question the notion of monogamy as a natural state. Possibly Skeets could not control his primal urge. Well, that's for damn sure, idiot, she reprimanded herself. Still, he had so much going for him maybe she might overlook this tiny little flaw. Overlook? She felt ashamed at the thought. How can she overlook her true love screwing other women?

She had first sought refuge at the Dillo Doe and visited with Lizzie Ortega, the bartender and her best friend. Lizzie had tried cheering her and had even encouraged a few of the painfully horny UT men in their bid for Gena's attentions. She explained, when Gena protested, a little "strange" might take her mind off Skeets. Gena had left in a huff but returned again the next night and apologized. She knew Lizzie had her best interest at heart.

Then Fritz, the Dillo Doe manager, started in on her. First with amorous intent, and finally in desperation he said, "Gena, you spend so much time in the Dillo Doe, you might as well work here and make a little money." She had refused his offer also.

Her problem was the lovelorn Dr. Charles Higdens, her graduate studies advisor. Higdens remained an emotional mess after his much younger wife had left him for one of his most promising graduate students. He felt a real kinship with Gena when, after his inquiry into her morose outlook, he learned she had kicked her musician lover out of her house. She knew "Dr. Lovelorn," as Lizzie called him, had a real crush on her, which made their counseling sessions very uncomfortable. But her loneliness and desperation and the abject pleading in his eyes when he'd asked, made her accept his invitation for dinner.

A pleasant looking man, about ten years older, he possessed few social skills. Still, over the dinner table he seemed quite at ease as they discussed her upcoming thesis on "Comparative Origins of Modern American Country and Western Lyrics." He conceded the originality of the thesis, but he had doubts about available research materials to prove it.

"But if we work closely together, we might get the job done." He beamed at the "closely" thought.

At her front door he fumbled miserably. He desperately wanted to kiss her, but settled for her peck on his cheek before he left. She went inside, quickly undressed, raked up PK, and plunged into bed hoping sleep would clear her muddled mind.

Charles had again invited her for dinner on their next outing but did not specify a destination. To her surprise, he pulled into the driveway of a small but attractive bungalow with a view of downtown Austin and Town Lake and announced, "Welcome to Chez Higdens." He had set a table for two on the veranda overlooking the twinkling lights of the city reflecting off the lake's surface. Ligustrum bushes heavy with blooms scented the air with pure sweetness, and the chimneyed candelabra flames stood stately, unaffected by the gentle evening breeze. An extremely pleasant Pinot Noir went down easily from a wine glass, which never ran dry. He had roasted quail stuffed with pâte de foi gras. The cherry richness of his Cumberland Sauce blended with the Pinot Noir and elicited a moan of pleasure from Gena. "When we hunted quail back home, they never tasted this good. Where did you learn to cook like this?"

"Man does not live by books alone."

After dinner they sat on a porch swing with their wine glasses, and the pulsing rhythm of Ravel's "Bolero" soon lulled her into acquiescence.

Tonight, Gena simmered on her quandary as long as she could and showed up at the Dillo Doe about eight o'clock. She approached the bar apprehensively, and Lizzie asked what was bothering her.

"I gave Dr. Lovelorn a mercy fuck last night. How could I do that? God, what an idiot I am." Gena dropped her head into her hands.

"You have somewhat clouded your vision of the future, right?" Lizzie lit a cigarette and blew smoke skyward. "Now how do you get rid of him since he's your graduate advisor and holds your whole academic future in his hands." She paused. "Was he any good?"

"Geez, Lizzie, how could you ask such a thing? I'm in terrible trouble here."

"Just for my future reference. You can't have all the fun." Lizzie laughed out loud as she mixed the next order of drinks for one of the few occupied tables.

Gena's cell phone launched into "Boot Scoutin' Boogie." "Oh, my god, it's probably Dr. Lovelorn. What am I gonna do?" She pulled the phone from her back jeans pocket and looked at the screen. " 'Out of Area?' Who would this be? Hello. . . . Yes, I am Gena Koster. Who is this? . . . Skeets and Jesse? Yes, I know a Skeets and Jesse. Why? . . . *Mucho problemas . . .*" She shrugged at Lizzie. "They're trying to speak English. Something about Skeets and Jesse."

Lizzie reached for the phone. *"¿Bueno? . . . No I am Gena's friend, Lizzie. I speak Spanish. . . . Ok, let me talk to her. . . Angelita Ramos? I am Lizzie . . . Yes, I understand. What's the problem with Skeets and Jesse? . . . motorcycle accident . . . Tolencita east of Guadalajara? . . . in Jail? . . . El Jefe? . . . might kill them? . . . Good God. Can't you get the police to help? . . . He is the police? . . . Casa de Masa? Okay. I understand they need help quickly."*

"What?" Gena stood up excitedly and reached for her phone.

"Some woman named Angelita Ramos said Skeets and Jesse had a motorcycle accident. Her family nursed them back to health, but now a guy named El Jefe has them in jail, and she's afraid he's gonna kill them. They need help, bad."

"God, how could this happen? Where are they?" The shrillness in Gena's voice could filet fish..

"She said in a little town east of Guadalajara called Tolencita."

Quito and Bosco sensed a new level of hatred toward El Jefe in Angelita after he brought her home Sunday evening. Immediately after Bosco showed Angelita the avocado inscribed plate, the two left by the back door of Casa de Masa and took back streets in case El Jefe watched them. They arrived at the *Oficina de Larga Distancia* separately and left separately. Returning, they huddled in the *casita* that Angelita had purchased recently, next door to Casa de Masa. The owners of the little house had died and their children, who now lived in Guadalajara, had no use for it. The furniture remained and the bedroom had an oversized window facing the center of La Plaza through which the bedridden father had watched the town's activities. Everyone who passed the window acknowledged him when the curtains were open, a salutation he returned until shortly before his death. Angelita planned to enlarge Casa de Masa and the *casita* would become a room for patrons' special occasions.

Her voice vacillated between desperation and hope when she told Quito about the phone call and conversation with a friend of Gena's. She felt sure help would come, although she did not know in what form.

"What should we do for Jesse and Skeets?" Quito asked.

"Bosco, you will tell them when you take la comida tomorrow about our conversation with Gena, and that she will send help. Then we must wait." Angelita knew the pure agony of waiting. She had waited years to destroy El Jefe. Her mind

churned on how they could overcome El Jefe and the *policia's* advantage. There must be a way to help Jesse and Skeets.

Lobo remained confused. The one motorcycle transponder had remained stationary about fifteen miles out of Tolencita for days now. The bikes are parked or the transponder had been removed and destroyed. Either way he had no notion of what the two riders did or where they went. "There's really something strange about those two *hombres* bein' in Tolencita." He mumbled aloud as he tapped on the Loran screen.

Lobo switched frequencies and picked up the dot on the screen of another transponder an agent had slipped into the lining of one of the suitcases hauling cocaine from Guadalajara to Tolencita. He had watched the suitcase and transponder bounce back and forth weekly between the two locations for over a month. Currently, the suitcase remained in Tolencita. He zoomed in on the GPS screen, and saw it remained at the police station. "We got us some really dirty cops in that little town." He put the Wolf Wagon into gear and growled out onto the highway and followed a van headed for Mexico City. He dialed a new frequency on the short wave radio and picked up the microphone. "Wolf Wagon to control. Come back."

After a garble of background noise, a voice. "Control to W.W. What's up?"

"Listen, good buddy, could you check on the Tolencita situation, and tell me if we're gonna move on it soon ? Come back."

After a long gargling pause, the voice again. "Negative, WW, the locals say those drugs do not come our way, so we're out of it."

Lobo's brow furrowed, and he shook his head. "They don't need our help? Come back."

"That's affirmative."

"I'm on my way to Mexico City following a mule to his pickup point. I think I'll swing back through Guadalajara and trail a load north. Come back."

"We'll see what we can dig up that's worth the trip. Out."

Chapter 30

Skeets spent a sleepless night, not so much from his pain or Jesse's groaning in his sleep, but from the realization their plight seemed insurmountable. As he lay in the dark and stench of the jail cell, his mind ricocheted around the possible scenarios that might befall them at the hands of the crooked police chief. There seemed no possible escape from their manifest fate. He understood the fear and dread of just how soon he might meet his end, but the most burdensome thought of never seeing Gena occurred again; not to hug her, to apologize, and tell her how very much he loved her. A great sense of loss welled in him, and he fought off tears by struggling to stand and walking through the pain in his knee. He was still limping slowly around the cell when the church bells tolled early mass.

He had not seen or heard anything more from the guards or El Jefe since they had let Bosco out of the cell last evening. Sounds of the town coming to life drifted through the window with the faint glow of morning light. Jesse had slept through the night in torpor from physical pain and mental exhaustion. Skeets finally returned to bed and drifted into sleep and midmorning sounds in the hall awoke him. Bosco carried a tray of food down the hall followed by the guard who had pummeled Jesse.

The guard wore a toothy grin as he unlocked the cell door. *"Buenos dias, amigos. ¿Did you have a pleasant evening?"*

Jesse must have awakened from the noise. *"No thanks to you, asshole."*

"Oh, still the belligerent one. I need some exercise this morning. ¿Would you like another massage?" The guard drew his baton and pointed at Jesse.

Skeets held his hand up. "Easy, man. Why don't you let us eat our food?"

Bosco interrupted, almost shouting. *"I'll bring you a plate of food if you let them alone."*

The guard laughed out loud. *"Now see. This boy knows politeness."* Bosco cringed when the guard tapped him on the head lightly with the baton before he put it back in its holster-loop. *"Hurry up, muchacho, I'm hungry,"* he said through the bars as he locked the door behind him.

The tray held two plates of *chilaquiles* with salsa, tortillas, a pot of coffee and two cups. Jesse managed to sit up on his own and hungrily accepted the plate Bosco offered. Bosco made sure the guard had left before he whispered, *"My sister and I called your friend last night and talked to Señorita Gena and another woman named Lizzie. They know you are in trouble here in jail, and they said they would get help for you."*

"What exactly did she say?" Skeets put his hands on Bosco's shoulders ready to shake information out of him.

"Amigo, can you tell us exactly what she said?" Jesse lifted his head from his plate and gave Bosco a reassuring smile.

"Lizzie spoke Spanish, so I let her talk to Angelita." Bosco still had a fearful look as he glanced back and forth between the two prisoners. *"I don't know what they said, but they understand you need help urgently."*

Skeets shook his head in desperation, paused for a moment, and looked at Jesse. "Tell Bosco I'm sorry if I sounded upset. Thank him for the brave things he does to help us."

"He knows you're not angry." Jesse turned to Bosco and told him what Skeets had said and then looked back at Skeets. "I guess I'm used to all this physical abuse as I'm feelin' a little better this morning. I only hurt when I laugh."

A broad smile cut across Skeets face when he realized Jesse might get his sense of humor back. "I'll try to be a little more serious while we sit here and consider our imminent demise."

El Jefe waited across La Plaza from Casa de Masa for the arrival of Carlos Algo's two goons. Normally he would sit at the counter and visit with Angelita at this time, but their relationship was a bit strained since he locked up the two gringos, hauled her to his house, and forced himself on her last night. When she knew his intentions, she extracted a promise to let the gringos go today. He quickly forgot his promise when he climaxed, like most promises made in the heat of passion.

One of El Jefe's men held a parking place for Algo's Mercedes Benz in front of the cantina. The two stiffs always dressed in expensive suits, ties and hats like Hollywood gangsters, and they did not like to walk in the heat and risk sweating. He saw the black Mercedes nose into La Plaza and smooth slowly around to the other side and park in the designated gangster slot. El Jefe pulled in beside the car before the two occupants could get out.

He smiled broadly and with a grand gesture toward the cantina door said, "¿How about some comida?"

Their conversation over lunch included boisterous anecdotes of sexual encounters and other subjects offensive to anyone else in the restaurant. At one point, El Jefe asked why they had not waited until tomorrow to come so they could pick up last week's and tonight's delivery. They both shrugged. One said, *"Carlos said he needed the package tonight. I guess we'll come back next Tuesday and pick up two deliveries at once."*

The second *desperado* said, *"Yeah, save a trip. This cantina's the only thing good about this miserable place."*

Angelita remained in the kitchen during the whole meal, which Chiquita served. They drank a cup of coffee with honey soaked *sopapillas* for dessert when El Jefe told them about these two gringos he had jailed, and how he had confiscated their Harley-Davidson Motorcycles.

"¿Are they musicians?" one of the two asked over the rim of his coffee cup.

"Yeah. ¿How did you know?" El Jefe raised his eyebrows in surprise.

"We know them from Guanajuato. Actually we have unfinished business with them." The speaker rubbed a place on his face, which looked like a gravel-burn.

"¿How do you know these guys? El Jefe still had his surprised look.

"They fucked Carlos' twins."

El Jefe had met Algo's twins once when Carlos had come to Tolencita himself. A look of compete admiration came over El Jefe's face when he remembered the spectacular looking girls. *"¿They fucked the famous Algo twins?"* A rumble of laughter rolled up through him and exploded into the room.

The two goons looked a little surprised but caught the joke and joined in. *"We'd all like a little bit of them too, right?"* The nods of agreement and laughter continued until Angelita finally peeked into the room to check them out.

The prisoner's hearts leaped with anticipation when a guard came down the hall and announced they had visitors. "The cavalry's arrived, bro. I don't know what Gena did, but it really worked. It's probably somebody from the consulate, right?" Skeets stood in anticipation.

El Jefe led the group, along with another guard, followed by Carlos Algo's two henchmen who smiled like they'd just found an Easter egg. The shock of the goons outside the cell sent Skeets reeling back to his cot.

"Greetings, amigos, we bring you a personal message from Carlos Algo." The larger desperado took off his coat and tie as the guard unlocked the cell.

The other pointed at Skeets. *"You're the one who knocked me down the stairs."* He turned to Jesse. *"You kicked me in the ass."* He followed the leader, took off his coat, and rolled up his sleeves.

"Kicked your ass?" El Jefe howled with laughter.

"It's not funny, amigo. He had on pointed cowboy boots."

El Jefe couldn't get his breath for laughing. *"¿He didn't kill you?¿Just kicked your ass?"* The guard swung the door open, and the group entered the cell and locked the door behind. Two of the guards picked Skeets up and dragged him over to Algo's men.

Skeets shouted, "Come on guys. We got nothing against you guys. We just wanted to get away from Algo." With no warning, a beefy fist smashed into his face. His knees buckled under him, and blood squirted from his nose and dripped from his chin. Jesse moved to help Skeets, but the third guard drew his baton and menaced him into submission. The two guards raised Skeets, and the second of the two thugs landed three rapid-fire punches to the stomach. Skeets puked on the floor. They threw him back on his cot and turned to Jesse, who now cowered in the corner of his bed and whimpered. The two guards grabbed him under the arms and dragged him screaming to the center of the cell, then turned him around and bent him over. The two gangsters took turns kicking him in the ass until they tired. Blood seeped through Jessie's pants. He could scream no more and collapsed. One of the thugs pulled his head up from the floor. "I'm sure Carlos will want to see you personally, amigos." He let the head drop with a thud.

Gena took the first Continental Airlines flight to Houston Monday morning and connected with their noon flight to Guadalajara. She had more difficulty traveling to the bus depot in Guadalajara. She needed an interpreter so the cab driver understood she would take a bus out of Guadalajara to Tolencita. The city traffic gridlocked and the fumes from the cars made her nauseous. The taxi driver detoured around the traffic, then wanted twice the fare she had been quoted after they arrived at the bus terminal. She paid reluctantly and rushed into the terminal. The weekly bus to Tolencita was preparing to pull out of the terminal when she shouted down the driver. People who had not bathed recently crowded the ancient, graffiti covered bus, which had torn upholstery, no air conditioning, and carried mostly men who leered at her with unblinking eyes. The bus had crates with chickens and a small pig that looked concerned over his future strapped to the roof

She wore motorcycle clothes since there might be Harley riding at some point – black jeans and a midriff tank top with the Harley-Davidson logo. The heat made her black leather Harley jacket uncomfortable, but it covered the tank top, so she dared not take the coat off in front of all these men. She had pulled her ponytail through the back of her Harley ball cap. Mirrored sunglasses and motorcycle boots completed the ensemble. Men seemed unable to take their eyes off the lady in black.

When she had calculated the distance of about one hundred miles, she had not considered all the stops in small towns and along the roadside to pickup and discharge passengers. Unloading the chickens and pig took some time. The crooked road meandered through hills as they faded from green to brown, leveling into the desert. Finally, only Joshua trees, small mesquites, and scrub brush covered the semiarid landscape.

The hot desert air poured through the open windows and made her sweat under the jacket. In self-defense, she pulled the ball cap down over her eyes and tried to sleep. She jostled awake when the bus turned onto the Tolencita road and watched the setting sun throw shadows over the scenery until they entered the small town. The bus stopped beside a church to discharge passengers on the plaza that Angelita had mentioned. She stretched the travel stiffness from her body and took down the rolling bag from the overhead rack. A handful of passengers got off the bus, so she followed them. A man handed her bag down as she stepped from the bus stairs.

The driver had opened the baggage doors and handed out luggage to the passengers. A policeman with the bearing of authority waited until the driver gave him three suitcases. He had tall good looks and made no secret of his interest in her. Before he picked up the suitcases, he walked toward her and said, "We don't get many tourists here in Tolencita."

She smiled. "I'm not a tourist. Just visiting friends."

He paused a moment. "Will they pick you up?"

"They said the bus usually arrives late, so I will call them. Is there a restaurant or cantina close?" She spoke nonchalantly.

"That's Casa de Masa across La Plaza." He pointed in the direction. "Can I give you a ride?"

"No thank you. A little walk would suit me right now."

"You're sure?" His smile glowed with reassurance.

"Positive."

"By the way, I'm El Jefe."

"El Jefe's a peculiar name,.."

"What's your name?"

She thought for a moment and took the easier course and said over her shoulder as she walked away, "Gena."

When she stepped through the barroom doors at Casa de Masa, the room fell silent and everyone stared at her. A few tables had diners, a woman and teenage boy stood behind a bar seated with patrons, and kitchen sounds and aromas came from a side door. She wondered what was the problem, and then remembered she still had her mirrored sunglasses on. When she removed them, the discomfort of all the eyes fixed on her only intensified. A little unnerved, she moved toward the bar, but as she approached, the teenager ran into the kitchen. Instantly, a beautiful woman came out drying her hands. Two teenagers followed behind as she rushed toward her. "Gena?"

"Angelita?"

They hugged in desperation. The two women stood in the cantina in an embrace, which transcended language to the level of complete understanding. After a time Angelita lifted her head with eyes brimming. *"Gracias, Señorita Gena for coming to Tolencita."*

Gena shook off her emotion, released her hold, and left a comforting arm over Angelita's shoulders. She pointed to her mouth, "Senorita, I would feel better about this whole thing if I understood a word you said. I don't think junior high school Spanish will cut it down here."

Angelita looked down embarrassed, and Gena put her finger under the woman's chin, raised the face, and for the first time adequately appreciated its beauty. "Girl, your face could jail a thousand gringos."

"No entiendo, Señorita."

A murmur of astonishment went through the cantina patrons, still wide-eyed at the vision of Gena, and Angelita's acceptance of her. Angelita realized for the first time they had an audience and took Gena's hand and led her into the kitchen. She ordered some food from Gustavo, the cook, and told Bosco to bring Gena's dinner next door. She told Quito, *"Go get the doctor. Hurry. Bring him back with you."* Quito wondered who was sick, but he ran out of the kitchen on his errand.

Angelita brought Gena into the casita through the rear door and took her bag into the bedroom. Gena followed her and saw a bed facing a large curtained window. The lights turned the bedroom bright as day. Whoever slept here was afraid of the dark, Gena thought. A dresser with a mirror and a chair sat across the room. She looked out the window at the steps across the street leading up to the level of La Plaza with the huge wrought iron gazebo centered behind.

Bosco delivering a plate of food for her dinner pleasantly surprised Gena. She had not eaten since the Houston airport. The aromas of the beautifully displayed food almost made her swoon. After a few bites she said, "If you cooked food like this in Austin, you'd die rich." Angelita smiled, but Gena could tell she did not understand. Gena decided to try her Spanish. "*¿Como esta* Skeets and Jesse?"

"*Oh, Señorita, they are in real trouble. El Jefe has beaten them badly. Bosco said they could not eat when he took their dinner tonight. We must do something. We must get them out before El Jefe beats them to death.*" Angelita frowned in anger, hatred, and sympathy – emotions of frustration and anguish.

Gena listened at the Spanish version with almost no comprehension except for "*El Jefe*" and "*muerte*" which meant the police officer she met tonight wanted Skeets and Jesse dead. The back door opened and Quito brought the doctor in, carrying his black bag.

Angelita greeted the doctor. "*Thank you for coming doctor. We have a terrible problem.*"

"*Who is sick?*" The doctor looked around the room and his stare lingered on Gena.

"*Pardon me, doctor, for not introducing Señorita Gena from Texas.*" She pointed toward Gena by way of introduction.

Gena smiled and held out her hand to the doctor. "A pleasure. I apologize in advance for not speaking Spanish."

"*Mucho gusto, Señorita,* and I apologize for how poorly I speak English." He gave an amicable smile as he sat in the chair offered by Angelita.

"I think maybe Angelita asked you over to translate for us because we must save my friends in the jail." Gena smiled and looked down at her plate. "I hope you don't mind me eating, 'cause I'm starving."

"*¿Doctor, would you like dinner?*" Angelita rose in anticipation of ordering food for the doctor.

"*No, no, thank you. I've eaten, but I might take a beer.*"

Angelita sent Quito for three beers and then explained the problem. When she had finished, the doctor looked concerned. "*If this is a problem with El Jefe, I don't know if I should get involved. People who cross El Jefe don't do well here in Tolencita.*"

"*Please, doctor, all I need you for is translating and please do not to tell anyone about this conversation.*" Angelita's pleading moved Gena to ask about the doctor's concern.

"I told Angelita I should not get involved in a problem with El Jefe,." He looked down at the floor, a little ashamed.

"Angelita says this El Jefe's a really bad guy. Why do you people put up with him?" Gena furrowed her eyebrows with the question.

"It's very complicated. He is a very dangerous man when he is angry." He shook his head in resignation. "I am just here until I finish my residency, but these poor people have suffered with his oppression for over a decade. It's truly a sad situation."

"Sounds like this guy's way overdue for his comeuppance. We must figure a way to accomplish it." Gena brimmed with confidence on the outside, but despair had crept into her like a virus.

Angelita told El Jefe's story from the beginning. She even told of her rape and the rape of many other young girls in the community, and how El Jefe paraded his sexual exploitation in front of the townspeople, shaming them and taking away their self-esteem. About how he brags over the radio tower to other *Federales* of how badly he treats the Tolencitans. How her father had tried to redeem her honor, and El Jefe had almost killed him and left his mind crippled. How he took whatever money he wanted from the people as his *mordida*. She told of the prisoners and townspeople who had disappeared. She told with difficulty how she used his sexual appetite to gain control over him with her submission. *"But now I love one of the men in jail. I think he loves me."* Tears welled in her eyes as she finished her story.

The doctor shook his head in disbelief when he finished the translation. "As an outsider, I had no idea what a tyrant he was."

Gena sagged at the problem they faced. "We must destroy him. But how?"

"There must be a way of destroying any respect and fear the Tolencitans have for him." The doctor's expression showed him an ally.

When Angelita heard the translation, she pointed at the doctor's crotch and said. *"All of his pride is in his britches."*

The doctor laughed and translated. Gena joined in the laughter. "Maybe we should just cut his dick off."

Angelita covered her mouth in mock embarrassment after the translation. She thought for a minute and looked at Gena. *"You must take care. As beautiful as you are, he will try having his way with you also. Last night I slept with him and he promised he would let them go today, but he lied. He may use you as ransom for their freedom, or even use force."*

Gena patted Angelita in sympathy for what she'd had endured in her failed attempt for Jesse and Skeets' freedom. Then Gena rubbed her forehead as she considered the problem. After a pause, she said, "Hey, wait a minute. That's not a bad idea. Why not use me as bait for a trap."

"What kind of trap?" The doctor looked perplexed.

"We can figure this out, but it's gonna take a shot of tequila and lots more beer."

Chapter 31

A pall of gloom blanketed Skeets. The cell, though larger than most, felt oppressive and more claustrophobic than before. The thunder mug sent a mind-numbing stench into the room. Neither he nor Jesse could move since Carlos Algo's henchmen had beaten them. The night had passed slowly with shooting pains accenting the slightest movement. Skeets' nose no longer bleed but felt broken. He wished he had a mirror to assess the damage. His leg moved better, but the soreness in his stomach made each breath an agony and eating almost impossible. He glanced at Jesse, who lay on his stomach because the ass kicking had rendered the area too sore to touch, much less to lie on. Hunger gnawed at Skeets since he had passed up the meal Bosco had brought the evening before. Now the time approached noon, much later than Bosco's normal arrival.

Skeets rose on one elbow. "I don't think I'll decline another meal if I'm ever offered one again. I'm more than a little hungry."

Jesse, his face in his arms made a muffled reply. "Maybe they don't feed dead people."

"I'll admit we're part way there, but we aren't to the givin' up stage, are we?" Skeets swung his legs over the edge of the cot and sat up with difficulty. He looked over at Jesse and could not determine his condition with him lying on his stomach.

Jesse moved a little and mumbled. "Maybe not, but I'm definitely in the need-some-good-news stage. You don't think El Jefe will turn us over to Carlos Algo, do you?"

"I've given up on figuring out what El Jefe will do. His options seem unlimited." Holdng his stomach with one hand, Skeets stood and moved toward the thunder mug. "Man, I'm not sure I can get close enough to use this stinking thing."

"Yeah, our cup runeth over, that's for sure." Jesse rolled over on his side with a groan. The cut behind his ear had scabbed over, so he took off the filthy bandana bandage.

The church bell tolled one o'clock when they heard Bosco and a guard in the hall. The guard unlocked the cell door and shoved Bosco inside. *"Hurry up. my food's getting cold."* He slammed the door behind the boy and strode back toward the front of the jail.

Bosco set the tray down on Skeets' cot, looked out the cell bars, and made sure the guard had left. He held his finger to his lips and cautioned the prisoners to be quiet. Bosco sat on Skeets' cot, handed him a bowl of tortillas, and showed him a small recorder hidden beneath. *"Shhhh. We bought this recorder this morning for you."*

Jesse grabbed at the recorder, and Bosco pulled back. *"You must hide the recorder until I leave. Do not let the guards know you have it. Eat something so they will not be suspicious. You need your strength back, amigos."*

Their hunger overrode their pain, and they wolfed down a sizable portion of the meal. The guard came for Bosco and locked the cell door behind them. Once certain the guard had left, Skeets removed the recorder they had hidden in his guitar case and sat on Jesse's cot.

"Maybe somebody up there likes us but He's confused. " Skeets stared down at the cassette recorder with a notepad and ballpoint pen taped to the back but with no note of explanation. "A recorder's nice, but I'm afraid we've seen the last of our recording days. Maybe we're supposed to dictate our last will and testament."

"Even a welcome-basket of fruit might be more in order. I just don't see how a cassette recorder is of much use," Jesse added.

Skeets saw a portion of the cassette tape rolled onto the second spool and rewound it. Before he could press "Play," he heard the security door open again and someone come down the hall. He shoved the recorder under his shirt just before El Jefe walked past their cell with a coffee can. Jefe opened the last cell and went inside. They could hear him move something around, then a loud curse, followed by the strong smell of coffee. Several minutes later he locked the other cell and walked past their cell with a plastic shopping bag and the coffee can.

When the security door locked, they leaned together and listened. The security door opened before they could start the tape. Quickly they hid the recorder. "Jesus, I can't believe this." Skeets hissed. El Jefe again appeared with another coffee can. He repeated his previous visit.

As the chief cleared the security door, Jesse said, "Jefe's going on a caffeine jag if he keeps this up."

They waited in case El Jefe showed up again. Finally, Skeets risked starting the recorder. A hissing noise on the tape preceded Gena's voice. "Well, isn't this just wonderful." Gena Koster's voice called up a lump in Skeet's throat that blocked his windpipe. "You two great guys are locked up tighter than Fort Knox in a premier example of the Mexican penal system, and frankly I'd give Jimmy Carter a better chance at reelection than you boys of ever improving your tan."

"Son, I knew she's a little upset with you, but this is purely cold." Jesse looked concerned.

"Shhhhh. There's more."

Gena's voice continued after a pause. "Okay, you're in there, we're out here in Casa de Masa, and the complete sociopath, El Jefe and his men stand between us. We've come up with a plan to cut El Jefe's nuts off – figuratively speaking, but you must do your part. First, get well because you gotta be movin' good when the time comes. I can use my feminine wiles and maybe get El Jefe to leave you alone, but don't worry about me. I don't have time for explanation, so listen up. If you never wrote a hit song in your life, this is the time. Since you have very little to do, write "The Ballad of El Jefe's New Lover." Here's how the song should go . . ." The two stayed huddled and listened at Gena's instructions.

The short wave radios crackled and hummed at *policia* and *Federale* stations all over Central Mexico. "*¡Atención. ¡Atención.*" Heads sagged in regret at the sound of El Jefe's voice once again. *"This is the Tuesday evening report from Tolencita, the city of opportunity. The weather is beautiful, as usual. Our record-breaking number of crime free days continues. No violent crime. No domestic disturbances. No drug trafficking. We hold our record up against any other city in Mexico. The wonderful Tolencitans continue in their generous contributions to the Policia retirement fund. SPECIAL NEWS BULLETIN – We have captured two notorious gringo smugglers and confiscated two Harley-Davidson Motorcycles brought into Mexico unlawfully. We will auction these motorcycles to the highest bidder. Consider this an opportunity for police and Federal motorcycle units to upgrade their fleet. Perfect for funerals, parades, and occasions of state. Call in your bids to 475- 2HD RIDE. This is El Jefe speaking from where the women are beautiful, and I am accommodating. Wishing every police and Federale station was the equal of mine. Paz. Fuera."*

Lobo grinned as the Wolf Wagon's short wave radio went silent after El Jefe's report. "So that's what's happened to those two *hombres*. Sounds like they're in more'n a little trouble." He normally monitored the *Federale* short wave communication frequency, but for a month he had paid particular attention to the "El Jefe Tolencita Evening Report." Among other things El Jefe always gave him a laugh or two, but he also listened for information about his drug distribution center. He had just pulled into the truck stop on the outskirts of Guadalajara where he parked the Wolf Wagon. He shut the truck down, pulled his duffel bag from the sleeping compartment, locked up, and sat at his customary seat in the café. Another man joined him and, after a cup of coffee, the two drove away in a white Ford pickup.

PART FIVE

"LA BALADA DE LA AMADA NUEVO DEL JEFE"
"The Ballad of El Jefe's New Lover"
Bill Stephens, composer

Chapter 32

Alfonso Diego, *Ministerio de Cultura* for the great state of Jalisco, lunched each Friday with Humberto Cortez, *Ministerio de Turismo* for the City of Guadalajara. At lunch, they plotted how they could best line their pockets from their respective governmental budgets. *"It's synergy in action,"* as Diego often said. *"Two heads being better than one."*

About nine months before, they had met at *Restaurante Jacala,* not the poshest of eateries in Guadajalara, but favored by businessmen and government officials who needed a certain ambiance for conducting business and running the affairs of state. Rather than freestanding tables with a view of all in the establishment, its high-backed, leather banquettes, circular in design, afforded little if any scrutiny of diners by the restaurant's other guests. Jacala's acoustic sound level, a low murmur rather than the normal roar of a restaurant of its size, allowed discreet conversations.

Normally, a few tequilas before the meal oiled the two ministers' conversation, but on this particular day Jacala's proprietor had brought his personal pulque barrel from his agave farm just north of Guadalajara for the edification of his customers. He stationed the barrel in a room separate from the main dining room and seated regular customers in this inner sanctum, which allowed free access for the contents of the barrel.

This sweet bubbling mass of cactus juice compelled the two men of culture, who grew more creative with each cup dipped from the barrel. Early on, after he finished his third cup of pulque, Cortez made a grand gesture indicating global thinking. *"Today we should think on a larger scale. There are opportunities yet untapped for our self-help agendas."*

Much later, after the echo of their first triple *grito* died, the idea formed. Diego spilled his pulque as he shouted, *"A contest. We will stage a competition."* The other guests released a cacophony of shouted *gritos,* more in honor of pulque, than a response for the anonymous notion hurled into the room by one of the other *pulquedores.*

"A competition? For what?" Cortez leaned forward with his brow furrowed.

"We will stage a contest and find the best mariachi band in all of Mexico." Diego rested back in his chair, loosed a grito punctuating the concept, and received another chorus of responses from fellow pulque lovers around the room.

"Think of it." Diego gestured grandly. "Television, radio and posters would fill the airwaves and building walls announcing the contest."

"The 'fees' from these alone could be huge." Cortez held his pulque cup up for a toast.

"We will need local contests for determining who will compete in Guadalajara." Diego got up with great difficulty for another try at the pulque barrel.

"But that would require a lot of work and expense, wouldn't it?" Cortez's face contorted into a thoughtful countenance.

Diego returned to the table with brimming cups and said, *"You're right. Better they send us their entry fees in advance and get here as best they can.*" Both men laughed outrageously at the prospect of entry fees.

"*Maybe we will have a couple of days of tryouts and pick the bands that will compete on the final night in Jalisco Stadium before the cameras of national television.*" Diego pulled out a pen and pad and recorded these wonderful ideas before they dissolved into *pulque.*

"*Our personal take from hotels, restaurants, transport-tation, tickets, media and the contestants themselves, will make us very wealthy men.*" The thought made Cortez sit quietly while he toted up their potential take for the "*First Annual Jalisco Fiesta de Mariachis.*"

"*And the best part?*"

"*The best part?*"

"*We will do it all again next year.*" The two men lofted *gritos* easily heard on the sidewalk outside.

Years later, *los señores* Cortez and Diego would agree no blame should be placed for the ill conceived "Jalisco Fiesta de Mariachis," as it was born of pulque.

The meeting with the doctor had run well into the night and Angelita suggested Gena should stay in the casita, since this would give El Jefe more access. Gena slept undisturbed from exhaustion and awoke to the smell of coffee and fresh tortillas in the kitchen. Reality slowly returned and drifted over her like a mantle. Lilting, good-humored conversation between Angelita and her brothers sifted through the door of the bedroom. Angelita came into the room with a cup of coffee and clothing. "*Good morning. These clothes will be more suitable in the cantina,*" she explained.

Gena understood, smiled, and accepted the Mexican peasant blouse and skirt. The previous night they had discussed Gena's Harley dress code. The doctor had explained the ancient Tolencita legend of "La Negra," the story of a very beautiful unmarried woman who lived by herself. The town had named her "La Negra" because she dressed only in black. The jealous wives felt her much too friendly with their husbands. So they banded together and drove her out of the little village. As they harried her toward the edge of town, she turned on them and in a rage swore one day she would return and seduce every husband in Tolencita and take them away with her. The doctor said when Gena came into town dressed in black, the townspeople probably remembered the legend. Gena laughed. "That explains why all the women frowned and all the men smiled."

The three agreed they must attack El Jefe through sexual appetite and ego with Gena the bait. They would launch their plot this morning. Angelita went back into the kitchen and finished breakfast. Gena sat on the edge of the bed and for the first time looked at the brightly colored peasant skirt and white blouse. Angelita had left sandals on the floor, and a beautiful scarf for Gena's hair. The uniform for the siege of El Jefe, she thought. The dresser held a washbasin, soap, and towels in readiness. She pulled the oversized UT Longhorns T-shirt over her head and stood naked before the mirror and inspected her weapons. Her body was firm but still had a feminine softness unblemished by sun. Everything was there, but a wave of self-doubt flowed over her. What if El Jefe wouldn't do what was required? What if he wasn't interested? What if she couldn't go through with the plan? What if the plan didn't work? She slowly washed herself. The water streamed over her face, dripped from her chin, and disappeared into the canyon between her breasts. She looked herself in the eyes and said out loud, "You *must* make this work."

El Jefe had spent a restless night excited by thoughts of the woman from the bus. He had needed Angelita for tension release. Up early, he drove his morning rounds aimlessly and wondered why the woman had come to visit the Ramos family. It added up to one thing. She's here to help the gringos. This would put some restrictions on what he could do with the bastards, which he hated. His agitation sent him storming back to the jail. The sleeping guard fell over backwards in his chair when his boss entered. The guard scrambled up and stood at semi-attention. El Jefe cursed him soundly for lack of diligence on the job. He wanted to see the prisoners, so the guard grabbed the keys and led his boss through the security door and down the hall.

Morning light left the cell in semi-darkness, and the two prisoners lay on their cots feigning sleep. The stench in the cell was overpowering. El Jefe grabbed the guard's nightstick and beat on the bars. "Wake up, you *pinche* bastards." The two sat up with difficulty but said nothing. "There's a pretty *gringa* in town named Gena. She wears Harley-Davidson clothes. Who is she?"

Skeets spoke up immediately. "We don't know anyone by that description."

"You stupid *pinche cabrónes*. You always make things hard. If you had listened the first time and gone home, you wouldn't even be in here." He pulled his pistol. *"Open the cell door. We're gonna beat the truth out of these assholes."*

Skeets stood and held up his hands. "Okay, okay. She's a friend of ours, and she will hire us a lawyer."

"A lawyer? Did you say, 'a lawyer'?" El Jefe doubled over laughing. "A lawyer. We don't need no stinkin' lawyers in Tolencita." His laughter tailed off as he and the guard went down the hall and back through the security door.

Later, El Jefe stood transfixed just inside the swinging door of Casa de Masa as his parts became stone. Gena, hair tied up and wearing the bare midriff peasant blouse, busily scrubbed the sediment of Tolencitan culture collected over the past years on the cantina's bar. Her wealth of cream colored mammary struggled and rooted like pigs in silage under the peasant blouse, their only restraint.

Gena scrubbed the bar just in front of the cantina's only two customers. They sat at each of two tables and stared unblinking – occasionally lifting their pulque with no glance in its direction. Each had the look of a bleacher full of fans that waited impatiently for a high fly ball to reenter earth's gravity and fall close enough for a try. If anything fell from the blouse, the frenzy to claim it would certainly break bones.

El Jefe, recovered himself slightly, straightened his ever-present sunglasses, hitched up his gun belt and cleared his throat. Before he could speak he rose from the floor and exploded into the middle of the room head first, knocking down chairs and sliding between the legs of a table with someone on his back. One of his *policia* rushing to make a report about the prisoners had rounded the corner at full tilt, failed to see his superior standing inside the Casa de Masa doorway, and had run into Jefe's backside.

The two lay still for a moment before El Jefe leaped up, launching the table thundering into the two customers who had still not taken their eyes from the spectacle of Gena's breasts. The customers toppled from their seats, landed on their backs, but still stared at Gena. The revolution had finally begun; El Jefe knew he needed quick action. He drew his pistol and fired two shots at the floor in the general direction of his policeman who sensed the error of his ways and crawled like a startled javelina for the door.

The bullets ricocheted on each side of him and set off such an anguished howl El Jefe looked more closely before firing again. He saw his fellow policeman's butt approach the door. In four bounds he stood behind his cohort and, with one deft kick, sent him through the opened doors and into a lifetime of anal problems.

"*Imbécil estúpido.*" El Jefe's neck veins approached hemorrhage as he shouted after the fleeing *policia*. He brushed off his uniform and heard the laughter. He spun on his heel and saw Angelita and Gena hug each other in their mirth. The hair raised on his neck. He flew across the room in a flash, grabbed Gena's blouse, and half dragged her across the bar. His temples throbbed, and he drew his arm across his body to backhand her.

Before he could swing, Angelita laid her arm between them and smiled sweetly as she asked, *"Would you like a tequila, Jefe?"*

Eight months passed since the ministers had conceived the *"First Annual Jalisco Fiesta de Mariachis."* The "local" weekly bus started its long Wednesday journey toward Guadalajara in Saltillo and wound its way south through the villages and towns, but this trip seemed different. Mariachis and their instruments crowded out the usual farmers, pigs, chickens, and produce. This posed no problem early in the trip, but as the bus proceeded, each town produced another mariachi band crammed into the limited space. First, all luggage migrated onto the bus roof beside the one crate of chickens, then the *guitarron* bass guitars moved up and finally the guitars. The fiddle players and trumpeters played for the bus full of musicians who sang at a volume only tequila could produce.

The mood, fueled by tequila, had remained celebratory as the bus turned onto the Tolencita road. The sun, now directly overhead, rendered the bus hot enough to bake bread. At siesta time, the singing faded into a tequila stupor with a rhythm section of snoring. This peaceful scene ended abruptly when the bus groaned, hunched, shivered, sighed, farted and stopped – its engine dead.

The passengers groaned and stirred while shouting expletives as they finally evacuated the bus. They hollered and scurried around with no particular purpose when they saw the driver walking toward Tolencita. Someone called for the driver to return, which he did. The passengers offered to push the bus, since the road had a slight slope toward Tolencita anyway. Later, they would admit that tequila could cause mistakes of this magnitude.

They knew the bus company would simply send a wrecker and haul the bus back to Saltillo and their central shop. This would become the passengers' problem since next week's bus might already be full on arrival. A burly *guitarron* player said, *"If we can get this piece of shit into Tolencita for repairs, we can get to the ' Jalisco Fiesta de Mariachis' contest on time."*

Most of the musicians wore their vaquero suits, and when they perceived this new endeavor might soil their only such costume, they removed their shirts. At first the bus disagreed with the pushing idea, but as the mass of mankind at its posterior increased, it grudgingly responded to the shouts of *"Vámonos!" "Empujen!, hombres." "Arre!."* and crept forward. As the bus slowly gained speed, encouraged by *gritos* and shouts of victory, the motivators could take turns walking, pushing, and shouting, with, of course, an occasional shot of tequila.

Several miles passed without incident until they reached the road's only curve. The tight-radius turn slowed the bus. Before regaining its speed, the bus descended into a low water crossing over a small stream and lurched to a stop at a *topes* speed bump.

The joyful shouts quickly became expletives as the passengers tried with no success to dislodge the bus. Reason returned as the tequila's euphoria wore off, and the thoughtful among them saw the uphill road stretching toward Tolencita. The prospect eroded their resolve.

No vehicle traffic capable of a rescue or tow seemed imminent, so they unloaded their instruments, donned their big hats, and began the walk into Tolencita uncertain how they would continue their journey.

Chapter 33

Lobo had left Guadalajara early in a "Company" pickup truck and arrived in Tolencita mid- morning. He stationed himself near the police station and watched Tolencitans go about their daily shopping, trading and visiting with friends. He was impressed with the cleanliness of the town and by the lack of beggars and other signs of poverty. Tolencita was what El Jefe reported on his shortwave radio.

He had watched the jail from the pickup during the morning and noted who came and went from the station. He had seen the man who must be El Jefe, and counted four other policemen. About ten o'clock, a teenage boy entered the jail with what looked like a tray of food. Lobo could see the backside of the jail and noted the line of high, open, barred windows, which he assumed, marked the jail cells. With the boy inside, Lobo walked over and stood under the first window. There was no conversation from inside. The wall consisted of plastered concrete blocks. He laughed at the design "They couldn't hold a sick whore in this place." He continued down the back wall and listened under each window until both Spanish and English conversation came from the third.

When the boy left with the tray, Lobo started the pickup truck and idled toward La Plaza, following at a distance. He parked close by when he saw the boy go into Casa de Masa. He had a substantial appetite since he had missed breakfast. Inside, he sat at a table facing both the bar and the kitchen. A gorgeous *Norteña* woman worked behind the bar in a peasant blouse while serving the men seated at the bar who ogled her blouse more than their food. A pretty Mexican woman brought a menu and later took his order. The teenager came out from the kitchen and cleared a table. Lobo called him over. *"¿Do you feed the jail prisoners?"* Bosco nodded agreement. *"¿Are there two gringo prisoners in there?"*

"Si, Señor, my friends, Skeets and Jesse are in there."

"¿How are they doing?"

"Not good, señor. The policia have beaten them up badly." Bosco showed concern for his friends. *"¿Do you know Skeets and Jesse?"*

"No, not really. ¿Why would the police beat them up?" Lobo leaned back and looked at the woman behind the bar.

"El Jefe, the police chef is a very bad man, Señor."

"I've heard that. Gracias, amigo." Lobo stood and walked toward the bar.

Gena had watched the tall, lanky, mustached American as he talked with Bosco. He wore faded jeans and a tank top with the word Lobo on it, and he had a wolf head tattooed on his shoulder. A crumpled straw cowboy hat sat on his head. As he approached the bar, she said, "Did you enjoy your lunch, Wolf Man? You look a little out of place in here."

Lobo smiled broadly. "I reckon we both do."

"You come through here often?" She took his money and made change in the cash drawer under the counter.

"First time. Just checking on a couple of friends of mine." His mustache curled up with his grin.

"I guess we have something in common." She handed him his change.

"Their names Skeets and Jesse?" He still grinned.

Her chin dropped. "How did you know that?"

"Figurin' out things is what I do, so I just took a stab at it."

"You know they're in jail, right?"

"Yes, ma'am, and I'm gonna help 'em get out." Lobo nodded a confirmation of his pronouncement.

She paused for a moment with an amazed look on her face. She looked around the room. "We can't talk here."

El Jefe sat in his car with the three suitcases bound for Guadalajara and waited for the arrival of the bus from Saltillo. It was later than ever before. In his rearview mirror, he saw a large group of what looked like mariachis carrying their bags and instruments into the town. He said, *"Jesus, Mary, and Joseph, what the hell is this?"* He got out of the car and looked back down the road. The first of the group approached La Plaza, and they definitely wore big hats, vaquero costumes, and carried guitars. They huffed their way into the plaza sweaty and bedraggled. Jefe accosted them. *"¿Where the hell did all you guys come from?"*

"We were on our way to the 'Jalisco Fiesta de Mariachis' when the bus broke down about ten miles back, so we walked. ¿ Is there somewhere we can we can get water?" The musician almost collapsed onto the curb. The rest of the musicians saw the trees, water fountain, and gazebo of La Plaza and trotted over for a drink and some shade. La Plaza quickly went into mariachi overload.

El Jefe drove around La Plaza on his way back to the police station with the empty suitcases. He looked at all the musicians and wondered how he could get his life and his town back to normal. He had two gringos in jail he must dispose of, a beautiful gringa had arrived to keep him from it, his lover hated him, he was horny, and he was asshole deep in mariachis. Life in Tolencita had gotten complicated, and he had lost patience.

He thought he heard guitar music as he got out of the car at the police station and stopped to see if more mariachis invaded from this direction. He carried the suitcases inside and got the guard to open the security door. He stopped at the gringos' cell. "Were you guys just playing the guitar?"

The two lay on their cots and the guitar case stood in its normal place. After a pause Skeets said, "I broke it over one of your guy's head, remember." He pointed at the dent in the case.

Jesse lifted his head. "Actually, Jefe, we're not quite back into playing shape yet."

The police chief kicked one of the suitcases down toward cell 5. "The way my day is going, I might come back here and beat the shit out of you two just to improve my attitude." He trundled down the hall, unlocked cell 5 and threw the three bags inside. Back in the police anteroom, he told the guard on duty to call the bus company and tell them their bus broke down ten miles south of town. *"Oh yeah, and tell them to send another bus over here to round up all these damn mariachis. I want them out of town."*

As El Jefe drove up to the front of Casa de Masa, he saw a tall, tattooed gringo come out, get in a Ford pickup, and drive off. El Jefe wondered who the hell he was and added the stranger's identity to his growing list of problems. He turned around and saw a few mariachis in La Plaza with their instruments out singing for tips from the locals. The sound of four mariachi groups playing and singing different songs at the same time drove him inside the cantina. The room had filled with mariachis sitting, standing, and leaning on the bar admiring Gena. He pushed his way aggressively through the crowd to the bar where he knocked two gawkers aside. Gena opened beer bottles, poured tequila shots, and took money while Chiquita and Angelita tried to keep up with the food orders. He hailed Gena and demanded a beer and a tequila shot. He shouted over the din of the customers, "I need to talk to you – now."

Gena straightened her blouse in a show of modesty. "I'm just a little busy right now."

"I can fix that." He turned and shouted to the room to shut up. Most who saw his uniform, silenced immediately, but one with his back to El Jefe kept talking. Jefe pulled his pistol and hit the man over the head. Blood coursed down his face as he slumped forward. *"Atencion, hombres. I don't know why you're here, but we have laws here in Tolencita. We do not allow drunkenness or loud noise. We have a very large jail and you will find yourself in it if you break the law. I've called for a bus to pick you up. Now, I want everyone out of here immediately. Vamonos, hombres."* He brandished his pistol over his head and everyone rushed for the door. After the mad scramble of musicians and their instruments banging into each other had subsided and the barroom doors flopped back and forth, El Jefe turned to Gena. "Are you too busy to talk now?"

"You're a real charmer aren't you?" She leaned against the back bar with a stern face, arms akimbo.

"I have important business to talk to you about. I don't want to wait." He sat on a bar stool, and chased his tequila shot with the beer. He looked at her with unblinking eyes. "You came here to try to help your friends, Skeets and Jesse, right? To get a lawyer? A lawyer." He couldn't hold back his laughter. Angelita came out from the kitchen with three plates of food and found the tables empty. She frowned at El Jefe, took the plates back into the kitchen, returned, and took off her apron.

Gena motioned for Angelita to join them. "You don't have lawyers here?"

"Lady, we don't have no court here." He kept laughing.

Gena's face went rigid with anger. "So who decides their fate?"

"I do."

"What about the law?"

"In Tolencita there is only one law. Me." Jefe rocked back and swelled with arrogance.

"So what will you do with them?"

"That depends." A wicked smile flitted across his face. "On many things."

"Can I see them?"

"No."

"Why not?"

"They're in solitary confinement for attacking a guard."

Gena leaned over the bar. Her blouse opened and showed the fullness therein. "So how do I get them out?" Angelita grinned as El Jefe locked his gaze on Gena's bosom.

After a long pause, during which he never looked up, he stammered, "We will negotiate that."

"There's really nothing I wouldn't do." She tried but could not make eye contact.

For Skeets the day had passed more quickly than the others. He had coaxed Jesse out of bed, and the two of them interspersed song writing with walking around the cell for exercise and recovery. They had used up half the note pad on lyric rejects. The laborious process required the lyrics metered and rhymed in English, and then Jesse must translate them into Spanish. Jesse cursed, sputtered, and ripped pages out of the book as he struggled at holding the lyrics' meaning while rhyming the Spanish words. Occasionally they burst out laughing when a humorous lyric fell into place. Distant mariachi music drifted through the window and gave them the opportunity for practicing the lyrics with Skeets' guitar without the guards hearing.

Throughout the day, Gena's message gnawed at Skeets. Gena using her "feminine wiles on El Jefe " nagged him raw. The thought of El Jefe having his way with her made him frantic. He ripped out a notebook page and wrote a note for Gena.

Bosco brought news of the day with their dinner. He told them about the stranger with the wolf tattoo on his shoulder and asked about them, about the mariachis, and about El Jefe clearing them out of Casa de Masa so he could talk to Señorita Gena alone. Skeets stood and paced around the cell. "Somehow, someway, I'll kill the bastard." He gave Bosco the note he had written for Gena. "Amigo, this is for Gena."

Jesse sat on his cot with his dinner plate and processed the information about Lobo. "Son, for the life of me I can't come up with a reason why Lobo would be in Tolencita. More'n that, how'd he knew we're in here."

"It's mental telepathy maybe, cause I've sent out lots of vibes hoping someone would help us." Skeets shook his head in awe.

Jesse looked up from his plate. "Yeah, I've said a few prayers myself."

The mariachis heeded the police chief's warning, so Angelita had Gustavo cook a big pot of chili con carne and dozens of enchiladas and tamales. With Gena, Quito, and Bosco, she served the food on paper plates under the gazebo. Their gratitude overwhelmed Angelita. Several of the groups got together and serenaded en mass. The more enterprising of the men had bought cases of *cerveza* at *El Mercado*, and something of a fiesta broke out. Soon a mariachi choir belted out classic old *rancheros* accompanied by dozens of fiddles, guitars, guitarons, and trumpets. Tolencitans came from all over town and danced and sang along with the musicians. One of the old timers commented this is just like the good old days before El Jefe, except more mariachis.

El Jefe's police car and the police pickup pushed their way through the crowd with sirens blaring and parked in the street. Jefe got out and shoved his way into the gazebo where he shouted down the mariachis who, one by one, quit playing and singing. *"You are violating our ordinance against public intoxication and disturbing the peace."* A groan of discontent came from the Tolencitans. *"Everybody go home. The fiesta's over."* The townspeople and mariachis stood in groups and looked confused over why anyone would stop a fiesta. Jefe added, *"I've got enough problems without all this noise. So get on home – all of you."*

This left the mariachis in a quandary since they had no homes. Some had too many beers and moved unsteadily about and mumbled curses under their breath. El Jefe pointed them out and his policemen dragged them off and deposited them in the pickup. Others continued toking on beers and getting a little *borracho*.

Their song was coming along too slowly, so Skeets and Jesse continued on the lyrics after Bosco left. They heard a commotion as the security door opened and a group of mariachis and their instruments came down the hall and into the first cell. Right behind them came another group, locked into the next cell. Shortly, a third group jammed into the cell on the other side of them.

"Looks like we have a band and backup singers for our recording session," Jesse said.

Angelita and Gena sat and nursed a beer at the dining table in the casita. A small table lamp lit the room, which still held the smell of the morning's breakfast. They relaxed for the first time that day, and they jumped at the knock on the back door. Angelita got up, identified the visitor, and ushered the doctor into the dining room. They exchanged greetings and he produced a pharmacy bottle with white pills. "Our pharmacy is limited, but I found these secobarbitol. I think three pills per person will knock them out long enough."

"We must grind them into food or something, right?" Gena tapped one of the pills into her hand.

"You should put them in something where they will swallow it all." The doctor translated for Angelita.

"We can send beer over. They won't leave any beer.," Angelita suggested.

"Great idea. Alcohol intensifies the effect of the drug." The doctor tapped his watch. *"Remember, this will take about twenty minutes for effect."* He asked Gena. "When do you plan the escape?"

"Angelita says people crowd into the plaza on Friday evenings, so that's our target."

"Okay, I'll borrow the trailer for Friday. Good luck." The doctor rose, and Angelita let him out the back door.

Gena took Skeets' note from her waistband and reread it: "God, I'm glad you're here. I've done nothing since we left Austin but think about what an asshole I am, and how much I love you. Watch this El Jefe guy. I would rather spend the rest of my life in this prison than let him put one finger on you. I love you, Skeets."

She put her head in her hands and sobbed.

Chapter 34

The din of drunken mariachis made sleep impossible. Jesse made friends with the men in the adjacent cells and explained how he and Skeets must record a song they had written, and they could use help from the mariachis as a back up band and singers. The mariachis radiated a most agreeable *cervesa* mood, and Skeets worked first with the guitar players and showed them the chords and rhythm pattern. The guitarists in turn taught the *guitaronistas* the bass line. The fiddle players came up with a pretty nifty background obbligato, and the trumpets laid down a three-part harmony underpinning, which added brilliant punctuation. By eleven o'clock they finished several run-throughs, and Skeets and Jesse smiled and nodded in appreciation. The guards in the jail's anteroom enjoyed the concert also.

While Skeets worked with the instrumental arrangement, Jesse had made several copies of the lyrics for the song's chorus and given them to the mariachis in the cells on both sides. They waited until they knew the police chief would not return, and the guard slept, before they sang the lyrics. Skeets and Jesse performed the song for the mariachis a little after midnight and cued the singers' entrance on the chorus. They quieted the mariachis laughter, *gritos* and applause before they woke the guard. Fearing discovery, they decided on recording without further practice. Jesse held the cassette recorder in front of him, pressed "Record," and Skeets counted off. "The Ballad of El Jefe's New Lover" drifted though the windows and into the night air. They recorded the song four more times with three-minute spaces between, before the end of the tape.

The next morning El Jefe arrived at the jail later than usual. The sleeping guard was jarred into reality when his boss kicked his leaning chair out from under him. When El Jefe menaced a kick toward the same location of anal insult that the guard had received at Casa de Masa, he went into a mad scramble across the floor. He stood with his backside against the wall and saluted Jefe. The chief snapped his fingers. *"Show me the prisoners."*

As the door swung open, the stench of the jail cells assaulted El Jefe, who recoiled as if he had encountered a fire-breathing demon. He held his nose in the crook of his arm and looked at the prisoners. The snoring deafened him and the sight of dozens of mariachis lying on the floor, draped on the cots, and propped against the bars repulsed him. *"Get these son-of-a-bitching mariachis out of here. I don't want to feed them. If I never see another mariachi, it will be too soon."* He cleared the security door and stopped. *"Hose down those cells and get this stinkin' smell out of here."* He turned and stomped out of the jail.

His two gringo prisoners were a lot of trouble, El Jefe thought as he drove to Casa de Masa. In the past only he and the policemen knew about the prisoners, which made their disposal easier. Now the Ramos family, the norteña, and dozens of mariachis knew about the gringos in his jail. This posed a problem. Maybe he might get *something* out of them, though. Possibly he could put the old *chorizo* into the beautiful Texas woman by offering Skeets' and Jesse's release. Just the thought made him reach down and loosen the crotch of his *pantalones*. He'd much prefer leaving them as coyote bait in the desert, but a man can only do what a man can do, he thought.

Gena, Angelita, and her two brothers carried pots and pans of what looked like food out of Casa de Masa when he parked. *"¿What's gong on?"* he demanded. The three walked across the street toward the plaza. El Jefe followed them and shouted, *"I said, '¿What's going on?'"*

Angelita stopped, turned, and said, *"We cooked breakfast for the mariachis – but it's none of your business."*

"You can't do that." El Jefe moved up the steps toward Angelita.

"¿Why, is it against El Jefe's law?" Angelita's sat her pot down and confronted him.

"They're like stray dogs. If you feed them, they'll never leave." El Jefe motioned around the plaza at the mariachis lying on every park bench, all over the gazebo floor, and down the street at a band of several dozen returning from their night in jail.

Angelita stood for a moment and looked at El Jefe in disgust, then stuck out the big pot of coffee she carried. "Here, make yourself useful." She motioned with her head, and everyone followed. In the gazebo, they spread out fresh tortillas, *chorizo* and eggs, and *carne guisada* stew. El Jefe slammed his pot of coffee down and stomped off toward the cantina. The smell of coffee and food resurrected the mariachis, and they bowed and scraped their gratitude as they came through the line.

Angelita conversed easily with the musicians, learned about their hometowns, and where they were going. They said they must arrive in Guadalajara in time for the trial concerts where the bands would compete for the Sunday night contest televised nationally from Jalisco Stadium. Most of them had run out of money and a few had called their families and friends for a ride home. The younger ones with no family responsibility had joined together into a band of about twenty musicians. The lead singers told Angelita they really enjoyed playing together, and if the bus arrived in time, they would continue on to Guadalajara and compete.

"*¿Do you need money for your journey?*" she asked.

They hung their heads and kicked imaginary rocks with their boots. "*Yes, Señorita, a little money would help.*"

Angelita and Bosco joined a dozen Mariachis who stood in front of Gena. "*Tell Gena I have an idea for tomorrow night.*"

El Jefe had eaten half of his *chilaquiles* when the four returned from the plaza with two mariachis carrying the pots and pans. When the musicians came out of the kitchen, Jefe gave them a look, and they scurried back out the door.

Gena took up her station behind the bar and watched the man finish his complimentary breakfast. "More coffee, Jefe?" She wore a good-natured smile.

He looked surprised at her cordial demeanor. "Why, yes, Señorita, thank you." His mind raced over the thought of her warming toward him.

She brought the coffee pot, leaned over the counter, and filled his cup. "Would you like milk?"

His gaze locked on the treasures of the blouse. "Milk? Yes, milk is good."

Gena moved away and returned with a pitcher of hot milk. "So, will you let my friends out of jail today?"

He gave no immediate answer. Then he looked up quickly with a frown. "What? What did you say? Let your friends out of jail today? Are you *loca*? Why would I?"

"You ask a lot of questions, Jefe. If you're the law like you say, you could just let them go, right? What have they done to you?"

"They attacked me and my officers, *and* they are notorious smugglers. I have the contraband to prove it." El Jefe nodded with satisfaction.

"Notorious?"

"*¡Absolutamente.* At least they will be when I get through with them."

"How much would their freedom cost?" She leaned lower over the bar.

"How much money?" His eyes riveted on her.

"Yes."

"You don't have enough money."

"I may have treasures you never dreamed of." She modestly corrected her blouse and leaned against the back bar. Her hair was radiant, her creamy complexion flawless, and her compact body perfectly shaped – hidden only by one layer of cloth.

Her perfume drifted toward him when she stood. His eyes closed as he groaned inwardly in sensual pleasure. "Possibly, but how would I collect these treasures?"

"I've heard you're quite a man. You should have no problem." After a long pause, she spoke again. "Come here tomorrow morning. Tell me how you will guarantee the release of my friends, and I will gratefully show you what a Texas girl can do." She turned and walked slowly into the kitchen.

The guard cursed as he scrubbed and rinsed the cell floors. Jesse shouted at him, *"Amigo, we'll scrub the floor if you let us use you water hose for a bath."* The guard thought for a moment, then handed them the broom through the bars. They took turns scrubbing their cell as the guard squirted water on the floor from the hall. Finally, the guard handed the hose through the bars and Skeets rinsed the floor off while the water run through the floor drain.

The guard approved. *"¡Bueno. Now empty the honey pot."* He dropped the broom and hose and drew his pistol.

Both men growled. *"Ah, man, give us a break."* Jesse shrugged. The guard motioned Skeets back against the far wall. He pointed the pistol at Jesse. *"Pick up the shit pot."*

Jesse obeyed but held the thunder mug as far as possible from his nose. "Man, this is what I get for speaking Spanish, right?" The guard opened the cell door, let Jesse into the hall, and relocked the cell. Jesse dumped the pot into a toilet across the hall, rinsed it, and carried it back into their cell. The guard locked Jesse in the next cell with the broom and hose. While Jesse scrubbed, the guard moved Skeets to a third cell. On his second honey pot trip, Jesse picked up a small piece of soap from the lavatory. With the cells clean, they stripped off their clothes, lathered up, and rinsed off with the hose. They laughed at the simple pleasure of cleanliness. Skeet said, "Bro, I feel almost human again." They put on their shorts, washed their clothes with the soap, and hung them on the cross bars to dry.

El Jefe sat at his desk and thought about a ruse for releasing the gringos the Norteña would believe. He knew he could take anything from her he wanted by force, but her gratefully bestowing her favors brought a special thrill of anticipation. The phone woke him from his reverie. "Bueno."

"Carlos Algo here. I will come there next Tuesday with my men for two deliveries. I also want the two gringos in your jail."

El Jefe laughed into the phone. *"Imposible, Carlos. They are under arrest for smuggling."*

"Forget 'imposible.' I will pay you five hundred dollars US for each of them."

"One thousand each."

"Done. You know they will not return, right?"

"I will miss them greatly, but such is the way of the world." El Jefe nodded his pleasure at solving at least one of his problems.

Chapter 35

Josefina, the burro, brayed with pleasure when the Young Boys took her from the pen this morning. Days had passed with little or no activity around the farm. Her privates had gotten raw from old Flaco nuzzling her rear end constantly. The Old Man and the Young Boys led her into the field where they hitched her to the plow. A good day for fieldwork, she thought. White puffy clouds often shaded the sun, and a nice breeze helped cool her. The corn stood higher than her head now and scratched her itchy places as she passed.

Josefina pulled the plow for The Old Man, while the Young Boys ran behind and pulled the uprooted weeds. The exercise felt good and produced a good honest sweat. Normally they left her standing in the field when they went into the house for lunch, but today they unhooked her and brought her back with them – a very nice courtesy, she thought.

The Young Boys tied her in the shade beside the house. One of them brought her a bucket of corn. She loved corn. Possibly corn would help cure the stomach problem she developed last night after eating hay. Maybe the People in the House finally realized what a superior burro they had. She had just dozed off after finishing her corn when the Young Boys brought two buckets of water. One boy poured water on her while the other scrubbed her with a bar of soap and a brush. Oh, MY GOD, how good the thick rich lather felt. And the scrubbing. The scrubbing made her shiver with pleasure. She could see all the flies scurry around as they avoided the tsunami of soapsuds. The boys rinsed her with the second bucket, brought rags, and dried her off. No horse ever had a better rubdown after a workout, she thought. She smiled that special burro smile and thought, I knew it. If you do things right and do them often enough, you'll be rewarded.

A pickup truck and trailer pulled into the yard, and the doctor got out. "It's not much of a trailer, but it's the only one I could borrow." Angelita's father came out of the house and inspected the trailer along with his sons and the doctor. About eight feet long and four feet wide, the trailer could easily hold Josefina. The slat-sideboards measured about three feet high. Two bald tires were outboard of the trailer, which had not seen paint in decades.

"*Not much to look at, but good enough if you watch those tires,*" the elder Ramos said. "*You know Josefina's never been loaded on a trailer before. She might make trouble.*"

"*Let's hope not. Surely the four of us can load her.*" The doctor swung the back gate open. "*Okay let's try it.*"

Quito untied Josefina and led her around the trailer.

Josefina thought, 'How can this happen? Not pull the cart, but ride in it, like horses?' She had almost given up hope. All the years of hard work, all the extra effort, never complaining, and all the meticulous personal hygiene had finally paid off. She now was the equal of horses. She paused at the rear of the trailer considering the magnitude of the occasion. The People looked at each other, concerned about something. She put one hoof on the trailer and raised herself, followed with a second, and with the bearing of royalty ascending a throne, moved slowly into her crowning achievement. She held her head high and slowly swayed back and forth as if acknowledging the cheering of crowds.

"Not a problem." The doctor moved quickly and closed the gate behind Josefina before she changed her mind. He shook Ramos' hand and thanked him while Quito and Bosco climbed into the cab. About halfway into town the doctor pulled off the road and stopped to check the trailer tires.

The richness of the corn and the stomach problem Josefina had experienced since last night combined and required she relieve herself. A burro of her quality and position in life would not possibly befoul her trailer, so she backed up as far as she could and let it fly over the rear trailer gate.

The hand-written poster nailed on a tree at the base of the stairs across the street from Angelita's new casita read:

TONIGHT
FREE
MARIACHI BENEFIT CONCERT
HERE
8:00 O'CLOCK

That morning Angelita had explained to the mariachis they should assemble for a performance in the narrow street between the plaza and Casa de Masa at about seven-thirty tonight. The Tolencitans could sit on the steps and all the way back up into the plaza Gazebo like an amphitheater. They would pass the hat and collect money for their Jalisco Fiesta de Mariachis trip.

After the lunch run, Angelita sat at a table with Gena, who had grown weary of her regulars who sipped beer at the bar and paid homage to her cleavage. Language problems made conversation difficult, but both were concerned about El Jefe's absence that morning. They hoped he would release Skeets and Jesse if Gena would bestow her favors on him, but he did not show. At this point, their whole plan was a bust and the two sat in separate worlds of anguish and wondered about the police chief's intentions, and how they could save the men they loved.

El Jefe had paced his office since mid-morning thinking of a plausible prisoner exchange plan, which would not, in fact, exchange any prisoners. He could easily gain the Norteña's confidence if he actually handed them over, but he also wanted Algo's two thousand dollars. He knew she would not go for anything fishy. He finally realized he lacked enough information for a plan. For instance, when and where would his dalliance with the Norteña occur? But the idea that he must accommodate someone else's desires made him increasingly angry. He had never accommodated anybody else on anything, and he didn't like the thought. He finally stuffed on his hat and stomped out of the office and said aloud, *"To hell with this shit."*

He told the guard on the way out of the anteroom, *"Call the bus company and tell them if they don't get a bus here pretty soon, I will start shooting mariachis."* He got in his car, roared over to Casa de Masa, screeched to a stop and strode into the cantina. "Get out of here and don't come back." he shouted at the four men at the bar. They took a chance at one more gulp of beer before running out the door. He looked around the room and spied Angelita and the Norteña at a corner table. He pointed at Gena and shouted, "Come here."

In no hurry, she stood and thought; never let them see you sweat. She moved with confidence toward the bar. "Did you want to see me, Jefe?"

He leaned forward and in a lowered voice said, "You want me to give you a plan? Okay, here's my plan. I will arrest you as an accomplice in the gringo smuggling ring. I'll lock you in the cell next to your friends, and fuck you twice a day in front of them. Now do you have a better plan?"

Gena's head spun in disbelief. How could everything go so wrong? This asshole is an animal, not a man. She paused, and with will power, showed no fear in her eyes and no tremble in her voice. "Well, doesn't that sound romantic? Rape is your idea of a good time?"

"It's my idea of getting what I want. I *always* get what I want." He crouched over the bar and hissed out the words.

"I thought you might *want* something a little more civilized. More enjoyable." She leaned against the back bar and played with the drawstring of her blouse.

"And what might that be?" His eyes followed her fingers.

"Why don't you come back here about seven tonight. Let's have a few drinks, go somewhere, and relax. Have fun." She smiled as sweetly as she could. "I have to help Angelita now, but later we can spend all night together."

Angelita had gone into the kitchen when El Jefe arrived, but she feared Gena might be in trouble and walked back into the dining room. *"¿What is the problem, Jefe?"*

"¿Problem? There is no problem." He looked menacingly at Gena. "Tonight." He stood up and left.

Gena steadied herself against the bar, fell forward with her head in her hands. "I can't believe what a completely depraved animal this bastard is."

Lobo left Guadalajara about noon in the Wolf Wagon. Shortly after, he turned on the GPS to check the location of the drug suitcases. The transponder showed them in Tolencita, at the jailhouse. More for amusement than anything else, he switched over to the motorcycle transponder and saw it move toward Tolencita. He watched the small dot move across the screen, then stop. "What the hell is going on? Somebody must be moving the motorcycles, but I thought they already were in Tolencita." He shook his head in consternation.

Angelita had suggested Lobo could drop off the Wolf Wagon trailer at the Ramos farm entrance. When he continued toward Tolencita in the Wolf-head tractor, the GPS showed the motorcycle transponder close. He zoomed in for a close up, slowed as he approached the indicated location, pulled off, and stopped. He looked around the area and saw no motorcycles. He looked for tire tracks as he walked back and forth on the roadside. No hidden motorcycles appeared when he looked under the scrubby trees. Something smelled funny. When he looked down, he had stepped in fresh manure. He cursed and rubbed his boot in the grass to get the manure off and saw a glitter in the pile. With a stick, he poked in the manure, and found the transponder. He nodded at the revelation and said out loud, "Yes, sir, these electronic marvels are certainly amazing. They can even locate a donkey turd for you."

Skeets and Jesse had spent an anxious day waiting for what they hoped would be their escape. They had asked the guards about their Harleys and gotten the reply, "You mean Jefe's Harleys? They're in the garage next door." But nothing had happened. The bath and clean clothes still made them feel better, but the wait did not help their attitudes. Neither had spoken lately, when they heard the security door open. El Jefe stood outside their cell grinning like a tetanus victim. "Good afternoon, *amigos*, is your day going well?"

"We've had better days." Jesse spoke warily.

"I will have a great evening, but I thought I must ask your advice on something." El Jefe leaned against the cell bars casually.

"Our advice?" Skeets moved against the cell wall opposite Jefe.

"Your girlfriend, Gena, has agreed to fuck me tonight if I let you guys out of jail. I just wanted to know about any little thing she particularly likes for her special pleasure."

Skeets lunged across the cell, through the bars, and barely missed Jefe's throat as he jumped back. Skeets' arms clawed the air as animal sounds growled out of him. "You dirty rotten cocksucker. God, let me kill this evil bastard."

"No? Nothing? I thought maybe a little S & M. Not the play like kind – the real thing. What do you think?" Jefe chortled.

Skeets banged his head against the bars and screamed, "Oh, God, I knew this would happen. Why did I get her involved?"

Jesse put his arms around Skeets and dragged him back toward his cot.

Chapter 36

Angelita finished plating the food for the policemen and told Bosco. *"Take these to the police station for the guards. Then run back as fast as you can. I will be in the casita and give you four beers for them with their dinner. ¿Do you understand?"* Bosco nodded, placed the tray on his shoulder, and left through the cantina's back door.

She took four beers from the bar, and from the kitchen the mortar and pestle normally for grinding herbs. In the casita, she counted out twelve pills from the bottle, thought for a moment and then dropped four more into the mortar for good measure. She ground them into a fine powder, dumped the powder onto a plate, divided it into four portions, and spooned the barbiturate into the four beers. The bottles fizzed and fritzed as the powder coursed downward and completely dissolved before reaching the bottom. Bosco burst through the back door and announced the policemen wanted their beer *pronto*. Angelita handed him the bottles. *"Stay until they finish their dinner. Then bring back the plates and tell me what happened. Andale, Chico."*

A group of mariachis stopped Bosco as he hurried past the plaza. *"¿How much for the beers, amigo?"* the guitar player asked.

"They are not for sale. I am delivering them to the police station." Bosco tried to move on but the musical group surrounded him.

The fiddle player handed Bosco a fifty-peso bill. *"We are very thirsty, muchacho."*

Bosco thought for a moment about all he could buy with a fifty-peso bill. *"Okay, here."* He stuffed the fifty-peso bill into his pants and ran back through the front door of the cantina. The bar was empty, so he quickly opened four more beers and ran down the street toward the police station.

The musicians had just finished their beers when a young couple, obviously very much in love, approached them. The young man held out a ten-peso bill and requested they sing, "Coo Coo Roo Coo Coo, Paloma," for his "little turtledove." The musicians tuned up for a moment and began the languid strains of the old love song. The two lovers looked longingly into each other's eyes until the second verse, when things went wrong. The singer faltered along singing, "Coo ... Cooo . . .Roooo . . . CoooCuCu . . .Rooooo ..." His eyes glazed. He dropped on his knees and fell forward onto his guitar. The cadence of the other musicians had slowed along with the singer, and they melted slowly into a pile at the feet of the lovers. The young boy looked sadly at his turtledove and said, "Maybe we should have requested a livelier tune."

Bosco finished washing the policemen's dinner plates and went looking for Angelita. She seemed very excited when she asked, *"¿So? . . . ¿What happened?"*

"Nothing happened. They ate their dinner, and I came back. ¿Why?" Bosco backed away a little and wondered what had gone wrong with his sister.

"¿They didn't get sleepy?" She had panic in her voice.

"No. ¿Why should they? They talked about how El Jefe ordered them to break up a Mariachi Benefit Concert at eight o'clock." Bosco's eyes grew bigger as his sister's excitement mounted.

"Mary, Mother of God, what has gone wrong?" Her mind spun as she thought of all the possibilities. Maybe the powder works slower than expected. I must see for myself. She stuck her head into the dining room. Gena sat at a corner table with her back toward the kitchen and drank tequila and beer with El Jefe. She couldn't get Gena's attention, so she ducked back through the kitchen, out the back door, and into her Volkswagen. She could see the crowd form on the stairs as she drove by the plaza. After a sliding stop at the police station, she rushed inside. Her entrance brought a start to the four *Policia* who lounged around the anteroom. One of them made an unseemly gesture and whistled at Angelita. She stammered, *"I just wanted to make sure Bosco brought you hombres a beer tonight."*

"Si, gracias, Señorita." one of the more gracious of the group offered.

"¿So everything is fine then?" She looked for signs of sleepiness from each of them. Not even a yawn.

"We will be in La Plaza at eight o'clock to break up the concert," said the one who had whistled at her.

"¿Why?"

"El Jefe told us to."

Her mind raced as she ran from the police station. Everything had gone wrong. She must stop Gena before she made a mistake.

Gena had told Chiquita she must keep El Jefe's tequila shot glass full. El Jefe came through the door, and Gena motioned him toward a table in the corner. She had bathed, perfumed, and wore a clean peasant blouse and skirt. Her hair fell loosely past her shoulders. A bowl of *chicharrones* sat on the table, especially prepared by Gustavo with lots of pepper sauce. He guaranteed the *chicharrones* would make El Jefe thirsty. El Jefe smiled and nodded his approval when Chiquita arrived with a shot of tequila and two beers as they sat down.

Gena's perfume smelled alluring, but not overpowering. El Jefe took in a deep breath. "You look particularly delightful tonight." His hand moved under the table and rested on her thigh.

"Isn't this more pleasant than a jail cell?" She laid her hand over his. "Try the chicharrones. Gustavo made them especially for you."

El Jefe lifted his shot glass. "Salud." He chased the tequila with his beer and a handful of the fiery fried pigskins. He winced and immediately hoisted his beer to quench the fire. Chiquita arrived with another tequila shot.

Gena raised her beer bottle. "¡Salud! Jefe." He knocked back the shot and chased it with the rest of his beer and more *chicharrones*. Chiquita immediately brought another shot and beer. He grabbed the beer and chugged until the fire in his mouth went out.

After the fourth beer and tequila shot, Gena saw the sheen and dilated pupils in the eyes of a *boracho*. She moved his hand down below her skirt and up the inside of her thigh. He stiffened and gulped audibly. "What soft skin you have, Señorita."

She could hear the crowd noise and the mariachis tuning their instruments through the cantina door. She put her hand on his crotch. "Jefe, you seem glad to see me. What can we do about this thing?" His head bobbed, but he said nothing. She led him by the hand through the kitchen, out the back door, and crossed over into the casita.

El Jefe looked around the room. "How did you know about this place?"

"Angelita lets me stay here." She motioned him toward the table and brought him a cold beer and a tequila shot. "Sit here while I change into more comfortable clothes." She moved his hand lightly across her bosom and disappeared through a door. Within moments she returned in a silk robe with nothing under it. He lurched forward and grabbed both her breasts. She gently took his hands away. "Easy, Jefe, we have all night. Here let me help." She unbuttoned his shirt, then stepped around him and pulled the shirt over his arms. She could easily reach his holstered pistol. Her inner trembling loosed a flutter in her hands. Excitement made breathing difficult, and she forced slow measured breaths. This asshole would never see the fear clawing at her heart. She must succeed. Skeets needed her.

He laughed. "You think about my pistol, but don't worry yourself. It's unloaded."

She moved around in front again. "I'm not worried about that pistol." She unbuckled and put his gun belt on the table, and unzipped his pants. He sat down while she pulled his boots off. He stood again, and she hooked her thumbs under his shorts and pulled pants and underwear down together. She gasped, "Oh my, Jefe. You *are* quite a man." He loosed a drunken laugh. She grabbed his hand and said, "Follow me."

Angelita's Volkswagen careered around the corner into the plaza and almost skidded into the crowd. They scattered in every direction. *"My God, the whole town must have come."* She put the car in reverse, backed down to the last cross street, and executed a broad-slide turn. Downshifting, she popped the clutch, and the little car leaped forward, swerved around the next corner, and careened between the traffic and parked cars until she reached the street behind Casa de Masa. The car skidded before stopping, and she leaped out and ran inside the restaurant. No Gena and El Jefe. Now what.

"It's too dark in here. I can't see nuthin'. Where are you?" El Jefe's voice sounded a little uncertain in the pitch-black bedroom. He inched forward, unsteady on tequila knees.

"But Jefe, I'm right here." She took his hand again.

"Oh, here you are.." El Jefe felt around and grabbed for Gena. "Where is the bed?"

Gena tugged on his hand. "Just a little further. Right, now just stand here while I pull down the cover and turn on the light."

"Señorita – the smell – surely it's not you?" El Jefe took a step and almost toppled onto his face.

Skeets had paced the cell all afternoon; shouted and pounded the bars until exhaustion and hoarseness overtook him. Jesse had tried consoling him but gave up as nothing he said relieved any of Skeets' anguish over being helpless to protect the one thing in his life he loved. The two sat on the edge of their cots with their heads between their knees, hands clasped behind their heads. The only sound was Skeets' occasional moan and sob.

A huge animal-like roar rent the air outside the building. Both their heads popped up, looking at each other. The building shuddered as if a huge beast shook it. The wall of their cell crumbled as concrete blocks dislodged and fell on the floor.

Jesse grabbed Skeets and pulled him against the far side of the cell. "Holy, shit, man. It's an earthquake." Another earsplitting roar, and their cell wall collapsed.

The two prisoners stood in complete amazement. "Great God Almighty. What's happening?" The giant head of a wolf filled the hole where the wall had been, growling, eyes flashing, and flames shooting from its nostrils, They heard a truck door swing open, and Lobo stepped into the cell holding an Uzi machine gun. "You hombres look like you could use a lift."

The four guards stood at the jail door ready to leave for La Plaza when the police station shook after what sounded like a blast. They rushed back, unlocked the security door, and ran down the hall. The air in the hall filled with concrete dust, and pieces of debris spread over the floor in the gringos' cell. They slid to a stop and recoiled against the opposite wall, stunned at the sight of a truck-sized wolf roaring and spitting fire. One of the guards reached for his pistol when a voice like a wolf's growl rumbled out of the cell. *"Freeze, hombres. Put your hands in the air, turn around, lean against the wall, and spread your feet. You, the ugly one, use your left hand, unhook your keys, and slide them under the cell door."* Without looking at Skeets and Jesse, Lobo said, "One of you hombres mind unlocking the cell door?"

Skeets had rallied from his shock. "You don't have to ask me twice."

"Man, I can't think of anybody I'd rather see 'cept maybe the U.S. Marines. How the hell did you even know about us?" Jesse followed Skeets out the cell door and helped collect the policmen's key rings and guns.

"It's a long story I'll share with you over a beer, but right now you've got a couple of pretty women a mite concerned about you. How about a little broadcasting?" Skeets had unlocked the adjacent cell, and Lobo said, "One of you stay with me and help get these gentlemen undressed and ready for bed."

Skeets hollered after Jesse, "Hurry, man, I've gottta find Gena before it's too late." Jesse rounded up the cassette recorder and a set of keys. He ran through the security door and into El Jefe's office. He fumbled with the short-wave transmitter until he found the power switch. Lights flashed on and dial indicators moved into readiness. He jerked open drawers until he found a roll of cellophane tape and taped down the microphone "On" switch. After moving the recorder's switch into "Auto Reverse," he punched "Play " and placed the microphone in front of the recorder's speaker. "The Ballad of El Jefe's New Lover" flowed out into the room and over the airwaves.

Jesse rifled through the guards' desk until he found their wallets and the Harley keys. He saw a pile of batons, gun belts, uniforms, and shoes at the far end of the hall as he ran toward their cell. The adjacent cell held the four guards huddled naked in the center.

Lobo saw Jesse's questioning look at the naked guards. "You never know where one of these hombres will hide a key."

Jesse grabbed a baton and pointed toward the guard who had beaten him. "I need a little quality time with this evil son-of-a-bitch."

"Come On, Jesse. We've got to find Gena." Skeets grabbed his guitar and ran out the hole in the wall.

Lobo turned to the guards. *"If I see you outside this cell, you're dead meat. ¿Sabe?"*

Skeets and Jesse ran to the garage door in front of the jail, swung the doors wide, and mounted their bikes. The two Harleys roared out in front of the Wolf Wagon toward La Plaza. Lobo flipped a switch on the dash and flames belched from the flame-nozzles under the truck. He laughed and shouted, "God, I just love them flame throwers."

A *Federale* in Guadalajara checked his watch and thought maybe he had been spared El Jefe's Evening Report just this once. He sagged a little when the short wave crackled. *"Santa Maria preserve us."* But mariachis were singing a song he had never heard. He listened to the lyrics and doubled over laughing. He called a friend in another *Federale* station. *"Are you listening to this?"* Switchboards lit up all across Central Mexico as the word spread.

Angelita had come out of Casa de Masa and wished she knew exactly what she should do. Fiesta was in the plaza air.

Tolencitans crowded onto the stairs and jammed all the way back into the gazebo. The sun had set behind the buildings, and dusk turned to darkness. La Plaza's lights provided pale illumination as the mariachis milled around the narrow street and tuned their instruments in anticipation of their concert. She had no idea what she could do, so she signaled a downbeat for the mariachis.

Out of gratitude for all the people of Tolencita had done for them, the mariachis had written new lyrics for *"Caminos de Guanajuato"* and changed the song's name to *"Caminos de Tolencita."* They had substituted a theme of "life really is good" for the negative original lyrics' feeling that "life really sucks."

Tolencitans laughed, clapped with the music, and danced. The mariachis ended the song and expected a thunderous ovation, but instead a collective gasp echoed down the street. The crowd stared wide-eyed behind them. The mariachis turned and saw the open curtains of the casita's big window. Brilliant light bathed the room, and in the center of the tableau, a naked, fully erect El Jefe stood behind Josefina the burro.

Josefina had been impressed beyond comprehension as the Young Boys led her into her new stall. Never in history had any horse ever had a stall of such size, design, and quality of craftsmanship. She felt both deserving and humbled by the extravagance. There *were* disadvantages. She had been tied uncomfortably tight to the hitching post. Night had seemed darker than she could remember. She felt movement behind her in the darkness and thought, *'How did that old fool Flaco get into my new stall? Outrageous. Flaco should not reap the benefits of all my years of uncomplaining hard work. It's just too much.'* Sunrise came instantly, and the bright light startled her. *'Okay, that's it.'* Gracefully, she bucked up her rear and buried both hind hooves in El Jefe's balls.

The crowd's mood changed from shock, into disbelief, into outrage. A roar of disapproval built. Shouts of *"¡Bestial."* ricocheted around the plaza. When Josefina kicked El Jefe, he flew backward and slammed his head into the wall behind and slithered down the wall unconscious. A cheer of approval went up from the crowd. A large stone arched over the crowd in slow motion, hung in the air, and crashed through the window. A roar went up, and a group of men rushed across the street, broke out the rest of the glass, and climbed into the casita. Shouts grew from the crowd, "Mátelo. Mátelo." They heard the chant, "Kill El Jefe," and pummeled and kicked him. They vented every outrage he had ever perpetrated on them. The men dragged him out through the front door and lifted him above the crowd. The crowd went wild. Cheers continued when they brought Josefina out. A chant built, *"Libertad. Libertad. Libertad."* A rancher produced a couple of ropes, and they bound El Jefe's hands and feet. A man shouted, *"Una procession."* The men threw El Jefe, stomach down, across Josefina's back and tied him tightly both directions. He could not get loose or fall off. A man with a machete cut fronds from a palm tree. The palm fond wavers preceded Josefina and the parade commenced. The Mariachis fell in behind playing *"La Marcha de Zacatecas."* The crowd followed chanting, *"El Jefe es muerto. El Jefe es muerto."*

'Oh, has there ever been such a day as this in the life of a burro?' thought Josefina. They have entrusted a precious cargo to me, and even given a parade honoring all the wonderful things I've done. She pranced like a pony, head high, and nodded regally, left and right, at her cheering subjects. She glanced up into the stars and thought, *'Whoever up there that's been messin' with me, finally got things right.'*

PART SIX

"¡VÁMONOS!"
"Gotta Go" Bill Stephens, Composer

Chapter 37

The throng in La Plaza parted like the Red Sea when the two Harleys and The Wolf Wagon arrived, but the vehicles had to fall in line behind the palm wavers, Josefina, the mariachis, and the people dancing along in the parade. Lobo fired the flamethrowers for occasional dramatic impact, and the crowd gasped in delight. Three quarters around the square, Skeets and Jesse saw Gena, Angelita, and the brothers in front of Casa de Masa, as they leaped, waved, and shouted their jubilant emotion across La Plaza.

Skeets got off his bike but hesitated before approaching Gena. She ran to him, jumped to grab his neck, and wrapped her legs around him. Skeets grimaced in pain from his bruised stomach and ribs and then laughed. "I've never had anything hurt this good."

Jesse held Angelita and kissed her tears of joy away. "I don't know how you two pulled this off, but you are definitely miracle workers." The reunions of hugs, kisses, apologizes, and explanations lasted until the parade completed another circuit of the plaza.

When El Jefe passed them, Skeets pulled one of the guard's pistols from his pants pocket and said through gritted teeth, "I'm gonna kill this rotten piece of shit right now."

Gena reached and held his gun hand. "You don't want to spoil a good party, do you?"

"Yeah, but . . ."

Gena held her finger to his lips. "Let the locals handle their problems."

Jesse pointed at the naked El Jefe draped across Josefina with his butt over the starboard side. "I reckon his moon shined all over La Plaza tonight."

Angelita put her arms around Quito and Bosco. *"Our father has unfinished business with El Jefe. ¿Do you agree?"* The two boys nodded agreement. They took Josefina's lead rope and hurried her down a back street out of sight of the plaza and out to the highway.

As the *Fiesta Libertad* raged on, the mariachis called for Skeets and Jesse to join them in the gazebo. The leader asked, *"¿Why don't we sing 'The Ballad of Jefe's New Lover'?"*

Quito clucked at Josefina and patted her immaculately clean flank. *"Go on girl. You know the way. Go on home, now"* At first Josefina seemed not to understand, but when she heard the mariachis strike up "The Ballad of El Jefe's New Lover" she knew she must parade again and pranced off toward the Ramos Farm and into the darkness.

A loud voice outside the farmhouse awoke Señor Ramos. Only a bright sliver of sun rested on the horizon, but he could make out Josefina with something on her back. He heard a shout. *"Get me off this goddamn burro."* He moved closer and saw a naked El Jefe tied to the burro's back. He looked bloody, bruised, and covered in scratches and scrapes from mesquite and huisache thorns. *"Untie me you miserable peasant. Your daughter did this to me. I'll kill the bitch if it's the last thing I do."*

Sr. Ramos said nothing, but went back inside and dressed. He returned with Bosco's baseball bat and a shovel and led Josefina out into the field.

The spotlights of Jalisco Stadium came up on a stage filled with mariachis milling about uncertainly. The television producer cued a wide shot of the group, then moved in tight on the master of ceremonies. The MC's voice boomed over the stadium speakers. *"Damas y Señores, we have a hardship late entry tonight. They are the largest group to perform, and they have had great difficulty getting here, so please welcome Mariachis de Tolencita, singing an original song, "The Ballad of El Jefe's New Lover."*

The mariachis, emboldened by the crowd's reception, moved to the microphones. The crowd cheered again at the deep, full instrumental introduction rolling out into the stadium.

Ballad of El Jefe's New Lover
(Sung to Marty Robbins' "El Paso")

Chorus
El Jefe the Don Juan of old Tolencita
Loved Jose-fi-na the beau-ti-ful bur-ro
He loved her big eyes, vel-vet ears and long tail
But mostly he loved giv-ing her the cho-ri-zo

Verse

When Jefe first saw her his heart skipped a beat
Car-ing and lov-ing her eyes cast a spell
He knew with-out her his life was in-com-plete
Her first touch caused his pan-ta-lones to swell
Nuzz-ling him soft-ly made El Je-fe grin
She laid back her head and just bra. . . .yed

Vámonos!

Her love-ly voice and her song made Je-fe's head spin
He hugged her and kissed her the whole night he stayed
Sounds of the lovers were loud through the streets and woke up
the town
They looked and they won-dered who was a dy-in'
They saw Jefe and Josee in a lov-ers' em-brace
Oh the people were an-gry at such a dis-grace.

Chorus

El Jefe the Don Juan of old Tolencita
Loved Jose-fi-na the beau-ty-ful bur-ro
He loved her big eyes, vel-vet ears and long tail
But mostly he loved giv-ing her the cho-ri-zo

Verse

Jefe could not give up his lov-er the bur-ro.
Tolen-ci-tans pried the two lov-ers apart
Jefe fought for Josee and to save his cho-ri-zo
But the two lov-ers were doomed from the start.
Of this evil uni-on what could any-one say
They locked up El Je-fe in Ja....il
Je-fe moaned and groaned for Jo-se-fi-na all day
One night while the town was still sleep-in' 'ol Je-fe stole a-way.
They looked and won-dered till no one was try-in'
They say when the des-ert winds are a blow-in'
Jefe and Jo-se-fina can be heard still a goin'

Chorus

El Jefe the Don Juan of old Tolencita
Loved Jose-fi-na the beau-ty-ful bur-ro
He loved her big eyes, vel-vet ears and long tail
But mostly he loved giv-ing her the cho-ri-zo

The bus pulled up to La Plaza and the driver unloaded the luggage. Three suitcases remained unclaimed. The driver looked around for El Jefe, who was never late. A man in a suit and tie walked toward him.

"*¿Are these bags for El Jefe?*" the man asked in a very authoritarian voice.

"*Yes. Why do you ask?*"

The man pulled his identification from his coat pocket. "*I'm with the Federal Police President's Strike Force.*"

The black Mercedes nosed into a parking place in front of Casa de Masa. The locked doors held a sign announcing, "*Closed for Remodeling.*" The three men read the notice and looked at each other. One of Carlos Algo's goons groaned, "*I'm starved, and this place is closed?*"

Algo looked at his two hefty companions. "*You two pigs could afford to miss a few meals. Forget eating. Let's go get our packages and those two gringos.*"

"*¿What are you going to do with those two guys?*" The second hood looked concerned about this trip.

Algo said, "*You idiot. ¿Why do you think we brought those two shovels?*"

They pulled up in front of the police station and got out. Inside a uniformed police guard behind a desk said, "*Buenas tardes.*"

Algo looked around the room. "*¿Where's El Jefe?*

"*He had to run an errand. He told me to give you anything you needed.*" The policeman looked at them pleasantly.

Carlos and his goons glanced at each other and wondered what to do. Finally, Carlos said, "*We came to pick up some packages and two passengers. ¿Can you do this?*"

"*Yes.*" The guard looked at them expectantly. Carlos nodded at the bigger of the two hoods. He took two receipt slips from his pocket and gave them to the guard, who said, "*Wait here.*" He got up and unlocked the security door. In a minute he returned with the two packages. He sat down at his desk again, held the packages and receipts above his shoulder, and read the code numbers aloud.

In El Jefe's office the hidden cameraman framed the video on the three crooks as they took the packages and receipts. He nodded to the other men in the office.

El Jefe's office door and the security door both swung open, and SWAT Team officers ran through with AK47's trained on the dope dealers. The guard shouted, *"Put your hands in the air. You are under arrest for narcotics trafficking."*

The SWAT officer guarding the security door said, *"¿Where do you want to put them? It's crowded back in the cells."*

The guard smiled. *"Cuff 'em and put 'em on the floor. The prison bus will arrive soon."*

A group of *Federales* sat around an office in the Guadalajara Federal Police Building. The officer, who had replaced the captain arrested for narcotics trafficking, pointed at the short wave radio. *"I kind of miss 'El Jefe's Evening Report.'"* A chorus of moans and curses arose from the other officers, who felt differently. *"Still,"* said the new Captain, *"We don't know what happened to him. Maybe we should go over to Tolencita and investigate."*

"He must have heard about the drug bust and rode off into the sunset on Josefina, his new lover," someone replied. The other officers convulsed into laughter.

The construction for enlarging Casa de Masa was complete, and the deeply mortgaged new owners, Gustavo and Chiquita, looked on proudly as the mayor and his aldermen walked into the new meeting room to consider applications for the new Tolencita Chief of Police.

Josefina stood under the new shed built in her own enclosure and grinned that special burro grin at Flaco, who munched on hay in the old pen. She nodded approval at her water trough filled with sparkling clear water and the corn in the feed bin. She loved corn. *'It's not as lovely as my townhouse,'* she thought, *'but a small place in the country is nice.'*

The check from the Mexico record company who bought the rights to "The Ballad of El Jefe's New Lover" made the down payment on the new equipment and furnishings for Casa de Masa Mexican Restaurant. The neon flashed into the night on Austin's East 6th Street proclaiming, "It's The Real Thing." An advertising sandwich board stood at the door and announced, "TONIGHT -SKEETS AND JESSE- TEXMEX MUSIC AT ITS BEST " Below they had pasted a blowup of a *Texas Weekly* article excerpt:

CASA DE MASA – The most authentic Mexican food in Austin. The Chili Relleno is a must. Large poblano pepper stuffed with shredded pork, almonds, raisins, and citron; deep fried in egg batter and served in a lightly herbed tomato broth. Live performers blend C&W with Mexican mariachi music for an evening of authentic entertainment.

A banner hung diagonally across the sandwich board announced: FIRST ANNIVERSARY CELEBRATION.

Gena and Angelita surveyed the packed dining room and bar. The log-beamed ceiling, authentic stuccoed walls, and the mural of peasants harvesting corn and pulque, painted by a UT art student, looked identical with the photograph from which she had worked. A sense of pride always welled in both women when they felt the ambiance of the room. They never tired of the compliments of new patrons about the interior look and the aromas wafting from the kitchen. Hispanic waiters wore white shirts, black ties, and long white aprons over black pants and moved briskly about the dining room.

Gena smiled thinking about two of the waiters, Alfonso and Beto, who served the food prepared in the kitchen by their wives Ariana and Blanca and made more money than they ever thought possible. She knew the two families would someday establish their own restaurant in Guanajuato with their savings and help from their friends at Casa de Masa.

Private lessons from Jesse's English/Spanish-teacher mom had Angelita comfortable with her new language. The owners crossed the dining room into the bar where Skeets and Jesse had just finished a set. Those waiting for a dinner table packed the bar along with the crowd who regularly came only for the music. The bartender, Lizzie Ortiz, Gena's best friend, worked head down and backside up trying to stay abreast of the drink orders. Gena and Angelita pushed their way up to the bar. Gena gave Lizzie the high sign. "You look like a girl who could use help."

Lizzie twirled the cocktail shaker and did a quick bump and grind. "Naw, this is no hill for a stepper. I'm an ol' Dillo Doe girl, remember?" She gave an overt wink at a tall mustached man seated at the bar who wore an old crushed straw cowboy hat and a black Tee with sleeves short enough to show a tattoo of a wolf's head.

A front row table of UT college girls enjoyed a very large time drinking, singing, and occasionally jumping up to line dance. Two of them, a really attractive blonde and an equally beautiful brunette, knew the words to every song Skeets and Jesse sang. In fact, they knew Skeets and Jesse quite well. Gena and Angelita watched the interplay between the singers and the girls with interest. "Those girls are very friendly, don't you think?" Angelita asked without looking at Gena. "Should we worry?"

"Nah, I don't think so." Gena looked at the girls with continued interest.

"You don't think so? They're very pretty, those two." Angelita's face showed concern.

"Not to worry. I have the Harley keys." Their chuckle elevated into a knowing laugh.

They would normally jump from the stage at the end of a set, but Skeets put his arm around Jesse, and they both waved at Gena and Angelita. "Listen up all you music lovers out there. We have an important announcement." The crowd noise lowered. "Some of you may not know the brains behind this operation, so please meet Gena and Angelita. Come on up here, ladies." They waved at the two women who tried to modestly back away, but the crowd's encouragement finally moved them toward the stage.

Jesse took the microphone. "Few people know this, but these two ladies saved our lives once." A question rustled through the patrons. "No. I mean literally. We were in big trouble down in Mexico, and they came to the rescue. Now you've got to marry a woman who saves your life, right? So please help us celebrate our very first anniversary tonight." A minor pandemonium broke loose.

Skeets took the microphone. "In honor of the occasion, Jesse and I wrote a special song so these ladies know how much we love them. We call it, "Vámonos!"

Vámonos!

Refrain

**Been wanderin' the deserts of old Mexico
Missin' your love and the warmth of you close.
Can I ever reclaim what we had long ago
Got to try, gotta get back, gotta go. Vámonos.**

Verse

**What might have been was erased by my lies
There was noth-ing I could do for the hurt in your eyes**

Vámonos!

I've traveled the back roads trying to forget
The loss of your smile and the touch of your lips
While I'm roamin' and wanderin' 'neath Mexico skies

Refrain

Been wanderin' the deserts of old Mexico
Missin' your love and the warmth of you close.
Can I ever reclaim what we had long ago
Got to try, gotta get back, gotta go. Vámonos.

Verse

You turned your back and you walked away
Now you're gone from my life and I search night and
day
For that spark in my soul to light my way home
To bask in your love and the feel of you close
This endless desert never more to roam

Refrain

Been wanderin' the deserts of old Mexico
Missin' your love and the warmth of you close.
Can I ever reclaim what we had long ago
Got to try, gotta get back, gotta go. Vámonos.

Coda

Gotta go, gotta hurry, gotta go. Vámonos.
Gotta go. Vámonos.

*** End ***

ACKNOWLEDGEMENTS

It's been my privilege to ride my Harley-Davidson with the Los Compadres coast-to-coast, border-to-border, and over 12,000 miles in Mexico. We've enjoyed many adventures together, and my life is far richer for having their friendship. However, all of the scenes and adventures in this book are purely the product of my imagination.

The members of Daedalus Writers Group: Cindy Leal-Massey, Ned Bailey, Linda Schuler, Florence Weinberg, Diana Lopez and Jim Peyton, all accomplished authors, and Kay, my wife, waded through chapter after chapter, applying the polish to the Vámonos! manuscript

My long time friend John Mills, author and artist, contributed immeasurably with support, graphic design, and book design; while Cheryl, my daughter, provided photography.

To these and many others who helped along the way I offer my deepest appreciation.

www.ingramcontent.com/pod-product-compliance
Lightning Source LLC
Chambersburg PA
CBHW050549260626
47157CB00002B/497